I AM A STRANGER
IN A STRANGE LAND

Tio's Story

By Leon LeBlanc

Based on true events

Copyright © 2017 Leon LeBlanc

All rights reserved.

ISBN: 1543156134
ISBN-13: 978-1543156133

In memory of my father, Max LeBlanc

FOREWORD

In August 2011, I travelled to Lancaster, England, along with my daughter and wife, for a two-week sojourn. My purpose was twofold. My daughter had enrolled as part of an exchange program, at the Lancaster University where she expected to complete her third year of an Honour's Degree program at the Western University in London, Ontario, Canada. We had travelled to England on two previous occasions and my daughter, then an English and History major, had fallen in love with the English landscape.

However, I had a secondary reason for the visit besides a reconnaissance mission to see the influences, good, bad or ugly, which my daughter would be exposed to, during the school year which she planned to spend at Lancaster University.

I wanted to troll the northern English countryside, redolent of manicured greenery, old stone fences, quaint coffee shops and old markets. I wanted a close encounter with a few car boot sales and other collectables which I may see in quaint towns or villages. Most of all, I wanted to browse for endless hours in used book stores, foraging for books on law, history or cricket, which glory days had long gone.

A few days after our arrival in England, after my family and I had snacked on an English breakfast and following successive days of generous servings of Haddock and French fries, we were picked up by my cousin, Leon and his wife, Pauline, who had generously driven a considerable distance for a tour of northern England. As we drove along well paved but narrow streets, past verdant pastures and quaint farmhouses, and after thinking of a thousand ways to discreetly ask my cousin if he would be kind enough to be gentle on the car's accelerator, given that I did not relish the thought of going gently into that good night, Leon spoke about his plans to write a novel based on the life of his late father, who was one of my mother's younger brothers.

His reason for advising me stemmed from the fact that I maintained an abiding interest in history and had indeed, written a biography of the late Edward Oliver LeBlanc, one of our family's most illustrious members, who had been the first Premier of the former British colony of Dominica. I was immediately interested to hear of his plans, given that the life and experiences of my mother's siblings who had migrated to England in the 1950s, were still very much of a mystery.

As Leon outlined his plans, I became more interested and advised him that not only would it be important to write about his father's personal odyssey but also that he was in a unique position to write it. My only concern, which remained unexpressed, was whether the IT specialist which he was, could muster the creative energy to write about his chosen topic in a manner which would appeal to a broad cross-section of the reading public.

Upon reading this wonderful work, I am happy to declare that my fears were unfounded. Leon has deployed a lyricism which I did not know he possessed in writing the story of his father, whose story will resonate in the minds of all those who have had to seek a life in the diaspora. At times lyrical, at times poignant, and without any exaggerated sentimentalism, Leon has provided a riveting account of a man who was the embodiment of every man, whether Arthur Miller's *Willy Loman* or Ralph Ellison's *Invisible Man*, who has struggled for self-actualization in an environment which, in simple parlance, doesn't appear to give a damn.

Tio, the hero of the book, came to England with plans to return to Dominica after a few years. A few years extended to over half a century and a lifetime of experiences that have been crystallized in his son's novel.

Leon's book, or Tio's story, will soon occupy, when I receive a copy, pride of place in my library, alongside copies of well-thumbed books such as *Beyond a Boundary* and *Rumpole of the Bailey*.

Justice Irving André

PREFACE

SOUTHAMPTON – MAY 1956

From tropical green, across the vast blue to brutal industrial grey. He was an incomer to a town of incomers, an outsider amongst many, from within the British Isles and without, he came to earn, to live and to leave.

He had been taught that *'to travel hopefully is a better thing than to arrive'*.

He had travelled hopeful of the opportunity to work hard, to earn enough money to return home in glory, to enhance his standing in life. Now he was upon dry land, where the sun stayed hidden and the cold chilled his bones.

He had arrived.

PART ONE

Dominica – 1956

CHAPTER 1

CLARA

Penville, Dominica, West Indies - February 1956

I caught a glimpse of him as he descended the road through Lower Penville upon which our house is situated. If I am truthful, and I try to be, I've been watching, waiting, more than is healthy, more than is dignified for a woman of my age. My mother, to whom I seem a constant source of disappointment, catches me as I gaze up the road, more in hope than expectation. A knowing look, a shake of the head, her point is made.

Yes, if indeed I were to be truthful, I've been waiting all day. Waiting, just as I did for his elder brother Gabriel years ago, before he decided that I was unworthy of further attention and to sail off to a distant land across the ocean whose gentle murmur I hear this very moment.

He looks weary today, and more than a little care-laden. So serious for such a young man. Too serious. His father, Ton Ton Pierre, a man respected across the north of the island and of some standing - not as an educated man, or even wealthy beyond his peers, but as a fine carpenter and a skilled musician - says he should be more like some of his brothers. I assume by that he means he should drink more liquor. Or perhaps what he really means is Tio should be more like his father. Let me tell you something, if he was like his father, I would not be waiting for him at all.

My own beloved father, dearly departed for some nine years, left us this modest residence as an inheritance. It commands a view of the mighty Atlantic Ocean - magnificent on an evening such as this, but worrisome come hurricane season, being as it is, a little more exposed to the elements than some here in Penville.

I thank Providence - no, not Providence - I thank the Good Lord Himself that my father was able to leave this place to us as an inheritance. I cannot begin to tell you what it means to a woman such as myself and my ailing, ever-present, ever-disapproving mother. Life without it would surely have been unbearable.

An unmarried woman approaching thirty - okay, over thirty, as my mother takes it upon herself to remind me daily - has only her dignity, her charm, her reputation and her wits, such as they are, and such as they manage to remain intact.

Everyone assumed - some very vocally – that my mother and I would not be able to maintain this house once my father died. We scraped by at first, she by doing seamstress work and working our modest plot of land, me by looking after the bright-eyed, bare-footed, knowledge-hungry children in the Vielle Case government school, a few miles away. I teach them the poems of Wordsworth, Sir John Squire, and others. They stand in their little semi-circle and I chastise them should they not remember their lines.

Lately, some of the children's parents have taken to chastising me. What use, they ask, are such poems, when the children have a far greater need to learn what is necessary to survive, to forge a living from the land? Why do their children come running home, crying that I have given them blows for forgetting their lines? What possible use is it to them to learn about the kings and queens of England, about King Henry and his six wives and such foolishness?

My attempts to placate seem to be working, though. I ask in return: you may work the land, but do you not want your children to achieve more? I have said this more than once and on no occasion could the parent answer me.

In truth, they have a point about the teaching of a land thousands of miles away that most of them will never visit, and even if they should do so, will probably never see the rolling hills and wide expanses as described so elegantly by Mr. William Wordsworth. But should I apologise for wanting to expand their minds and expose them to that which transcends their daily existence?

Such parents understand little how I love those children. Yes, love is not too strong a word. I have invested my life in them, and for that, I expect to see a return on my investment – namely, that from these humble beginnings they will go on to do great things.

I lift up thanks to the Almighty for a great many things in my life, such as my education. I was fortunate to achieve the 'upper standard' at school as a pupil. From there, the government school at Vielle Case was able to employ me full-time as a schoolteacher. Moreover, my modest salary is now sufficient for us not to have to worry.

I am also thankful for the diligence of my late father, whom I miss more than words can say. They say that a daughter seeks the likeness of her father in a husband. My father was a good man. I dare to hope that I have found such a man in Benoit Mourillon, Tio to those to whom he is close.

Those who don't like him simply don't know him. He will make a fine husband. For him to do so, this stubborn goat of a man must first propose marriage. Yes, that would surely be a start.

CHAPTER 2

TIO

As day gave way to night, Tio Mourillon descended the Lower Penville Road, weary from the day's toil. By the sweat of his brow he would eat bread. Lately, though, there had been plenty of sweat, but too little bread by way of reward.

On a good day, from the remote North of Dominica, it was possible to view some of the adjoining islands in the Windward chain of the Caribbean - firstly Marie Galante, beyond which sat Guadeloupe proper at the point at which the Atlantic met the Caribbean Sea. He gazed out seawards, seeing but not noticing how the sea shimmered at the command of the moon, so close at hand to him now, but soon to be seen no more. Nor did he perceive the beauty of his surroundings. He had seldom seen anything else. In years to come, Tio Mourillon would remember all of these things with a sense of longing.

People from his native villages, Upper and Lower Penville, hewn from African, Carib, and European stone, were disparagingly referred to in patois as 'Penvillian goat-la' - the 'goats of Penville' in English. The term, intended as an insult, was fitting – the people of this northernmost region of the island were indeed stubborn, but also resilient and adaptable in this mountainous region. After all, one man's stubbornness is another's admirable tenacity, proven daily through their ability to traverse the narrow tracks that snaked around the tropical mountain landscape, maintaining a footing above precipices both literal and metaphorical.

A languid lamp, fuelled by coconut oil - a habit they had formed during the war when kerosene was at a premium - shone faintly from Clara's porch, a land-bound lighthouse guiding him to safe harbour, a haven from the day's woes, where he knew that a warm welcome awaited. He needed to see a friendly face, perhaps even something to eat. Earlier, he had washed in the Dimitre River and had dried his shirt, knowing that he may well call at Clara's. He was not as smart as he liked to be, as he was brought up to be, but at least he was presentable.

Tio and Clara had an understanding. They were to be married, but only when he could make his way in the world, an understanding firmer in her mind than in his. Clara could so easily have reproached him for taking so long to propose marriage. She did not and for that he was thankful. Even so, he could not keep her waiting forever. Sooner or later he would have to make his mind up. She made no complaint. Instead, she waited.

She understood that he must provide for her, not she for him. A man must have pride and self-respect, he said. He knew of many men who would allow an educated woman like Clara to support them, while they spent her modest, hard earned salary on liquor and tobacco and perhaps mistresses. Tio Mourillon was not such a man. Even her mother, who held Tio in no great regard, said so.

She was seven years his senior, source of much amusement from his brothers and their know-nothing friends. He knew the way they ran off at the mouth. It used to bother him, but he knew better now. He reasoned that they spent one minute, maybe two, ridiculing something or someone, then they forgot about their quarry and moved onto the next hapless recipient of their derision. After all, why spend your life worrying about another's shallow passing thoughts? Why let them come between you and the things most important to you in this world?

He called out, thinking not to startle her.

"Clara?"

She may be on her own, and it would not be a good thing to approach her porch like some thief in the night.

"Tio, I didn't know you were going to pass by. Come in. You look exhausted."

"I'm a bit dirty. It's okay?"

"But of course. It's no problem."

"Perhaps it's better we sit out the front."

"If you prefer. Are you hungry? We have ground provision and some salt-fish. You want some?"

Assuming the question to be rhetorical, he did not answer. What else would he be other than hungry after such a day?

The world looked a little brighter once his stomach was full. There was much to talk about, but for now, it was good just to relax in the cool of the evening.

These days Tio found he was having to give more thought to reputation than ever before in his life. Last year he found himself at the wrong end of some awkward rumours of his being pursuing his father's latest woman. Clara had chosen to completely ignore the rumours as scurrilous gossip. Tio's father, Ton Ton Pierre, certainly did not ignore them and as a result, Tio had thought it wise to make himself scarce for two or three weeks until the furore died down.

Clara's history was far more straightforward. Tio's brother Gabriel was interested in her several years ago, but had for some reason decided no longer to be so, having led her along for over a year. This experience forged in Clara a steely restraint and a fixed-mindedness born from necessity and self-preservation.

She was his window to the world, as had her father been to his family in years previous. Where others might speculate what prevailed beyond the vast blue, Clara could speak with authority, not from having travelled there, but by it having travelled to her in the form of education. A conversation with her was never a descent into ignorance, but a step, perhaps several steps, into transcending enlightenment. If only he had had the chance to study to the upper standard. He would have grasped the opportunity with both hands and not let go.

Times past, on Sunday evenings she would read passages from famous books to Tio and some of his older siblings, Lipson and Everton. The brothers would often be boisterous and joke around, as all young men do, but sometimes they would pay attention and listen more intently than they ever cared to let on. Perhaps they thought it something they would have enjoyed more of had their mother not died several years ago. Or perhaps it was simply that they thought that it would give the appearance of being more educated in a time in which education was beginning to carry much social currency.

More likely, though, was that it gave them a glimpse of the world that existed beyond this small island. It was a time in which many young men uttered the phrase *'mwen mal'* – life is hard for me. Those same young men needed to expand their horizons to see and experience what existed beyond the Caribbean and perhaps even beyond the Atlantic. Yes, they laughed, joked and fooled around like all young men, but they most certainly listened. And after they listened, both Everton and Tio often fell silent, immersed in their own thoughts.

Every young man of Tio's age had either worked or considered working in neighbouring French and Dutch speaking islands, Martinique, Guadeloupe, St Maarten, possibly even Curacao or even the South American mainland, just as all had heard of the awful things that might easily befall a young West Indian male should he be bold enough to venture across to the United States. Lately, however, opportunities to work in the surrounding islands were drying up. Tio had to come up with new ideas about how to get ahead in life.

Clara's father had once bought a *chaloup*, a small boat, not knowing the first thing about fishing or sailing for that matter. Clara's mother, ever the optimist, had famously said that it would end up in tears. She turned out to be right. From then on, her mother used the anecdote to ensure any speculative idea was stillborn. For the entire duration of Clara's early life, she had seen how grinding pessimism had worn her father down. Clara was not her mother. She would not make such a mistake.

Clara watched in silence as he paced back and forth on the porch, clearly agitated, his post dinner calm having quickly evaporated. He would say what was on his mind soon enough, she thought, but not before the charade of her having to coax out the information.

"Well, did you see Desmond at the Geest launch?" asked Clara

Tio, having stopped pacing, now sat reclined in upon a chair, chin almost on his chest, arms folded, shaking his head periodically.

"Did it not go well?"

"Ask Desmond when you speak to him."

"Tio, I am asking you."

No answer.

"Tio, if you do not tell your story, who will?"

"I saw him when he was with all his important business friends."

"And?"

More head shaking.

"I barely got a word out. Mister call me up and down. He start shouting about how I am coming to him for hand-out and that nobody ever give him anything in life, and why should he give me something?"

Where once she had heard confidence and sure-footedness, she now heard hurt and humiliation at the hand of a close relative. And yet, was this not the same well to do cousin who had worked with Tio's own brother?

"I don't understand this, Tio. Does Desmond think you will be troublesome?"

"Clara, I don't know what mister think. The man spoke to me like I am *nothing*. I felt so *foolish*. What make it worse is it was in front of his important business friends who just stand there watching. I was hoping to do business with them in the future, and he shout at me like I was a piece of dirt. I've been thinking for days and days about how to talk about doing business."

Ah yes, the truck - the Bedford truck. Such a magnificent vehicle would be capable of traversing the difficult and inaccessible terrain around Penville and Vielle Case and transporting produce such as bananas from the villages in the North East of the island to the North West, most importantly to the Geest launch at Portsmouth. Gone would be the backbreaking days of carrying bunches of bananas on one's head for miles in all types of weather, fair and foul. Bananas would arrive fresh and intact in a timely manner. What could be better?

Such a vehicle would be an asset to the whole community, for trucks like these were invariably also used as makeshift buses. It would make Tio a man of some standing, and right now that would do his state of mind no harm at all.

"Clara, I have thought about this. I've done nothing but think about it. My father is the most skilled carpenter on the island; my older brothers are either carpenters or successful farmers. What am I?"

"You are a planter, for now, Tio. Gabriel and Everton may have started as carpenters, but they are in England right now. Who knows what they're doing? It is no shame to be a planter. In time, you will rise to be more."

"But what is there for me here? What chance will I ever have of getting up from the dust?"

"You are not in the dust. Life is hard, and hard for everyone right now. It will get better, though."

"When?"

"I can't answer that, Tio."

"I am as good as them. All of them. But how can I get anywhere in life? I only have an elementary education. Every Dick, Tom, and Harry is on the ladder climbing upwards, and I am not even on the first step. Men like mister, in his important position. Why should he talk to me so? Am I *nothing*?"

Clara, fearful of interrupting while he was in this state of mind, thought it best to stay silent for a while.

"Desmond has his place in this world. My brother has his. Where is mine?"

Clara hesitated.

"Tio, of course you are not nothing. I've said so to my mother and to many people. You tend your land diligently. You're a hard worker…"

"But I am not *getting* anywhere, Clara."

She wanted to say something meaningful, something profound to assuage his diminished pride, to convince him of his value. She wanted to say that his place in this world was here. No words came.

"What does your father say about all of this?"

"My father?" Tio looked at her, his eyes faintly glistening. "my father does not understand. There must be something better than this," he sighed, "there has to be."

"Are you still talking about the truck, Tio?"

He drew breath.

"I'm talking about going overseas to work, Clara."

"You mean like last year, to Guadeloupe? Or Martinique?"

"No, England."

The man who could become irritable and insufferable embarking upon even the smallest journey was going to travel half way across the world? Surely this was a joke.

"You mean go to England to stay?"

"No, no. Not live there, just go and work. Earn some money. One year, maybe two, then come back with enough money to buy the truck. England is open now."

Evidently, it must also be accepting unskilled workers. From what Tio was saying, he must no longer be below the threshold to emigrate. Not so very long ago, those such as his oldest brother Gabriel, who were contemplating the journey had to prove they had sufficient means to return. Things must have changed. How quickly the world was changing. How quickly *her* world was changing.

"Dominicans are not treated with respect in England, Tio. I have heard that in the places where they have rooms to stay they have signs saying …"

"I know what the signs say there, Clara, the ones that say no dog and no black man and no Irish man. I have read some of Gabriel's letters saying how it is beaucoup cold there and how you never see the sea once you get off the boat."

"And do you think you will be okay to live and work in England? What if they don't like you? What if you don't like them?"

"I don't need to go see the queen in her palace. I just need to work and earn money. And I have worked with lots of people I don't like."

Clara worried that she may be sounding a little desperate, or at very least taking too unfavourable a view upon the idea. She could almost hear her mother's voice now. Of course he is going, she would say, you are not married, what claim do you have on him?

"I don't recall where your brothers are staying in England. Do you?"

"Is he London?"

"No, it's not London. London is south. I think it is further in the North of England."

"Scotland?"

"No, no. Scotland is a different country altogether."

She knew this, she was sure, but it was momentarily evading her.

"Lincoln. It is called Lincoln, I think."

"Like the president?"

"I think so."

"So, are you thinking of joining Gabriel and Everton?"

"Yes. I'm waiting for a letter from Gabriel."

A letter? It was becoming increasingly clear that some parts of this conversation were not entirely spontaneous. What else was he not telling her?

"You may be waiting some time. Your brother doesn't like writing."

"Do you have any pictures or books about England, about Lincoln?"

"I have many books from England, but I don't think any are about Lincoln. Let me go see."

Clara disappeared indoors to rummage. Many of the books she possessed were given to her by a close English Creole friend before she left for England. Clara had managed to accumulate quite a library of English classic literature such as Shakespeare plays, sonnets, poetry books, encyclopaedias and some history books that contained some eye-watering references to the some of the Empire's colonial subjects.

Minutes after disappearing, Clara emerged with a book as promised. The book she had retrieved seemed far too small to contain any detailed maps or meaningful pictures.

"Here it is. It is the only thing on Lincoln I could find. I knew I had something."

"What is he?"

"A few poems."

"Poems?" The disappointment in his voice was audible.

"You sometimes like poetry."

"Here's one. The Brook, by Alfred, Lord Tennyson."

"What is he about?"

"It's about a brook, of course. A stream."

"Like here?"

"Yes, like here. Close your eyes and I'll read it to you."

"If I close my eyes, they will stay closed, I'm so tired."

"Close your eyes. Then you'll see the picture in your mind."

"I can hear what you are reading, Clara. Just read."

She checked to see if his eyes were closed.

"I'm not going to read all of it, or you *will* be asleep. I'll just read the best parts."

No further protest was forthcoming. His eyes remained open, however.

"Okay,

> *'I wind about, and in and out,*
> *with here a blossom sailing,*
> *And here and there a lusty trout,*
> *And here and there a grayling,*
>
> *'And here and there a foamy flake*
> *Upon me, as I travel*
> *With many a silver water-break*
> *Above the golden gravel,*
>
> *'And draw them all along, and flow*
> *To join the brimming river,*
> *For men may come and men may go,*
> *But I go on forever.*

> *'I steal by lawns and grassy plots,*
> *I slide by hazel covers;*
> *I move the sweet forget-me-nots*
> *That grow for happy lovers.'*

She wondered for a moment if she was trying his patience. He appeared relatively content compared to a few minutes ago, despite his refusal to close his eyes. It was as if the rhythm soothed him after so long and arduous a day. She continued.

> *'I slip, I slide, I gloom, I glance,*
> *Among my skimming swallows;*
> *I make the netted sunbeam dance*
> *Against my sandy shallows.*
>
> *'I murmur under moon and stars*
> *In brambly wildernesses;*
> *I linger by my shingly bars;*
> *I loiter round my cresses;*
>
> *'And out again I curve and flow*
> *To join the brimming river,*
> *For men may come and men may go,*
> *But I go on forever.'*

She paused, awaiting a response.

"Sounds like here."

"Perhaps a little like here, yes."

"Maybe England is just like here, but with English, not Dominicans."

"And colder."

"Yes, and colder."

"Where they drink tea like this." She feigned holding an imaginary tiny cup with her little finger cocked.

"What do you think a grayling is?"

"A grayling is a fish, I think. You like the poem?"

Tio shrugged.

"It's alright."

It was a poem about a stream in the countryside, but not in *his* countryside, or at least not yet. He would be going to a land where streams were so few and far between that poems were written about them. Here streams were so numerous there was one for every single day of the year.

Why leave the richness of his home environment for what may well be paucity in another land? She knew not to ask, for the answer was plain for all to see. He could not live on the beauty of his surroundings. He needed substance and the substance was to be found elsewhere.

"So, Tio Mourillon. What is it that you want to ask me since you arrived?"

He shuffled in his seat.

"I wanted … I'd like … will you wait for me, Clara?"

She paused for what seemed to him an eternity, simply staring at the floor. It was not the question she had hoped he would ask.

"You know …" she started in a faltering voice, "you know I'm not getting any younger, Tio? And you know that England is full of white women, and you will get lonely there when you stay with your brothers?"

"I'm not looking for a white woman, Clara. You're the woman I want, and when I can make my way in this world, I want us to be married when I come home."

"So, you are asking me to marry you?"

"Yes, I want us to marry and I want you to wait for me. Will you?"

Once again Clara gazed at the floor for yet another seeming eternity.

"But of course. I will marry you. I will wait for you. And I will help you go to England to make your way there, and to come back to be a man of business here. With a truck."

"Yes," he laughed for the first time that evening, "with a truck."

Before he left, they kissed on the porch of her house, this time, less worried about what anyone might say. After all, they could now tell anyone they were engaged should they care to comment. Clara the schoolteacher would not be marrying beneath her. She would be marrying a man who had travelled the world, soon to come back as a man of means - the owner of freight transport to Portsmouth - a businessman.

She had long awaited his proposal, just as she had once waited in vain for one from his brother. Now that it had finally arrived, it was tempered with the bitterness of his leaving, potentially for years.

As Tio Mourillon strode away from Clara's house, a thought lingered in his mind. Sometimes a person can think that they are wrestling with a decision, poring over each and every detail as if the whole thing is precariously balanced and could tip either way, when actually they are kidding themselves. In truth, they made that decision long ago.

Once he had disappeared into the teeming darkness, Evelyn, Clara's mother, edged out onto the porch, too soon for her to have been any distance away previously. She must have overheard most, if not all of the conversation.

"So," she sniffed, "England?"

"Yes, Mama ... England."

"I think the boy want to put some milk in his coffee!"

CHAPTER 3

FON BÈLÈ

Eighteen Years Earlier - 1938

Pierre Mourillon arose at 3 o'clock in the morning, lit the kerosene lamp in Fon Bèlè, his remote dwelling place near Penville, the northernmost village in Dominica. None of his eight children stirred as he began tending the stove, emptying it of yesterday's ashes, restocking it with fresh coconut husks in order to warm up the clothes iron. Had his wife Elmie not died last year, he could have tended to his own tasks. Had she not died, his daughters would have been able to attend school today rather than their schooling be so cruelly curtailed. Elmie would have been at Fon Bèlè to do her own work in their stead. Life had been hard before, but it was much harder now.

Fon Bèlè sat west of the track that snaked from Vielle Case to Lower, and then Upper Penville, within the embrace of a valley that had kept it sheltered from the worst excesses of hurricanes and tropical storms over the decades. Residents of Vielle Case and Penville had traditionally interacted far more with people from the neighbouring Marie Galante and southern Guadeloupe than with the rest of Dominica. Times, however, were changing, thought Pierre. The world was opening up. His children, he determined, would not be like himself, able to speak patois and French and only very rudimentary English. No, his children would grow up speaking English fluently, just as those islanders who lived in town and stuck their noses up in the air did.

Waiting for the heat of the stove to fully seep through to the iron, Pierre took the lamp outside, quickly performed his ablutions, then promptly returned to clean and then polish the shoes. Each of the uniforms he had washed and dried the previous day was then neatly pressed and folded. The Mourillon children would be nothing if not well presented.

'Your mother', he had said to each of the children, 'she was a clean woman'. A person may have an excuse for being poor, Pierre decreed, but never ever dirty. Nor would *his* children ever be punished for failing Head Teacher Mr. Sorhaindo's daily inspection.

Some of his children's shirts he had made himself, having figured out how to do so by reverse engineering one he had bought some time ago.

This morning, as on every weekday, the children would go directly south to join the track to Vielle Case, a journey of about three miles. Each child had a slate and pencil, each a uniform neatly wrapped, not to be worn until they had bathed. Torrential rain would not be sufficient excuse to fail uniform inspection, nor flooded rivers. At the Balthazar River, they would bathe and clean their teeth with guava tree twigs. Those who were exalted enough to possess shoes would put them on and neatly lace them up, all in time for 9 o'clock start.

All of the Mourillon children missed their dear departed mother. The ones Pierre worried about most were Lipson, Tio, and the youngest, Emile. All three were varying degrees of mute for weeks after her death. Tio's breathing problems by now, fortunately, seemed to have subsided, and Pierre was increasingly confident that his family's numbers would not be further diminished.

Tio smiled so rarely of late. Had he always been this way? Pierre could not remember noticing that before now. He was far too serious for an eight-year-old. It was not good to see such gravity in one so young. People do not like it.

In his own childhood, Pierre had bewailed the fact that his older brother had been educated to the upper standard, leaving him languishing with the task of working the land. Had he not been required to do so and leave school at twelve, who knows to what heights he may have ascended? But Pierre had not complained – well, not very often – and had taken hold of all the resources he had been given. He had graduated from the University of Life and exercised supreme stewardship over this place where there were no neighbours and no friends for miles, finding a way to survive in the place where not so long ago the Europeans could not.

Resourcefulness had been the key. Back in the early days a rusty nail, a bent nail, a tin can, a piece of wire – all had their uses and frequent reuses. The quintessential Dominican quality of trying to make the most of the little that life had handed over was never better manifested than in this man of the mountainous north.

Father Leutens, the parish priest in the neighbouring village of Vielle Case, had once regaled a young Pierre with the story of how God had asked Moses when he was by the burning bush 'What do you have in your hand?', referring to his staff. The reason the Almighty had asked such a question, Father Leutens expounded, was to illustrate that he should use what little he had and would he receive help with the rest.

At the heart of this struggle to achieve dominion over the land was the dwelling place Fon Bèlè. Pierre told anyone who would listen to the story of how he had eked out a foothold upon the land on which he now stood. He would tell them how he had not complained, but make no mistake, it had been hard. Now he was the most respected carpenter for many miles around, so much so that men came from the neighbouring islands of Martinique, Marie Galante and Guadeloupe commissioning him to do specialist work they would entrust to no other.

To that end, later that week a Monsieur Galbas would be travelling over from Vanibel in Guadeloupe, having tasked Pierre with crafting a gear and pinion for a new mill. Pierre Mourillon could not read a plan, although Monsieur Galbas may well choose to bring one. No, the end product would be arrived at by lively and animated discussion. He may not be educated, but need that mean that he could not be a scientific man?

And, most importantly, he had placed Monsieur Galbas under firm instructions that under no circumstances should he come without his 'friend', by which he meant white rum.

Pierre and his friend were indeed good friends, whether at home or amongst acquaintances down in Penville. Life must have its compensation for its unrelenting hardships, he said. A man must be able to enjoy himself once in a while. But after that, as the saying in patois went:

'Bal fini, violon en sak'

The party was over, and the musician had packed. Time to apply himself to his labours once more.

So once more Pierre applied himself to his work. Jobs like this were good money and much needed. In time, some of his oldest sons Gabriel and Everton may well become carpenters too, under his tutelage of course. As for the rest, he would see.

Shirts now ironed, he strode softly over to the children.

"Boy. Wake up."

Pierre prodded Tio, who responded with moans and coughs. Alphonse, thinking the instruction applied to him also, but was quick to settle down when his father placed him back in bed.

He allowed the almost closed eyed Tio to dress in nothing more than his shorts and then led his barely awake eight-year-old son out beyond their modest wooden dwelling. Down they went, into the valley, beyond his coffee plants, still further beyond the lime grove, toward the ocean.

There they drew to a halt. Pierre raised his booming voice, addressing his son in Patois.

> "*Ou saw mwen fanmi* – you are my family, so what is mine is also yours. The land here, it is - how you say? – it is your inheritance. It is handed down to my father by his father and from me to you, your brothers and your sisters. You will hand down your portion to son and daughter; they to their son and their daughter.
>
> "You must tend the land, work hard. Grow yam, sweet potato, plantain, banana, and mango. I will show you where are the boundaries. You must respect the boundaries. You can see that yours starts at the lime tree and goes down to the two rocks by the stream? After that, the land is your brother's. What is yours, you take care of. What is his, he takes care, not you.
>
> You should *not* sell the land. If you do, you must sell only to family.
>
> "If a man cannot pay you what he owes, he can come and work for you - one day if he is a carpenter, two days if he is a labourer. Soon Ton Sylvain will come work for me for three days and I will feed him

– good food, and plenty, but if I work for him he will pay me more because I am a carpenter.

"You must sell your yam, plantain, banana and mango in town, in Portsmouth, coffee also. Save your money. Pay for education for your children so they will become a teacher, work for the government – an engineer, maybe a doctor, so they work with people who don't even speak Patois. They will look after you when you are too old to plant yam and take it up from the ground.

"See these ears? Français! I have Frenchman's blood in me - from Bayonne. You see? I am not Frenchman. I am not African. I am Dominican! You understand?"

Tio arched his neck and met his father's gaze.

"*Ou saw mwen fanmi, garzon.* Tue es ma famille! Copran?"

You are my family. You understand?

Tio was by no means sure he did understand, but thought it wise to nod anyway. Pierre took him by the hand, led him back up the steep slope and into the house for a further hour's sleep, after which the boy would soon rise.

Outside Fon Bèlè he sat on a wooden stump and lit his clay pipe. His wife, he said to himself, she was a good woman. The best of him. He missed her.

No matter, his friend would console him later.

Sunday morning saw the Mourillon family in the glory of their Sunday finest – Pierre wearing a white cotton suit and sporting a matching trilby, carrying a walking cane, more for effect than support.

The stifling heat had earlier been punctured by a brief cloudburst as midday approached, leaving some cover in its wake and even a little breeze, making today at least tolerable.

Today was a good day. A day of rest from one's toils, a day to enjoy the fruits of them, even the fruit of his loins, as the priest often put it. His children - good looking - all of them, he said, and often, were also bedecked in white, as they shuffled slowly before him having departed from the Vielle Case parish church shortly after mass.

He bade his children halt. Something or someone by the side of the road caught his eye as his entourage descended the street. Three adolescent girls were sat with boys of a similar age. He could only assume they were walking out together or at least thinking of doing so. Approaching them, he tapped one of the girls on the shoulder with his walking cane.

"These boys," said Pierre in patois, "You are wasting your time with these boys. You need good, strong Mourillon boys instead."

Neither the girls nor the accompanying boys replied. Neither did any of them dare to even look up to meet his now intense gaze. The girl to whom he had spoken, Evelyn's daughter, appeared as if she was pretending to be unable to understand patois, but she understood alright. Why else was he able to see the tear running down her cheek this very moment? Yes, she understood perfectly.

Satisfied that his words had achieved their desired impact, he snorted and turned away from the youngsters, beckoning for his children to continue. The message was to be conveyed to their parents. The girls were merely a conduit, and if the message was a little unpalatable for them in the meantime, so be it.

Just in case the girls' parents had thought him conveniently tucked away, far from view at Fon Bèlè, Pierre was announcing that he too was a man to be reckoned with. Perhaps not be an educated man, nor a man of great land or immense riches, but surely, he was a man who was making his mark in this world, having started out with so little.

Those boys by the side of the road, thought Pierre as he strode into the distance triumphant, they were not strong and good looking like his boys.

Yes, he thought, today was indeed a good day.

CHAPTER 4

THE PATIENT

Roseau, Dominica, West Indies - March 1956

"I wonder how the English will respond to you, Tio."

"What do you mean, Clara?"

"I mean, they have very different ways there. If you say things like you say them here, it may cause a commotion."

"Like what?"

"Well, take for instance how you become vexed whenever you travel somewhere new. You won't be able to do that there. You will have one of those police officers wearing a big pointed hat come and tell you to be quiet."

"I don't know where you get all of these things from. How often do you see me in trouble with the police here?"

"I am just teasing you, Tio."

Both laughed at the thought of Tio being accosted by the police because of his ill humour. Then they were lost in their own thoughts once more.

Seated in a small patch of land adjacent Clara's property, Tio had determined to clear as much hard manual work as possible for her before leaving. Soon, he would no longer be on hand to do such work. She and her mother would have to do it from now on. For the rest, she would have to pay someone.

Tio sat a short distance away from Clara upon a small tree stump, machete in hand, stripping husks from a dozen or so coconuts in a pile.

"Do you think the English are so different to us, Clara?"

She detected uncertainty in his voice. He was normally quite opinionated about matters such as this. Perhaps he was having second thoughts. She paused in contemplation before speaking.

"I think if you were to ask many people around here, they will tell you the same thing – the ones that come here look down on us."

"But I'm not asking many people, Clara I'm asking you."

"I used to know this English Creole girl when I was staying in Roseau with my aunt. She lived a street away in Goodwill, but in a much bigger and nicer house than ours. She would stare at me, I would stare at her. I would see her the next day. She would stare at me, I would stare at her even more. One day I got mad and went up to her to tell her off. I started to shout at her. I asked her 'who do you think you are thinking you better than me?' I called her stuck up, I was going to call her every name under heaven. Do you know what she said to me?"

Tio shook his head.

"She said she wished she *was* me. How nice I looked, how she would like to be my friend.

"Boy, I'm telling you, I felt *so* small. I was going to tell her this and tell her that, and cuss her, and she was so nice and wanted to be my friend. We still are friends. She went to England. She hates it there, mostly because of the climate and the fact she is used to life here. She writes to me occasionally. She never let me forget how troublesome I was to her. She teased me about it all the time because she knew how bad I felt about it."

"So, what are you saying?"

"I'm saying it's harder to dislike some people when you meet them. I'm saying they breathe the same air as us. They feel hungry like we do, they feel pain like us. They have to go to the toilet just like we do," she laughed.

As Tio had said, he had not just asked anyone, he asked her. He knew she would give a considered, thoughtful answer. This was why he liked her.

"They don't go to the same toilets in America," he said, "They have one for white people, one for black."

"But you are not going to America. You are going to England."

He mulled over her words for a moment. He imagined she thought him foolish for asking philosophical questions when what was required was down to earth practicality.

There was a multitude of matters requiring attention. He must make arrangements for the care of his livestock and land. He had already initiated discussion with his brother Lipson, but the details must be hammered out. Then there were the references, the trip to Roseau to book and pay for the April journey, or perhaps send his friend Peter with the money. He would need far more warm clothes than he had, but there was no great call for them in Dominica so the shops did not stock many. If he bought them in Dominica they would be at a premium. Far better to buy them once he arrived – less packing, more readily available and above all, cheaper.

Tio could tell that something was on Clara's mind. She was paying close attention to the floor again. No point in prompting her, he thought, she would come out with it when she was ready.

"You know, I think you will get on with the English too well."

He knew what she was getting at, but played innocent.

"Too well? What do you mean?"

"I think you will find yourself an English woman for when you are lonely there. Doesn't your brother have one?"

Tio picked another coconut from the pile and placed another coconut husk between his legs. He thought to reply but said nothing. Then he realised that in saying nothing he had replied.

"You know I will not be able to come to Roseau to see you off?"

"I know."

"So, you will pass by and say goodbye before you leave?"

"Of course I…"

The first thing Tio was aware was an unfamiliar sound from the machete strike, then Clara's shocked expression. Everything then blurred. In the briefest of moments, when his vision cleared, everything was covered in blood – his blood. The machete had almost severed his thumb.

Clara was shouting something. Was it to him, to someone else? Her mother, Evelyn, had arrived. Tio was prostrate by now. Once again, his vision failed.

Sometimes pain can be so intense that it no longer hurts. Evelyn, whose physical strength surprised the dazed and injured young man, tore a strip of fabric from somewhere, probably her own clothes. By the time he could feel the tourniquet tightening, he was drifting in and out of consciousness. Then nothing.

"I bring the Englishman," announced Thomas indignantly, "he do nothing but shout at me all journey. I nearly throw him from the boat. I give him some rum. He sick all the time."

"You know he does not like to travel. Anyway, he in pain. Thomas, you know this."

Olivia's instinctive defence of her younger brother was forged by many years of surrogate parenthood.

"He chop him fool hand with the machete before him go to England. Englishman already forget how to chop coconut. Now I bring him here and he can't even go to England. I waste my time. He waste he money."

No doubt many others at home were already disparagingly referring to emigrants as Englishmen. In fairness, it had been the same with Tio's older brothers. Whether they had even embarked upon their journey was of no consequence. A joke perhaps, but a joke with an edge. Once departed, you were somehow less, not quite the real deal, no longer a bona fide islander.

"Thomas, you make me vex with you if you carry on so. He will go to England. He will rest here until he is okay. Has my father pay you?"

"Ton Ton Pierre give me enough money and enough words."

"And I will give you some more words. Do not be calling my brother an Englishman just because you don't like him. He is a Mourillon. He is from Penville."

"He *was* from Penville. The boy leave. He is an Englishman now."

Olivia drew breath, ready to shout at Thomas but managed to restrain herself. Tio's young travelling companion had delivered her brother from the north of the island safe and sound and for that she was grateful. At least now she could tend to him and hopefully, strengthen him sufficiently in preparation for the journey.

"You do not say who is he. His father say who. His mother say who."

"Where is he mother?"

A flash of anger in Olivia's eyes left the twenty-year-old Thomas in no uncertainty that it was time for him to beat a hasty retreat, no further conversation necessary.

Where indeed was his mother? Resting with all the saints was the answer, at least in part. The remaining part of the answer was that his mother was right there – she, Olivia, was had been his de facto mother from an early age.

Tio as a child had been small, wiry and beleaguered with asthma. As with all the Mourillon children, he had a temper and from time to time his manner could appear a little grave. The Mourillon boys were always fighting with the boys from Vielle Case and Thibaut, the neighbouring villages. Invariably they won.

One occasion upon which their father came home the worse for wear for drink, the children, wanting to avoid a beating, had hidden under their wooden house at Fon Bèlè. The young Tio saw this as yet another opportunity to frighten his younger brother Alphonse by making ghost noises as they lay there in the pitch dark, thinking it great fun to scare his younger brother witless. The fun ended abruptly when Alphonse reacted by shoving his large thumb from his large hand hard into Tio's eye. From that moment on there were no more ghost noises, just whimpers of pain, just as now.

Olivia had to nurse her brother for a solid week after, just as it seemed she would have to tend to him now.

Back then, as Tio convalesced, he had overheard Olivia speculating amongst the womenfolk that the younger Mourillon boys would likely lack tenderness towards their wives because of the absence of their mother. Momentarily she caught a glimpse of the look of confusion on the young Tio's face, but had been confident at the time that he was too young to understand the full meaning of what she was saying. That confidence soon waned, however, when he became withdrawn for several days after. From then on, she determined to put a bridle on her tongue, lest she upset her ever serious younger brother.

Serious as he may be, she would far rather suffer his frequent displays of ill humour, than see him sail across an ocean where she could be a mother to him no more.

But he would go, and she would cry for a while, but sooner or later she would reconcile herself to the thought that he was probably enjoying his adventures in a new and distant land.

For Tio, the three days prior to embarkation had been unspeakably fraught. It had started relatively straightforwardly with having to chase down his old head teacher, Clive Sorhaindo and then the police for references. The ever-precise Mr. Sorhaindo had provided his letter with the promptness and efficiency Tio would have expected. The police had also been punctual, supplying Tio's reference two days earlier. He had drawn up a rudimentary document signing over his crops and livestock to his brother Lipson under instruction that should he sell any of the above, a proportion of the proceeds should be forwarded onto Tio. Lipson would tend the land in Tio's stead.

All was relatively fine until the machete accident. Tio had sliced deeply into his left hand with a machete while stripping coconut husk. He had cut through to the bone. Everyone thought that he would lose his thumb completely. Evelyn Celestine's prompt action had prevented that loss. Her makeshift patching managed to stem the blood loss - evidently being a seamstress could come in quite useful. No longer bleeding, he was then rushed to Portsmouth where he was further cleaned up and given some momentary rest.

None who had seen the severity of the cut, with the notable exception of Tio's father, had thought he would be well enough to make the journey. Twenty-four hours before his scheduled departure Tio rallied. Everyone's frantic efforts had paid off. He would make the journey.

The journey from nearby Portsmouth to the island's capital, Roseau, was by boat. It was planned that he would stay with his eldest sister, Olivia, and her husband for one night as she was the only immediate member of his family living in Roseau.

As Tio stirred into consciousness, he was met with the comforting view of his sister's face.

"Tio! Bondieux, bondieux! Sit up now. I expect you to pass by much earlier."

Her tiny shack on the outskirts of Roseau had only two rooms worth mentioning. Small the dwelling may be, and modest too, but it bore the distinctive hallmark of the Mourillon family – tidiness.

"Brother, you look so pale. Come and sit up. I will go to the nurse and get you some new bandage."

"Philomena has packed the bandage. Two bandage. In the case."

Olivia removed the grubby dressing that smelled of fish and who knew what else, before painstakingly washing his hand with clean water and redressing it.

"There. No Mourillon boy going on the big important ship looking and smelling like a ruffian. You going on there looking tip top. And make sure Manuel carries your case when you getting on the ship."

"Okay."

"You must be hungry. Herminia who live next-door is making you some broth."

Tio scanned his surroundings.

"Where is your husband?"

"He is not here now. You can stay on the bed in this room until the morning. It is no problem."

"So why is he not here?"

Olivia had no appetite for discussing her husband's whereabouts with her upstart brother. It was barely five minutes ago that she was tending him through asthma attacks and wiping his nose, or so it seemed.

"Little brother, just leave it alone."

"Leave it alone?"

"Yes, leave it alone."

"But why do you want me to leave it alone?"

"Tio, I am not getting into a big conversation with you about this. I am just telling you. Leave it alone."

"Is he left you? Is he another woman?"

"He will be round here tomorrow for his meal. He is busy right now. He will be here."

Olivia's attempts at evasiveness left Tio to fill in the blanks. Up to now, he and everyone else in the family had been firmly under the impression that her move to Roseau had been an unmitigated success. After all, she had been the first to escape, if indeed she had escaped.

Years of duty and care, years of thwarted life opportunities, only to end up here – the most modest of dwellings, thought Tio, still in a state of torpor. She was here, though - this place where she could hear her neighbour's conversations and her neighbours could hear hers, against the sound of the gentle lapping of the Caribbean Sea in the not too distant background.

Was this as far as any of the Mourillon children could go? No, he would go further, even if he had to die trying. Right now, that seemed a distinct possibility.

"Olivia? Hello."

A woman's voice could be heard outside.

"I see your brother pass by."

"Yes. He cannot come and say hello. He chop his hand with a machete. He laying down now."

"No? Is he okay?"

"He will be okay. He just need some rest."

"I see he is not okay when he come in. I bring him some broth."

"Ah, that is so kind."

"And I bring him my husband coat from when he went to America. Does your brother have a coat? It will be cold in England."

The conversation continued for several minutes, Tio only catching snippets. He heard mention of the broth and could by now smell it. The by now intense aroma only served to torture him further, given his now intense hunger.

Finally, the neighbour bade his sister farewell, after which Olivia emerged, food in hand, received eagerly by the patient.

"So, another brother goes to England. Soon I have no brothers left here."

"It will be two years, maybe three. I will come back."

"What does Papa Pierre say?"

"About what?"

"About you leaving?"

"He says bring him back his other friend when I come home."

"You mean whiskey from Scotland?"

They laughed, but doing so brought on a surge of pain down the whole of Tio's arm.

He grimaced.

"Why did this have to happen at a time like this?"

"Perhaps it is a good thing."

"What? I nearly lose my hand. How is that a good thing?"

"Because you think about your hand, not about the journey."

"Every single person thinks I cannot make journeys. Every single one. And yet I've been to Marie Galante, Guadeloupe, to Martinique."

"Tio, those journeys are *tiny*. You are going to England. It takes weeks and weeks to get there. It is not like going to Guadeloupe."

"I will be okay going there. Just the same as I was okay going everywhere else."

His wilful amnesia was impressive, and it was quite apparent that no amount of disagreeing would convince him otherwise.

"You will not come back, I think."

"Olivia, why you say that to me?"

"Because I think you will not come back."

"But why? Gabriel and Everton have both said they will return."

"But they are married."

"And I am engaged to Clara."

Olivia sucked her teeth.

"You should not have promised to marry Clara. It is not fair to her."

"Is he because she's older than me?"

"Booooy, that nothing to do with it."

"What then?"

"Lickle brother, don't be sounding so with me. You not too old for me to give you some blows. I used to wipe your nose when you were a small boy."

Olivia drew breath, hesitated, then spoke.

"I do not think you love Clara, Tio."

Tio's expression was that of someone who had been struck.

"I have promised I will marry her. She has agreed to wait until I get back, so I am not treating her badly. Why do you say these things to me? Just because you are my sister, it does not mean you can just say what you like, you know."

"Tio, calm down. It is not good for you to get vexed like this. I am sorry. Maybe I should have said nothing. It is your business, not mine."

"But why do you say I do not love her?"

"I am saying nothing now. You just get upset."

"Olivia, I am already upset. Why did you say what you have said?"

Another pause.

"Because in all the time we have been talking, I have not heard you say you love her. You have told me you have made a promise, you have told me her age does not matter, but you have not said you love her. And that is like telling me that you don't"

Tio's exasperated silence hung in the air for a while.

"Tio, once you get there, you will change. England will change you. Even if you don't want it to. Do you think before our ancestor were brought here in chains they wake up one morning and say 'I want to be a Dominican'?"

"Olivia, what are you talking about chains? No-one is making me go to England. I make the decision."

"Brother, you do not understand what I am saying. I am saying that we are Dominican because we find ourselves here and we have to make a way here. Sometimes you become like where you are."

"I am not going to England to stay, Olivia. This is my home. It always will be. I will always be Dominican."

"A person cannot know the future, Tio. Fon Bèlè was my home. Now my home is in Roseau. You know, when I lived in Fon Bèlè, I thought a person who lived here in town were so much better than me. I do not think that now. I know better."

"And do you know better about England?"

Olivia smiled wryly.

"I know you will leave, Tio. I think you left a long time ago. I left Fon Bèlè many years before I did leave there. I make all your meals, I clean and mend your clothes, I tend your wound, I look after you when your brother stick his thumb in your eye. I did all these things. I did not complain."

Tio had never even given a moment's thought to what it must have been like for any of his sisters. They were just there. As Olivia had said, she had not complained. But it was conspicuous how she had left at the first given opportunity. And Philomena, favourite of all his sisters, she had filled Olivia's shoes immediately upon her departure. Surely, she would do the same, no doubt further afield than Roseau. Everyone, it seemed, was either leaving or plotting their departure.

"Your mind is across the water, Tio. It is right that you will go. I will be sad to see you leave because I may not see you again."

"I will come back."

"You cannot know that, brother. Only Papa Dieux can know such things. Come, eat some broth."

Here, now, in Olivia's home, Tio felt too ill for further debate. Bother him as it may that everyone seemed to believe he had behaved toward Clara in less than good faith, this debate would have to wait until another day. Everyone seemed to think they knew him better than he knew himself. Why? Were they saying the same things to Clara? It was infuriating.

For all of this, he knew Olivia was on his side, just as a mother would have been. She tended him, just as a mother would have tended him until confident that he had regained his strength sufficient to make the journey.

He felt a momentary surge of shame at having made a snap judgment about her circumstances, perhaps even having looked down on her without intending to.

Had his father perhaps given Olivia the same speech as he had given him when he was small – marking out a place in the world and tending it, no matter how small or humble? Why should his sister's place automatically be inferior simply because she was his father's daughter?

After all, this neighbour, whose face he had not seen, whose voice he had only ever heard, had shown kindness. She, never having met him, had fed him and given him a warm coat, once owned by her late husband. For all he knew, perhaps one day he may come to consider himself fortunate to fare as well as her.

Olivia had come away from Fon Bèlè, from Penville, from the rugged north, and ended up here in this tiny patch, with a seemingly absent husband and the most modest of dwellings. And yet for all that, she seemed happy, and the place – modest as it was – was hers. She had found her place in this world. It was time for Tio Mourillon to find his.

Colonial Office
15 Victoria Street
London SW1

23rd March 1956

MEMORANDUM

THE POSSIBILITIES OF EMPLOYING COLONIAL LABOUR IN THE UNITED KINGDOM, WITH NOTES ON THE NUMBER OF VACANCIES IN PRINCIPAL UNDERMANNED INDUSTRIES

Throughout the past 18 months, a great deal has been done, by redeployment of British labour and by the importation of foreign workers to remedy the current state of imbalance in the British labour force.

Since March 1948, progress has been made in building up the labour forces of industries within which the said imbalance lies, and this is now amongst the government's highest priorities. In spite of all of these efforts, however, agriculture, coalmining and iron and steel industries are still undermanned.

NOTES ON SEPARATE INDUSTRIES

IRON AND STEEL INDUSTRY

2,000 to 3,000 skilled workers (male) are urgently required, but the Trade Unions have throughout been opposed to the engagement of skilled foreign workers and it is to be doubted whether many West Indians would, in fact, possess the requisite skill for this work. Some West Indians were placed in employment as unskilled labourers, but there is no longer any real shortage of that class of worker.

IRON ORE MINES

There is an immediate demand for 400 unskilled men, but the mines are situated in out of the way places where there be little or no accommodation. The work is very unpopular with British workers.

P Jeffries

Ministry of Labour and National Service
Regional Office
Sunlight House
Quay Street
Manchester 3

2nd April 1956

Mr. Jeffries

As you know, there is some unemployment in the Colonies, and as there is alleged to be a manpower shortage in Britain, the idea has occurred to the Colonial Office that they should get rid of some of their troubles and give us some help in ours by a scheme of bringing Colonials into this country. The thing has been going the rounds for some time but now finally an Interdepartmental Committee has been set up and I understand that its first meeting is next week.

My personal view is that these people would be far more trouble than they are worth. As I understand it, they would come here voluntarily and under no obligation to take work in any particular industry. It is unlikely, therefore, that it would be possible to place them where they would be useful. They might very well cause difficulties with the trade unions, who are singularly insensitive to the ties of the Commonwealth when it comes to a threat of unemployment. If, therefore, we do agree to some people coming, it would have to be on the distinct understanding that we were doing this as a gesture to the Colonials and not because we thought it would help us very much.

From your point of view, therefore, are two points of note.

(a) The general position just stated, namely, that if we agree to anything it is out of altruism and not out of self-interest.

(b) To what extent any of these persons are an exception to the above rule, they must enter under the strict proviso of finding useful employment.

F Young Esq.

CHAPTER 5

UPSIDE DOWN

Atlantic Ocean - April 1956

Her Britannic Majesty's Principal Secretary of State for Foreign and Commonwealth Affairs Requests and requires in the Name of Her Majesty all those whom it may concern to allow the bearer to pass freely without let or hindrance, and to afford the bearer such assistance and protection as may be necessary.

The SS Auriga crept slowly and inexorably north-eastwards towards Spain. Built on the Clyde and named the Ruahine, it had been refurbished and renamed seven years ago was now in its last gasps of life as an Italian owned passenger cargo ship.

Its journey had started in April in La Guaira in Venezuela, from which it had island-hopped to Curaçao, Trinidad, Grenada and Martinique, before finally stopping at Roseau, Dominica. From there it was on to Antigua, Monserrat and finally its largest embarkation at Kingston, Jamaica. By then, there would be eleven hundred souls on board, finally setting off across the mighty Atlantic, first stop Vigo after approximately twenty days at sea, then on to Le Havre and finally disembarkation scheduled for May 13 at Southampton.

It had not been possible for anyone other than Olivia to wave Tio off, given that the Auriga anchored off Roseau, several hours from Portsmouth and the North. She bade him a tearful goodbye and gave his cousin and travelling companion, Manuel LeBlanc, strict instructions to take care of her younger brother.

Tio and Manuel boarded one of the small boats that ferried passengers from shore to the Auriga and had been astounded to see hundreds of fellow passengers also leaving.

Embarkation - tedious and chaotic in equal measures – required that each passenger state his or her line of work and their eventual destination upon arrival in England for entry into the ship's manifest. The Italian ship's clerk entered Tio's name as Benjamin Mourillon rather than Benoit, throwing Tio into a minor panic, thinking it may complicate his onward travel. The queue was too large and the clerk's English too poor to rectify the error, so the mistake stood. Tio was on board, that would have to do for now.

Labourers, seamstresses, housemaids, mechanics, carpenters, agricultural workers, masons, tailors, painters, clerks and planters such as Tio were all thrown into the melee. How, he wondered, would his tiny island that had almost been his whole world manage with all of these people leaving at once?

Tio had been required to visit his former head-teacher, Clive Sorhaindo, before setting off to Roseau. Despite now being an adult, Tio still held his former this sternest and most circumspect of men in some considerable awe.

Clive Sorhaindo, for his part, seemed genuinely pleased to see his former pupil. Although never effusive, he gladly conversed with Tio for some time about his thoughts and aspirations, and silently welled with pride as Tio regaled him with an account of his ambition to own a truck, how by way of venturing overseas he intended to fund it, how he was prepared to dig ditches if necessary, to work hard, to do anything to earn money and improve his station in life.

Mr. Sorhaindo's seeming omniscience was a source of both reassurance and foreboding for Tio.

Reassurance came in the form of encouragement that he was journeying to one of the world's great cultural epicentres. Throughout the entirety of his education, Tio had been raised on a daily scholarly diet of all that appertained to the heart of the Empire, the United Kingdom of England, Scotland, Wales and Northern Ireland. Every part of the kingdom was held in equal importance, but naturally, size, population, and sheer practicality dictated that the main concentration of power and prestige lay in England, the heart of which is London. There was an order of things and this, of course, was the right order.

And Tio must never forget that all of the sons and daughters of the Empire were equally loved. As such, they were to be allowed without let or hindrance into its bosom of the mother country, but naturally, their place within the family must reflect their aptitude, breeding, and station in life.

For sure, the world in which Tio Mourillon grew had seemed on the outskirts of the world. Now, finally, he would be journeying to the centre of it - or at least one of the centres. Where indeed was the centre, now he came to think about it? Some said Great Britain, some said France, some said the United States. Who cared? It was not here in Roseau, nor in Portsmouth, nor in any place where he heard daily *'mwen mal' - life is hard for me*, that was for sure.

"Young men such as yourself are in many ways pioneers, Benoit. In past years, pioneers were always thought to venture from east to west, but you are heading in the opposite direction."

A gentle pride rose up in Tio as his former teacher spoke. Praise from Mr. Sorhaindo was praise indeed. A simple but profound choice made, people seemingly held Tio in very different esteem. Yes, it was true that some took an altogether negative view of him leaving – quite why he could not say. Perhaps it was envy. Perhaps they thought Tio not so much to be enhancing himself, but deserting his compatriots.

Let them think what they want, thought Tio. Would any of them pay for, or even contribute to his upkeep in these hardest of times?

After all, according to a man whose standing and reputation was unimpeachable, whose opinion Tio truly respected, he was a pioneer.

As for foreboding, that came in the form of Mr. Sorhaindo's sage advice on how Tio must conduct himself, how he must be diligent, hard-working, how he must seek the company of the industrious, not the dissolute. He must not only be law-abiding but only ever seek the company of likeminded souls.

And yet, it seemed, there was something he was not saying, something he was distinctly reticent about. Perhaps this was because it contradicted the narrative he had fed Tio and his fellow pupils throughout their school years.

But now Tio was an adult, he had already been exposed to it. In this account of history, England had been an inattentive lover who had once thought Dominica worth fighting for against another suitor, France, only to neglect her once that fight had been won and everything of virtue taken.

France, by contrast, had bestowed marriage, wealth, and adoration upon Dominica's sisters, Martinique and Guadeloupe. Now, years later, it was as if some of Dominica's children were coming home to visit, perhaps even to stay, like the offspring of a long-forgotten mistress, unsure of their familial legitimacy.

Perhaps Mr. Sorhaindo wanted to say something to that effect. If so, he chose not to. Ever one for an apt quotation from classic literature, This most erudite of men waxed lyrical as in days of old.

"To travel hopefully is a better thing than to arrive, Benoit."

Tio felt a sudden momentary surge of panic as he searched his mind for the meaning, lest suddenly corporal punishment be dispensed. Then he stopped searching. It was quite obvious, really.

He may not like England when he got there.

Tio's father, Ton Ton Pierre, by contrast, opted to dispense advice as if writing a telegram.

"Vaplé ou ka Mourillon." Remember you are a Mourillon.

It made no sense. What else could he be?

Tio's father had never really been one for extended speeches. The only one he could ever recall was when he was a child, Pierre had spoken to him about the importance of the land Tio was to inherit, how he needed to tend it well, ensure it remained in the family, and respect its borders. No, his speeches were rare, but his father clearly inspected his instruction to be heard once but heeded forever.

He was to remember he was a Mourillon. What did that even mean?

Tio gained at least a hint of what it meant when his name was being entered into the passenger manifest. It had bothered Tio that his name was entered incorrectly. He did not know why. It just did. What, after all, did he have that was more important than his name? Wherever he went he would take it, all that it meant, who he was, whose he was.

Pain and discomfort from the wound from Tio's machete mishap had dominated the first few days of the journey. What made things worse was the constant overwhelming aroma of fish and chips emanating from the ship's galley so that combined with pain-induced nausea made it impossible for him to find his sea legs. Consequently, the contents of his stomach were poured daily into the Atlantic for eight consecutive days.

It was a mystery why the Italian crew should choose to make fish and chips the sole gastronomic offering to the captive passengers. All of the Caribbean islanders were used to a very different and far more varied diet. Perhaps the galley staff thought it would be helpful to acquaint West Indian palates with English food.

"We are preparing you for what you will eat in England," was the most they would offer when quizzed.

Whatever their thinking, the end effect was to give Tio a distaste for fish and chips and its smell for several years to come.

Now, as the low, dull throb that had coursed through Tio's hand gradually subsided, his consciousness could finally divert from the searing pain of the last few days to the journey ahead and what it may hold, as he and his travelling companion gazed out to sea from the taffrail at the stern of the SS Auriga.

"Who would have guessed that so much sea existed in this world?" asked Manuel.

"Not me."

Tio was dressed in white shorts, a calypso patterned shirt and robust leather sandals, Manuel more formally in beige cotton trousers, white shirt, and smart shoes.

"Days of sea. Weeks of sea!" exclaimed Manuel.

Tio was glad to simply be able to see the sea instead of the bottom of a vomit filled bucket.

"Why are we always here near the back of the boat?"

"The back of the boat is called the stern."

"Why are we always at the stern?"

"There are some people at the front of the… at the bow I don't want to meet right now."

"Tell me, now. Who is he?"

"It is that big Antiguan fellow. I owe mister some money at cards."

"Will he be troublesome?"

"Not if he nah see me. Anyway, there are plenty Dominicans if there is trouble."

Manuel gestured towards two men, Joseph and Ernest, within earshot, a small distance away. Tio did not mind Ernest, but he had little patience for Joseph and desperately hoped Manuel would not call them over.

Joseph Baptiste could never simply converse, he always had to dominate a conversation, if indeed a conversation was what it was – monologue might be a more appropriate word, dispersed with the occasional opening for anyone who was the butt of his jokes to grunt a response.

"We can't be fighting. The captain says we won't be allowed in England if there is trouble. He says they will take us to Jamaica and leave us there," said Tio.

"Bwoy, you really are a Penville goat. You think they will turn the ship around? Hah! Nobody is going anywhere."

"I may be a goat, but this goat knows how to keep his money in his pocket. Do you see me hiding from anyone?"

"True," Manuel laughed. "So, my friend, where are you going when you get to England? Is he London?"

"No, Lincoln."

"Lincoln? Is he big like London?"

"I don't know. My brothers are there working in a steel factory. I am joining them."

"So how did they know to get the job in the steel factory?"

Tio was about to speak, but evidently, his blank expression was sufficient answer for Manuel.

"Did they already know how to make steel?"

"Manuel, what are you talking about? Who in Dominica knows about making steel?"

"But that is my question, boy. How can they know to find work there if they don't already have the knowledge and the skill?"

"I don't know! They must teach you when you get there."

By now, the conversation had aroused the interest of the two Dominicans close by, Ernest and Joseph.

"What skill do your brother have?" asked Joseph.

"Gabriel is a carpenter. They are both carpenters."

"That make no sense," added Manuel, "how can you use wood in a steel factory?"

"I didn't say they are doing carpenter thing in the factory. Maybe that is just how they get the job first."

Tio was feeling quite defensive now. It seemed quite apparent that none of them actually knew how things worked in their destination country, but somehow all the conjecture was directed at him as if somehow he was the authority simply on the basis of having siblings already there.

"I don't think you can go and work in the steel factory, Tio. You must have skills like engineer to work there."

Joseph's quite vocal speculation was in danger of drawing Tio into a full-blown argument. He found the whole idea of sailing across the world and living thousands of miles from home precarious enough. His 'friends' were just heaping worry upon worry, as they were ever prone.

"England," pontificated Joseph, oblivious to Tio's irritation, "England have some of the most skilled engineer in the world. They invent the train and electricity and lots of tings."

"So what?" protested Tio, "my father is the most skilled carpenter in Dominica. People come from Guadeloupe and Martinique so he work for them."

Joseph knew better than to insult a friend's father. They could, by all means, show disregard for the offspring, but the parent was never to be disrespected.

"Look at this ship," continued Joseph regardless, "they build it in England. The officer tell me yesterday."

"He said they build the ship in Scotland," interjected Ernest.

"That's what I say."

"But Scotland isn't England! That is like saying Dominica is Antigua."

"Ernest, hear me, now! Why you vex me so when I'm telling a story about the ship?"

"Boy, tell the story. But Scotland isn't England."

"The officer tell me this ship is in New Zealand all the time before now."

"So?" Tio was distinctly unimpressed.

"So, I tell you they good engineer. They make a ship that sail upside down."

Everyone but Tio burst into laughter, but even he cracked a reluctant smile.

"You think I'm bloody stupid."

"Nah, boy. We think you Penvillian goat-la. Up in the north, in the mountain, where the air too thin."

"So Tio, your brothers," enquired Ernest, "they write to you about England?"

"Sometimes. Not much."

"And?"

"And what?"

"What do they say about England? Do they like it there?"

"They say the weather is very cold. Not like Dominica."

"Yes? And what else?"

"They say West Indians are not treated with respect there."

"Why?"

"I don't know. Anyway, why are you asking me these things? How should I know?"

Nothing further was said. Each of the men gazed seawards into the distance, each consumed in his own private thoughts.

"Everything is upside down," said Joseph, "We supposed to go to a better country, but the food is worse, the weather is worse. How do we know if everything is not worse?"

Footsteps approached from their rear. For a moment, Manuel worried they may belong to Antiguan feet.

"Mi scusi, fiammiferi?"

The four men stared absently at the Italian deck hand now before them.

"Matches?"

Ernest handed him a box of matches.

"Grazie."

The man lit his cigarette stub, nodded his thanks and went back to swabbing the deck as the four bemused passengers took their ease and looked on.

Manuel broke the silence.

"Maybe it is like you say, Joseph. The world is become upside down."

PART TWO

England - 1956

CHAPTER 6

ARRIVAL

London – May 1956

TIO

What have I done? What was I thinking? Absolutely everything is grey. The sky is grey, the towns are grey, the streets and the houses are grey. The expressions on people's faces are grey. Everything is grey!

I went to the market to buy some bananas today. What? The price they charge for one bunch of bananas here is more than the price I would charge for twenty bunches at home! How can that be?

When I complained, the man swear at me, he tell me to go back home and call me names. When I ask why he calls me those names, he says it is I who have the problem.

I do not understand these people. Why would anyone think you are a bad person when they have never met you, when they do not know you?

I had heard about this type of thing from my brother Gabriel before I came, and yet still I was unprepared.

Many of the people here do not like people like me. Some will say they do not like you; others say nothing, but you can see it in their eyes, you can hear it in their voices, and see it in their faces.

One thing you must understand about this place is that you cannot just walk down any street here. You come to a corner of a quiet street, you ask yourself 'is it safe for me to go down that street?' You tell yourself 'no', so you stick to where you think it is safe. This is not a good country for a Dominican to be alone.

Every now and then you will meet someone who is friendly, and they make you feel that it is safe here. But then you talk to someone who is unfriendly. How am I to know who is friendly and who is unfriendly before talking to them?

They say to me I am not wanted, that I should go back to where I come from. That is not what I was told in Dominica. There they tell me that England is open, that I am helping England build back up after the war. Which one is true?

I wish I did not need to ask anything from them. But I need everything from them. I need them to tell me the directions down each street; I need them to sell me the food I must eat; I need them to tell me where I can find a roof over my head to stay tonight. Everything. Things would be so much better if I wanted nothing, if I could be independent like my father at home.

Home. I wish I was back home. I wish that right now I was sat in front of Clara's house, eating ground provision and mountain chicken. I would even be able to tolerate the looks of contempt from her mother, who hates my guts, who thinks I am unworthy of her educated daughter.

I wonder what Clara is doing right now. I wonder if she is teaching her children at the government school. Her children admire her, just like everyone admired her father. She did not need to come to places such as this. She can make a living for herself in Dominica. If only I had had more than an elementary education, there would have been no need for me to stray so far away from home.

This is not the country that they speak about in her poems! I have never heard such poem as talk about everything being cold, grey and miserable.

Home. Things are so much better at home. We may not have much there, but we have family, and people there are kind and friendly. Well, maybe they are not all friendly, but at least we knew how to deal with those who are not. I do not know how to deal with people here.

Maybe I should have swallowed my pride, allowed my cousin Desmond to shout at me a little. I should have gone back to speak to him again, perhaps in private. That way he could not have humiliated me. He would not have found it so easy to shout at me if it was just the two of us.

I will not be staying here. That is for certain. No, I will not be staying. Why would anyone want to stay in such a place? If I could go home now, I would go. Let them call me all the names they want back in Penville. The names they will call me cannot be as bad as the names that strangers call me here.

At least I understand how the world works back home. The world makes sense there.

The daylight hours are longer here. When it does turn dark, the darkness does not fall so quickly as it does at home. I wish my old teacher Mr. Sorhaindo was here. He knows everything. He would be able to explain why all these things are.

It gets very cold here, especially in the evening. Let me tell you, I have never felt anything like it - and in May! What must it be like in winter? It is like nothing you have ever known before. It goes right through your bones. It makes your toes and your fingers hurt.

Now I understand why Gabriel wrote to me about the clothes I must bring. How do these people stay warm? He says that they have fires in their houses. How can you have a fire in a house without the house catching on fire also? There are so many things I do not understand about this country.

Did the Almighty ever intend for people to live in places such as this, where the sun almost never comes out from behind the clouds? And if the sun shines, people will even stop in the street and discuss it!

What have I come to? W*hat* possessed me to stray so far from home?

And yet, my brothers have survived here. How have they managed? I must ask them for advice. I must ask them how a man such as myself can live in this strange land.

LINCOLNSHIRE – ONE WEEK LATER

"You're the younger brother, aren't you?"

A young, fairly slim blonde woman in her late twenties whom Tio had just passed spoke so softly he barely realised she was speaking to him. She held a cigarette between her fingers and squinted as she drew upon it.

"Theo, is it?" she continued, she was leaning against the doorway of one of the terraced houses, some way from his destination. How odd it was to hear an affectionate name spoken by a complete stranger, thousands of miles from home.

"Tio. It is just a nickname. My name is Benoit."

His name seemed to be of little or no interest to her.

"You don't look much like him. Not bad looking. I can tell you're nothing like he is, though. Man of the world and all that."

Tio's slightly austere military style haircut he had sported at the beginning of the journey had given way to a softer look that suited him better.

He had no idea how to respond. The very existence of the conversation had upset what little sense of balance he possessed. She was obviously referring to one of his brothers, whether Gabriel or Everton was not yet apparent. Evidently, she knew of his impending arrival.

"Tell your brother that Marj says… just tell him she says hello."

"Which one?"

"Of course, how daft of me. Gabriel."

He nodded and went on his way.

The smoke-laden dining room of the two up, two down terraced house in Porter Street heaved with the scent of liquor, the clatter of dominoes and the sound of jovial men, one of whom was Everton, the rest locals.

It occurred to him that this was the first time that he had encountered Englishmen in any sort of social setting. How strange. They seemed just like anyone else, just English, or - more to the point - white. He had encountered some Englishmen in Dominica, of course, but by and large, they were professionals and therefore in positions of authority in the towns such as Portsmouth or Roseau.

On his incoming journey, he had been astounded to see Italian crew members of the SS Auriga doing menial jobs such as scrubbing the decks, throwing the food waste overboard, cleaning up vomit that had not quite made it overboard. His familiarity with the latter stemmed from much of the early part of his journey being sick over the rail.

Tio had expressed some wonderment earlier on the day of his arrival in the northern industrial town of Scunthorpe, watching a group of men digging a hole in the road. Actually, it was one man digging and four advising him as they drew hard on their Woodbine cigarettes.

Later that same day he had sought accommodation. His initial confidence in being able to obtain a roof over his head was quickly punctured after a couple of vain attempts. His first attempt was stymied after seeing a card saying VACANCIES in what looked like a respectable boarding house. The owner had seen him approach the door, suitcase in hand and had hurriedly rotated the card to read NO VACANCIES.

He thought his chances better at the second boarding house when a wizened looking woman in her late forties answered the door.

"Excuse me, madam, your sign says you have a room to rent. Is it still available?" The woman, wearing a flowered apron did not reply, but simply called someone in the rear of the dwelling.

"Harold!"

A scrawny unshaven man wearing a tatty waistcoat came to the door, perhaps fifteen or so years the woman's senior.

"Excuse me, sir, I was wondering if…"

"It's not available any more. There are no vacancies."

The man's demeanour was belligerent, his voice gruff. He came within a few inches of Tio's face. Tio had had little opportunity to wash since leaving London, but he was quite sure he was sure the intense, acrid smell of body odour was not coming from him.

"No?"

"No."

"The sign says there are vacancies."

"Me missus forgot to turn it round. Nothing here. You'll have to try somewhere else."

"Oh, okay. Thank you."

Tio had heard that an Englishman's home is his castle. Evidently, these castles were not accessible to all. Chastened and a little humiliated, he backed away. He could not stand his ground. Tio needed something that from him and it was within his gift to grant or withhold, and the man chose, perhaps even gloried, in doing the latter.

He retreated to a high-street café to mull his options over a hot beverage. Foreign sounds and voices met his ears, foreign aromas his nose, alien sights his eyes. He was in a whirlwind of confusion. Perhaps everyone at home was right. Perhaps he was the last man on earth who should have embarked upon such a journey. What must he have been thinking to have come here?

Think! There must be a way to obtain a roof over his head before dusk. But what? How? It was absolutely clear from the letter he had received before setting off that he would not be able to stay with his brothers. Tio took this as coded language to say that Gabriel must have a woman in tow.

If in doubt, ask a policeman. Upon leaving the café, he approached an extremely large police constable on the high street. The officer eyed him with a mixture of bemusement and surprise. Satisfied that he was neither criminal nor vagrant, the officer was as helpful as he could have hoped under the circumstances.

"I suggest you try Porter Street," he offered, "that's where the Arabs and Somalis usually find rooms. You'll have a much better chance there. Ask for a Nigerian bloke called Ali."

Tio thanked the officer and went on his way, heeding his advice.

Ali Kasim, a former merchant seaman was the first unambiguously friendly face he had seen all day. Ali was known to rent out rooms to all and sundry - Arabs, Africans of all nationalities, South Asians and occasionally West Indians. It just so happened that he had one available bed remaining. Had Tio asked only one day earlier, he was told, there would have had been no room at the inn.

Ali's broad effusive smile exposed several gold teeth. He had a deep voice, which was punctuated intermittently by a high-pitched laugh and a jovial nature. Once the rate had been agreed, he settled Tio into a heavily spice scented room, which for at least a while he would have to share with two Egyptian roommates. It was less than ideal to have to share, but tonight he would sleep safely with a roof over his head, and for that, he was extremely thankful.

Tio had known one or two West Africans who had come ashore in Dominica from various merchant vessels from time to time. They generally enjoyed the relaxed pace of life in the Caribbean for however long or short their stay was, but it had surprised Tio how little he had in common with them. He once ventured to mention this to one African sailor in his sixties who had given the insightful response that it was similar to Americans and English – there was a commonality to a point, but no further.

Ali, however, seemed very easy to talk to. He re-bandaged Tio's by now light dressing, helped him unpack and spent a good deal of time explaining how things worked in England. He explained to Tio how he needed to go to a place called the labour exchange and after that the works office, how he needed to take forms of identification such as his passport, his references, how he needed to insist that he did not want to be assigned to somewhere called the coke ovens, or at least try to insist.

Ali Kasim was an uncommonly kind man. Tio counted himself extremely fortunate to have met him. He strongly suspected that Ali allowed some people to take advantage of his kindness, given his many anecdotes of how he had been stolen from, mugged, and other times attacked seemingly for the fun of it. And yet, for all of this, he remained sanguine about it all as he shrugged and flashed his gold teeth and said 'C'est la vie'.

Newcomer or no newcomer, no-one was going to mug or assault Tio, he determined, nor would he allow the verbal abuse he had received so far to escalate without a fairly firm response. Gabriel and Everton had alluded only very briefly to anything of that sort in their letters. Neither were prolific writers, but they had mentioned that some of the locals were not very friendly and that he needed to be on his guard. Before and during the journey, he filled in gaps in the sparse details of their correspondence with the fruits of his own fertile imagination, the benefit of which was that none of his recent experiences in trying to find accommodation had greatly surprised him.

After his week-long sojourn in London, it had been a wearying couple of days to the point when he finally met his brothers, but it was not without its successes. His earlier visit this morning to the labour exchange had led to a further visit to the works office down on the steelworks, where he had obtained gainful employment.

True, he was a long way from home, but for a man who had never travelled further than neighbouring Martinique and Guadeloupe, he was finally beginning to adapt to his new environment.

And now, arriving at last at his brothers' abode, he was greeted by the clatter of dominoes - the first sight and sound reminiscent of home. That and his brother Everton, of course.

"Tio! Come, boy," Everton boomed, "sit yourself down here. Look, this is my younger brother. This fine gentleman who is giving me all his pennies tonight is John. And that gentleman there is John also. Pour my brother a drink, John."

English John One dutifully obliged.

Everton knew Tio rarely if ever drank, but this was a different country with different rules.

"Don't be looking at me so, little brother. Don't be telling me you nah gonna drink, man. *Everyone* in England drink. If you don't, you die of the cold here."

Everton did not have to oversell it. For this, once Tio really needed a drink, if not just to stop his mind racing for the first time since his arrival. Every sight and sound were utterly new.

Drink poured by John One, Everton continued.

"So, Ali Kasim tell me you have a job already?"

Evidently, the grapevine was as swift here as at home.

"I went down the work office today. I start tomorrow down something called the soot plant?"

"The sinter plant, you mean? And what you will be doing there?"

"Engineer."

The room fell silent, drinking and dominoes paused.

"You have a job as an engineer? I think you should be buying us de drinks, man."

"No way. Must be some sort of mistake," offered John Two, "did they give you a slip?"

"A what?"

"A piece of paper with the job details?"

"Yes, yes. Here is he."

English John Two examined the slip of paper, choked a laugh and handed it to Everton and John One, at which point they all burst into laughter.

"Lubrication engineer. It means a greaser!"

"Greaser? What is greaser?" Tio asked, bewildered.

"Well, put it this way," replied Everton, "don't go to work wearing your best Sunday collar and tie. It is one of the dirtiest job on the work."

Everton's comment prompted another roar of laughter, Tio clearly being the butt of the joke, bringing him to the realisation that not every recollection from home was a thing of warm nostalgia.

"Never mind, lad. Where there's muck there's brass," said John Two.

Tio gave John Two a blank look. He had often required the townspeople to repeat themselves throughout the past two days. He just could not understand what they were saying a lot of the time, their accents were so heavy.

"He means when somewhere is dirty you can earn money there."

"Oh."

"Tio, engineer your brother a drink of water and take it up to him. He need to be up for his night shift. He will be pleased to see you, boy."

Tio scoured the room in search of water.

"No, man. Tap is inside the house. You just turn the tap on."

"Should be no problem to a gifted engineer such as yourself," said John Two.

More laughter. Tio negotiated the indoor tap and made his way upstairs away from the smoke and the din. Two doors ajar, one closed, he peered into the rooms and saw the unmistakable imprint of his father's upbringing – tidiness.

'There is excuse for being poor, but no excuse for being dirty.' Once again, his father's words, seared into the being of all of his sons and daughters, echoed in his mind and gave the dark, alien environment a hint of home from home.

Tio knocked gently on the door before entering, glass in hand. His eldest brother Gabriel was already sat up in bed.

"Tio! Good to see you, boy. It's been a long time." They embraced briefly. "Bwoooyyy, look at what you do to your hand. I know what this foolishness is. You cut your hand with machete!"

Tio looked sheepish. It was indeed a careless thing to do.

"You had a good journey?"

Tio shrugged. "He was okay. It take forever."

"Yes, yes, yes. Long journey, boy, long journey. So, you barely off the boat and the train and already you find work?"

The conversation downstairs had evidently travelled upwards.

"Yes, on the soot… the sint…"

"The sinter plant. They call it Seraphim. You'll soon wish you had never heard that word. Dirty place, very dirty, and dirty job too. But not so dangerous like the ironworks or the mills. Not so much money, though."

It was not the news that Tio wanted to hear. He was not here to admire the scenery, and what scenery he had seen he had not been overly impressed with so far. He was here to earn money. Success or failure hinged solely upon his ability to do so. Working a dirty but relatively safe job was a start, he had already determined that it would be a holding position before obtaining whatever role best enabled him to accrue money quickly.

After that, he would return home, buy the Bedford truck, and establish himself as a man of importance in Dominica. A coherent plan was still intact within his mind, having at least survived the journey, but with one notable omission - he had barely given Clara a passing thought throughout the whole journey. He would write to her, no doubt, once he had found his bearings. What on earth he would say was a different matter.

"An Englishwoman outside said to say hello to you?"

"Yes? Did she tell you her name?"

"She did, but I forget."

"Boy, some messenger you. What did she look like?"

"Light coloured hair. Young, quite pretty."

"Ah. Must be Marjorie. Perhaps want to come and tell me how she doesn't like being married."

"She come to see you when she married?"

"Bwoy, listen to you, straight off the boat. Don't try to tell me that you going to be the first ever Dominican to come here and live like a monk. If you say you are, I will not believe you."

Manuel and Tio had speculated how they would spend their time in England. They discussed how if they been travelling to the United States, where many states had miscegenation laws, consorting with the local women would have affected their liberty, perhaps even their safety. To Tio's knowledge, no such laws existed in England. That said, he was not sure what ground rules existed here, nor, for that matter, the rules he was setting for himself. There would be plenty of time to think of all that.

"This is a *very* different country, boy. Women nah do as they told here like they do at home. Remember that."

"Don't you worry that her husband will come round and be troublesome?"

"No, boy. Not unless he come with plenty of his friends. They have a saying here – you make your bed, you lie in it. That's what she have to do. And I have a saying – I have lie in this bed, you are going to help me make it. Come."

Once done, both sat on the freshly made bed as Gabriel dressed.

"You bring plenty clothes to work in, lickle brother?"

Tio explained what clothes he had. Gabriel duly informed him that they would be completely inadequate for the English climate, and definitely unsuitable for the place in which he would be working. Not to worry, he said, Tio could go down to the army surplus store and buy some the next day.

Downstairs, Gabriel crafted some rudimentary sandwiches in the bottle strewn kitchen. He then wrapped them in foil and placed them in a sturdy looking tin, which he placed in a leather bag under the seat of his battered looking Raleigh bicycle. A brief swig of beer and the briefest of farewells later, he cycled off in the direction of the works entrance, little over a mile away.

Tio possessed neither the energy nor will to exchange jovialities with the assembled drinkers and domino players. Excuses made, he headed back to his lodgings. Ali had agreed to wake him in good time for his morning appointment at the works office, where he was to report for work. By the time he approached his bed, oblivious to the loud snoring of one of his Egyptian roommates, he was too tired even to undress. He fell asleep fully clothed on top of the bed, the rigours of the journey and subsequent search for accommodation having finally got the better of him.

Vielle Case Govt. School
Dominica BWI

To Whom it may concern.

This is to certify that I have known Tio Mourillon from the time he attended school at the age of five years.

During his school career, he had always proved to be diligent, obedient and respectful, and I never had any cause to punish him for breach of discipline. From the time he left school, I have never heard anything against his character and am pleased to recommend him for any job which can improve his status in life.

Clive Sorhaindo
Head Teacher

16 April 1956

CHAPTER 7

CATHEDRAL

"You not on your small island now, boy. We are in a very, *very* different place," Oswald Lawless, the Bajan, remarked to Tio as they stood at the entrance of Frodingham Melting Shop peering into the darkness that was penetrated by sporadic bursts of light and heat.

"Have you ever seen anything like this before?"

"No. Of course not," said Tio.

"I can't even see the end of the building."

The two Caribbean small islanders watched transfixed. It was the first time they had been in such a place. Gabriel and Ali Kasim had earlier tried to give Tio some forewarning of what he would likely encounter on his first day, but nothing he had said had prepared Tio for this.

Tio gazed down the long rectangular mill, which appeared to all the world a huge industrial cathedral. A cacophony of metal-upon-metal sounds accompanied by great behemoth machines doing he knew not what. Languid shafts of light pierced the dust-laden air and petered out at the sand floor. An overhead gantry crane transported a large iron ladle from which sparks flew in all directions from its molten steel contents.

A bare-chested man climbed down from a fork lift truck and strode towards another man wearing a flat cap and overalls. A torrent of screams and curses ensued, practically none of which could be comprehended by the two onlookers. They then disengaged, appearing to only narrowly avert a physical altercation.

Back in Dominica, Father Leutens, the only European Tio had known to any great extent, had warned him before his departure.

"You will not remain good Catholics if you go to England, Benoit. Most people there are not in the Catholic faith. You must guard yourselves against such things."

Tio had been unsure what 'such things' were. He had assumed at the time Father Leutens had been speaking about matters to do with women. Now, he seemed less sure. Perhaps this was what he meant.

Tio had thought he was coming to one of the great cradles of civilisation. This seemed less civilised than any place he had ever been. It was not so much civilisation before him as its very underbelly.

How could anyone survive in such a place? How did they not choke from the fumes within a few hours? Were some of the fumes toxic, just as the volcanic gases were at Trois Pitons back in Dominica? The questions kept coming, dizzying and unceasing.

The answer to at least one question was not encouraging. He already knew – some did not survive.

And yet, for all of that, his older brothers had been through all of this and were clearly still living to tell the tale. It must surely be achievable. But how?

Tio had planned to work in England for a while and leave. With liquid fire dancing across the air, would he even live to do so?

"This is what they don't tell you when you back at home when you sitting under the tree eating jelly coconut," said Oswald.

Tio released a mirthless laugh. No words came.

Earlier that morning, in what could loosely be described as an induction.

Tio, Oswald, and two English fellow co-starters had earlier been given the briefest of pep talks on safety in which they had been placed under no illusion that safety was, in fact, their own responsibility more so than anyone else's. They were given a list of things they should not do, the vast majority of which they could relate to in the slightest. Tips on what not to do near a slag runner were of little use if you neither knew what slag nor a runner were in the first place. Mike Astle's hurried answer was to be patient, they would find out in due time.

"Any questions?"

"Yes, I have some questions."

"Make them quick, Lawless. We have to be on our way."

"Do many people have accidents?"

"A few, yes."

"Is anyone killed here?"

"Don't laugh, lads. It's an important question. The answer is yes, certainly. It's a dangerous place, make no mistake about it. It's not for everyone."

"Do they lose arms and legs?"

"Yes."

"Fingers, feet?"

"Yes, of course."

"What happens if you get hurt?"

"Try not to."

"But what if you do?"

"It will be harder for you to earn money then. Try not to get hurt. I knew one chap who lost his right arm in the Heavy Section Mill, another who lost his left down Redbourn Melting Shop. Come Christmas, when either of them was given a pair of gloves for a present, they'd send each other the glove they didn't need. See? You have to make the most of things."

There was a murmur of nervous laughter throughout the room.

"Who will teach us what to do?"

"Stupid question. Blokes you'll be working with. Who else?"

"When do we get paid?"

"Tell you what. Let's start the job first before we start worrying about payday, eh?"

"Is there somewhere to eat?"

"Not where you're going. Bring your own snap with you."

"Do we get clothes and boots?"

"No."

"When do we get paid?"

"Enough questions. This way, lads."

At the Seraphim Plant, Tio was introduced to a lexicon of terms completely alien to him. His world was now a confusing array of crushers, coolers, conveyors, screens, hoppers and fans. Iron ore, limestone, and coke went in, sinter came out that could be loaded – or charged – into the furnace. It was not necessary for him to receive instruction on how any of it worked, given that he was unskilled labour. All he was required to know was that the plant had a multitude of moving parts and his job was to ensure that they kept moving, making sure he did not get trapped or injured in the process. Why? Because first of all, it would cause a production delay, and secondly, it would mean the loss of body parts.

If a conveyor motor, a fan or a roller was noisy or hot, his role was to note its location, ensure that an entry was made into the log so the maintenance fitters would attend whatever ailed the machinery. Armed with a grease gun, occasionally an oil can, a few minutes' instruction was sufficient. Within two or three days, Tio probably knew as much as he was ever going to about the job.

His occupation as a planter had required far more expertise and aptitude than this. At least that had required knowledge of horticulture, animal care, even commerce. What use was it to compare the two? Had that line of work paid enough, he would be back in Dominica raising poetry reciting children with Clara right now.

Getting used to the dirt took far longer than a few days. Industrial dirt, democratic dirt, affecting Englishman, Irishman, Somali, Bangladeshi, Ukrainian, Pole and West Indian equally, and seeping into his hands, his hair, his lungs, his eyes, his very being.

He had come here to work hard. Work was precisely what he was going to do. If he and his forefathers could survive - no, not just survive, but thrive - in the mountainous terrain of Penville, then he could do so here. The noise, the dirt, the danger, the ferocity of the environment, he would get used to. There was no choice.

The next day he went to Parker & White's Army Surplus Store and bought himself two pairs of decent work clothes. He would probably need three. He could come back for more in a few days if he needed to. He would only ever be a newcomer once. As each day on the works passed, everything would become more and more familiar and he would become more acclimatised.

The main thing, for now, was to ensure he returned to the Caribbean with no significant parts of his person missing.

CHAPTER 8

BRUTE AND BEASTLY

Wyn Owen strode up the Scunthorpe High Street unaccompanied. It was shortly after seven o'clock on a Thursday evening. He generally tried to avoid town around this hour. Someone spilling out of a pub, fuelled by liquid courage may easily try to confront him. The street had a distinct Wild West feel to it of late. Many of the pubs were quite raucous, strip clubs were springing up here and there. If someone were to try and confront him, it would have to be someone who did not know him - those who knew him generally liked and respected him, and even those few who neither liked nor respected him knew well enough not to go against the wishes of those who did.

The last thing he would want on an evening such as this was to become embroiled in any kind of unseemly fracas. A church elder, after all, should not be given to drunkenness, should not lack self-control, nor be greedy, nor violent. The members of his small Baptist church were more than confident that he fulfilled all the above criteria. Wyn, however, thought himself to fall at the last hurdle. It, therefore, begged the question: if the epistles to Timothy and Titus stated specifically that one must not be a brawler, what constituted one? Did it mean an incorrigible man who continuously engaged in violence or one who may perhaps have a propensity to lose control from time to time, but was determined to refrain? Those of his congregation with whom he had discussed this had told him it was the former, not the latter. But is not an alcoholic resolute to never drink, he had replied, up to the point until he or she does so? Surely, the principle was the same when one's weakness was violence. To this, he received the answer that even the Apostle Peter had been no shrinking violet from time to time.

To those of the congregation with whom he had conversed about this matter, the very fact he asked these questions so earnestly of himself showed that he was a good man, the very man they needed for the role as an elder. They also knew that working on the steelworks was no picnic. Moreover, the meekness required of Wyn was not synonymous with weakness, they said, but restrained strength.

Originally from Neath, South Wales, Wyn was part of the influx of skilled workers brought in to staff the Scunthorpe plant in the forties and fifties. Generations of experience such as his, gained from working at Port Talbot steelworks, was of great value to a booming steel town starved of manpower.

He and his wife had decided to answer the call for workers from the valleys to move to the Industrial North of England. They had both worried about leaving the picturesque, accessible beauty of the valleys for the agricultural blandness of Lincolnshire. Generally knowledgeable of history, the only fact he knew of Lincolnshire was that it was *'the most brute and beastly shire of the whole realm'*. A long-deceased monarch had coined the term, he vaguely recalled. In mitigation to this was that he and his family would be moving near the birthplace of the John and Charles Wesley, regarded by Wyn and his congregation as heroes of the faith.

Wyn's own grandfather had been a leading light of the Welsh Revival at the beginning of the twentieth century.

Likewise, his father had been integrally involved with a man called Rees Howells, famous in his time for his intercessory prayer ministry. Wyn Senior had not thought it unusual to rub shoulders with men like the Emperor Haile Selassie of Ethiopia, who visited Swansea in the mid-thirties. Surrounded by so great a cloud of witnesses, Wyn Owen walked.

Wyn Owen was not expected to live a life of insignificance. A man who is skilled with his hands, said Wyn Senior, may stand before kings. Wyn had replied that he had no skill or trade to boast of as such, so what king would he ever stand before? You have one, son, his father had replied, but it may take you some time to find out what it is, to find the area in which you excel above and beyond your peers.

Over many years Wyn had discovered his talent – he was a natural, but reluctant, leader. He voiced this frustration to his father. Ever the man for a scripture or an allegory or both, Wyn senior simply told him one man may chase a thousand, but two may chase ten thousand – a single person may achieve great things, but several unified may achieve exponentially more. Wyn had the ability to bring people together, said Wyn Senior, and that was not to be gainsaid.

Still, leadership, whether sought or imposed, was invariably lonely and isolating. Therefore, over the years Wyn did his level best not to seek promotion in any field of endeavour. So, on the steelworks he was a charge-hand instead of a foreman, in church he was an elder rather than a pastor.

Prominence should not be his chief concern, his father counselled. True leadership was in doing the right thing, no matter how unpopular, and eventually bringing people along with him. That was Wyn's unique gift, his father said.

Midway down the High Street, Wyn caught the bus that took him onto the Frodingham works. After he alighted, he walked the remaining distance to the South Ironworks.

In a makeshift communal area, he changed into his work clothes, transforming from private citizen and family man into employee and servant of United Steel Companies Ltd. Two decades of working in the iron and steel industry had rendered him impervious to the room's overpowering odours and unconscious of its distinctive cacophony. Of variations to the norm, however, he was very much conscious.

Today, something was not quite right, something in the air. There were quite a few new faces, some quite evidently were not from anywhere local. In the present climate, that could mean trouble.

A small but rowdy group announced themselves into the room. Shane Phillips and Iain McKay considered themselves pack leaders of sorts amongst the labourers. The influx of newcomers demanded a reassertion of the pecking order. More often than not, that usually meant someone getting hurt and the more public the spectacle, the better.

Phillips paced the entirety of a long wooden bench as if performing a military inspection. He neared a young Irishman seated upon the bench, whose back was turned to him. Two of the man's workmates stepped forward to warn Phillips away from their friend. He smiled wryly, then continued in the direction of the solitary man at the edge of the bench.

Before Wyn or anyone else could comprehend what was happening, there was an explosion of noise and rage. A large, powerfully built Nigerian man in a state of almost complete undress was suffering a hail of kicks and punches from Shane Phillips, himself even larger than the Nigerian.

The recipient of the blows was prostrate and was by now succumbing to a sickening assault. Accompanying each dull thud was a cry of pain, all but drowned out by fevered shouts and cheers. As Wyn pressed through the onlookers, he could see the man at the feet of his assailants, curled up in a foetal position.

Phillips wound his leg back, as if preparing to kick a ball. Wyn's instincts kicked in before he had a chance to consider any possible consequences. He threw his arms around Phillips, levering him away from his intended victim, to the collective groan of the crowd. It was a risky intervention to make with such a large and dangerous man.

A few unintelligible curses and threats were cast towards Wyn from Shane Phillips, and still more from Iain McKay. For all the visible display of anger, Wyn sensed that Phillips may perhaps be relieved that he had saved him from permanently damaging his victim, not through concern for the man himself. Anything further would likely cause serious harm, and serious harm would mean yet another stint in prison. It would be the second time within twelve months. Phillips had accomplished what he had wanted for now.

As the crowd filtered away, Wyn leaned over, about to assist the injured man, when suddenly he felt himself being shoved slowly, but forcefully away from the Nigerian.

Two West Indians, both looking tense and agitated, stood over the prostrate man, as if to indicate that they would take over from this point forward. Wyn recognised their faces as men who had worked on the ironworks for some considerable time – unlike the Nigerian. As if to gesture that he meant no harm, Wyn offered the palms of his hands. This seemed to assuage their anger, though why they should have been angry with him, he had no idea.

The two Caribbean islanders gingerly raised the injured man from the ground to the accompaniment of moans and blood-spattered coughs. His left eye was completely closed, his right eye half open and heavily bloodshot. The sound of raucous laughter rang out in the distance from those who gloried in what they had witnessed.

As the victim was assisted towards the exit, presumably in the direction of the medical centre, only the younger of the West Indians remained facing Wyn. No words were exchanged, only a nod from the younger man, which Wyn duly reciprocated.

Wyn understood that they were upset, but for the life of him could not see why they should be upset with him. Had he not put his own safety on the line to help the man? Perhaps, amidst all the confusion, they thought he was a participant in the assault.

No matter, he had not intervened for thanks. He barely knew why he intervened at all, given Phillips and McKay's fearsome reputations. Whatever he had done, he had done instinctively and he was not sorry.

Everton Mourillon had insisted on taking the injured man to the medical centre alone. Tio, he said, needed to get to his place of work, as he was starting his shift. Everton had just completed his. The distant triumphant laughter was the only thing of which Tio was conscious. And his anger at what he had seen and heard burned.

Eight days later, to Wyn's great relief, the Nigerian showed up for work. Thankfully, his injuries appeared less severe than had been suspected. Either that or he was made of sturdier stuff than most.

Wyn observed him from a distance in his bruised and bandaged state, each movement seemingly taking three times longer than it should.

"Couple of black eyes, mate? You can get something for that."

The man's tormentor, a thin emaciated looking individual wearing a flat cap, known as Skinny Pat, made his way over to Wyn.

"You hear what I asked him? I said have you got a couple of…"

"I heard you. You're very brave, Pat, considering he can barely move."

"What do you mean? It was only a joke. What do you mean? Do you like that sort, then?"

Wyn considered the question unworthy of a response, fixing instead his attention upon a commotion at the opposite end of the changing area.

At the opposite end of the changing room, Tio Mourillon and Oswald Lawless readied themselves for work. Both men saw Shane Phillips and Iain McKay enter the room and sit a short distance away from them.

The arrival of Phillips and McKay invoked very different responses from Tio and Oswald. Tio seethed quietly, restraining himself moment by moment, telling himself that he could not afford to lose his job by becoming embroiled in something ugly.

Oswald, by contrast, was by now conversing with Phillips and McKay, apparently trying his very best to ingratiate himself with them. He laughed along at whatever terms they used to demean him, echoing them to supposed greater hilarity. He mimicked monkey noises whenever he was called one. Tio would rather have died than debase himself in such a way. How could Oswald Lawless live with himself? Quite easily, apparently. His reward was encouragement and acceptance.

"You're alright, mate," McKay said to Oswald in his deep Scottish brogue, "not sure about your friend there, though."

"Oh, he's not my friend," Oswald had replied without a moment's thought, "he is from a different island. They barely even speak English there."

It was the only thing Oswald said that Tio agreed with. They were not friends, nor would they ever be.

As Tio's sense of indignation rose, he felt determined to say something. Discretion got the better of him. No, better to say nothing. Better to bite his tongue and just get through the day. His brothers had done it, surely, he could also.

Perhaps Tio should take a leaf out of Oswald's book right now, roll with the punches and just laugh at the whole situation. It seemed to work for him.

Who was he kidding? Tio could no more do that than pluck out his own eyes. He was not made that way. He was a Mourillon from Penville, the son of Pierre Mourillon, a man of character, who would stand even if he had to stand alone. So instead, he kept his counsel, determined to see the day through without incident.

Shane Phillips did not share Tio's goal of seeing out the day without incident. Quite the opposite. Catching sight of the Nigerian across the room, he was more than a little surprised to see him. Surely the beating he had handed out a week ago was clear enough a message. Evidently not. Slowly, he approached his recent victim, who by now was well aware of Phillips' presence, and yet his demeanour was inexplicably calm.

As Wyn watched Phillips approach from across the room, his heart began racing.

"Come back for a second helping, eh? I thought I told you not to show your face back in here again."

Phillips raised his hand in an exaggerated manner, then brought it down on the man's shoulder in a raucous slap.

"I'll let you off this time. Takes some nerve to come back after our last little conversation. You seem a bit nervous, a bit jumpy. Any particular reason for that?"

By now the room was almost silent.

"Speak up! I asked you a question. I know you wouldn't want to hurt my feelings by not answering. I'm sure everyone in the room would like to know the answer. So, I'm going to ask you the question once more. Is there any reason why you're looking so jumpy?"

The hapless recipient of Phillips' renewed attention murmured something barely audible.

"Speak up! I can't hear…"

In a blurred instant, the Nigerian pulled free from Phillips' grasp and threw a powdery substance into his tormentor's eyes, rendering not only Phillips but several in the immediate vicinity momentarily helpless.

It bought him sufficient time to strike several hard blows upon his onetime assailant. Phillips' expression of pained surprise was absolute. By the time anyone could intervene, Phillips was barely conscious. Notably, none of the onlookers had rushed to Phillips' assistance.

Neither did anyone mourn Phillips' public humiliation and defeat. Indeed, many secretly rejoiced. After all, perhaps sooner or later he may have turned his attention towards them.

Wyn had been wrong – evidently, the Nigerian could move after all. He searched around for Skinny Pat. He was nowhere to be seen until he returned two minutes later, accompanied by a shift foreman. He pointed out the Nigerian, nervously at first, then appeared to regain his confidence.

"That's him. That's the bloke I was talking about."

A few words were spoken, none of which Wyn could hear, after which all three men exited the changing area. As Skinny Pat, the Nigerian and the foreman were leaving, Wyn followed their procession across the room and found himself staring at the same young West Indian as he had encountered a week ago. Their eyes met briefly. They nodded to each other.

Tio did not know quite what to make of the man glancing across at him, the man who had restrained Phillips a week ago. Perhaps he wanted to differentiate himself from men like Phillips and his entourage. Perhaps he was trying to say he was different from the baying mob who had cheered the Nigerian's demise last week, but Tio had already figured that out. There was no way of knowing other than speaking to him, and Tio had no intention of doing that.

Wyn shrugged his shoulders. Things had a habit of balancing themselves out in this place. All part of the ebb and flow of daily life here. Just another day on the South Ironworks.

CHAPTER 9

'A WEEK ON SUNDAY'

Lincolnshire - December 1958

It was a truth, universally acknowledged, that a young man in possession of money in his pocket attending Jackson's American-style restaurant-cum-diner on Scunthorpe High Street must be in search of a date.

Should that same young man require a partner for an evening at the local dance hall on a Saturday evening or to take her to the cinema on a Sunday evening, it would have to be prearranged by Saturday afternoon at the very latest.

England, doing its level best to shake off the greyness of the early fifties, looked across to the optimism of the United States and its ubiquitous rock and roll culture. For a tanner – sixpence - the best jukebox in town blared out tunes like *'See You Later Alligator'* by Bill Haley and His Comets, and for something slower, the lofty falsetto of *'Only You'* by The Platters or the velvet tones of the king of romance, Nat King Cole singing his latest hit *'When I Fall in Love'*.

In Jackson's a boy or a girl from Scunthorpe was as close as he or she thought they would ever get to Hollywood, California or to New York City. Just as Cliff Richard was learning to mimic Elvis Presley at the time, a Northern English rocker might imagine himself as Kirk Douglas or Burt Lancaster meeting his Jayne Mansfield or Debra Paget beneath the hissing of high-standing steam-charged pipes for the concoction of black coffee to be served in a huge cup or tall glass mugs.

Tio Mourillon was a man on a mission. His brothers, Gabriel and Everton, knew that he was headed down to the restaurant, so any thought of an ignominious and empty-handed return was not to be countenanced. To that end, today he was looking a million dollars – or whatever the pound sterling equivalent of that was. He was dressed in his bright blue blazer from John Collier the tailors, light grey slacks, white shirt and tie and highly polished black shoes. The locals may opt for the Teddy Boy look, but the youngest of the travelling Mourillon brothers believed he could show them a thing or two in when it came to sartorial elegance.

He lacked no shortage of advice from his brothers, particularly Gabriel, on what his approach to the opposite sex ought to be.

"If you too nice to the women here they will walk all over you. They will take your money and wait until you get paid again before they your friend again. The women here, they never do as they told.

"The Englishmen, they have a saying: *'treat the women mean, so they stay keen'*. That is a *good* saying, boy, good saying."

As always with Gabriel, he had an anecdote to prove his point.

"You remember that Marjorie who you see when you first arrive here?"

How could Tio forget her? It seemed like whenever he wandered down the High Street, seemingly without a care in the world, Marjorie would come badgering him about Gabriel. It had attracted some very unwanted attention. The word round town was that she was having an affair with a black man, or at least was in the last throes of one, so her grabbing Tio's arm and speaking in hushed tones was the very last thing he needed.

"I try to be nice to her one time," continued Gabriel, "Whaaat! She start crying and making all sort of noise about some foolishness about her father. The woman would not shut up and stop crying. After that, I was never nice to her again. She still come around when I want to see her. No, boy, these women don't like a man who is weak."

And there it was, anecdotal proof. Who could argue with that?

Everton, on the other hand, was far more considered in his opinions and considerate in his ways. He was very much a social creature, by no means averse to hard drinking and gambling, but he was generally more relaxed and laissez faire about how to interact with the locals.

Tio had always looked up to Gabriel with a mixture of respect and awe. He could appear quiet and taciturn upon first meeting, but Tio always thought him to have absolute command of anything to which he turned his hand. Lately, however, he wondered if Gabriel placed too high priority on his indulgences. If he had a particular female in tow at any given time, nothing and no-one was to interfere with or interrupt his love life, not even family.

It was Gabriel who had advised Tio to come down to Jackson's to sow his wild oats. Gabriel, who was in his late thirties was too old for such a venue, it was the haunt of rock and roll teenagers and those who could pass as being young, and that included Tio because, as the locals said, it was hard to tell what a black man's age was anyway.

Gabriel had encouraged him to spread his wings a little. You are young, he had said, go and enjoy yourself a little. So Tio had come down to meeting places such as Jackson's for several months and enjoyed himself, and having fun was, well – fun. But Tio had occasionally wondered to what degree this lifestyle was really him. He and Gabriel were by no means opposites, but neither were they carbon copies.

Tio waited until her friends left for what he assumed was a visit to the powder room, before approaching the girl he had spotted at the bar.

"Hello."

A guarded response came back.

"Hello."

"Would you like to go for a walk?"

"No, I wouldn't. What sort of a girl do you take me for?"

"I don't know. What sort of girl are you?"

"One that doesn't go out with coloured blokes for a start."

Tio laughed.

"Really? And why is that?"

"Well, for starters I don't know the first thing about you, and secondly, I think I know what your *'go for a walk'* means."

"Ah, I see. Well, when I said to you *'do you want to go for a walk?'* what I actually meant was: do you want to go for a walk?"

"Okay, so why do you want to go for a walk?"

"So that I can get to know you."

"You can do that here, can't you?"

"Yes, I suppose you can. I just didn't want to do it with a crowd."

"Okay, so what's your name, then?"

"I am Tio Mourillon. How do you do?"

"That's a mouthful. My name's Judith. How old are you, Theo?"

"Not Theo. Tio."

"Okay, Tio. How old are you? I'm seventeen."

"I'm twenty-eight. I have been here for two and a half years."

"You're such a liar! You're never twenty-eight."

"No?"

"No. How old are you? Tell me the truth."

"I've told you the truth."

"Come on. I'm serious. Tell me the truth."

"Okay, if you prefer, I'm twenty-one then."

"That's more like it. Wasn't so hard, was it?"

"If you say so."

"I do. So why were you going to ask me on this *'walk'*?"

"I was going to ask you if you would like to come out dancing tomorrow evening. And just in case we are speaking two different language, when I say dancing, what I mean is – dancing."

"Maybe. I need to know a bit more about you first."

Encouraged by the first sign of a smile, he pressed ahead. By now her friends had returned and had gleefully occupied a newly available booth. All seemed amused at her having been approached by this exotic new suitor.

"So, what do you want to know?"

"What job do you do?"

"I'm a lubrication engineer on the steelworks."

"Hmmm, sounds fancy. How do I know you're not making that up?"

"Look, I have a slip from work. Here."

She examined the slip.

"I suppose that's what it says. This belongs to someone called Ben-waat... Mourillon. Is that how you pronounce it?"

"Benoit Mourillon. Yes, that's me. People call me Tio since I was a child. I'm surprised you can say my last name."

"I did a little French at school. I went to grammar school."

Tio had no real idea what a grammar school was, but assuming it was something notable he made sure he appeared suitably impressed.

"So, tomorrow. You are coming to the Baths?"

The Baths Hall was one of the main entertainment venues of the town, used – as one would expect – as a swimming pool, then boarded over to double up as a dancing venue.

"I might. What time?"

"Seven o'clock. Okay?"

"Okay then. See you there."

Content that his now refined patter was consistently producing the desired results, there was no reason for Tio to remain at the restaurant, leaving Judith to ponder the encounter.

The general rule, of which there was no shortage for young women of Judith's age, was that nice girls did not date black men. Should you do so, you were walking on the riskier side of life. You were possibly asking not to be treated well, or so the rumour went. Having said that, similar rumours abounded that listening to loud rock and roll music would send you deaf by forty, that a multitude of evils lay dormant on all public lavatory seats, that not being married by the age of twenty-one meant damnation to eternal spinsterhood. Self-evidently, not all rumours were reliable, some things you simply had to find out for yourself.

A deep, booming voice from across the High Street. Gabriel, Tio's brother.

"Tio, there is a letter from home."

He crossed the road and handed the unopened letter to his younger brother.

"So, you have not broken things up with Clara yet, boy?"

Tio mumbled an answer to the negative, leaving his smiling brother under distinct the impression he wanted to discuss it no further. The handwriting on the envelope was certainly Clara's.

The timing was not good. Opening it would force him to confront what he wanted to avoid. It would lay bare just how woefully he had neglected the woman to whom he was still engaged, the woman who had listened quietly as he had expressed his hopes and fears before travelling, who had suppressed her own fears about - about days such as this.

There was nothing else for it. Sooner or later he would have to face it. Perhaps later would be better. He was in too good a mood today. Why spoil it?

No, perhaps now was as good a time as any. He pulled into another café and ordered a cup of tea he neither needed nor wanted, then sat alone at the end table.

He studied the envelope once more, then pulled out the letter.

Lower Penville
Dominica BWI

Dear Tio,

I hope you are keeping well. Please pass on my warmest regards to all your brothers. I saw your father after Mass on Sunday. He looks well, as do all your brothers and sisters here. I asked him if he had received any letters from you. He said he had not received any.

It is also a long time since I received a letter from you. I do understand that you must be very busy in England, but I must raise a matter that is very important to me and I hope to you also.

Before you left, we discussed that we would get married upon your return to Dominica. You have now lived in England for three years, which is longer than you had originally planned, although you were not specific about how long you would be staying.

Do you intend to return soon? I would like to know whether you still consider us to be engaged to be married. I understand that things may sometimes be very difficult for Dominicans living in England, but I also hope you understand that I need to know how things truly are because not knowing is very painful for me.

Please forgive me if you think this letter is an intrusion, but I hope you understand why I needed to write to you after so long a silence.

Your loving fiancée
Clara Celestine

11 November 1958

Tio cursed himself for having opened the letter. Had he been in any doubt of her pain and anguish, he could at least have put it to the back of his mind. Now it was at the very forefront of his thoughts.

He knew he had hurt her. He could tell from what she had written. No, he could tell from what she had not written. If she had written a letter about all the ways that he had let her down, it would have been a long letter.

But she had not written that letter, she had written this one. And this one made him feel much worse.

This letter proved correct all the things that people had tortured her with for so long, about how he was not treating her right, how he was just using her - how could he now tell anyone that they were wrong?

But it was not like that, he protested.

Surely, the whole point of Tio Mourillon was that he was supposed to be the man who told the truth. Now, not even Clara could ever believe that he had done so. He knew that she would want to defend him. Now, she could not do so.

It is not easy, being happy, thought Tio. He wished that Clara was happy, but he knew that she was not. He wished he had not hurt her, but he had.

He needed time to think. There was no use in going out dancing and dating at such a time. He headed back to Jackson's café.

By the time he returned, the spring in his step was notably absent. Judith was still there, but by now she had moved over to the booth with her giggling friends.

She left her friends and joined him at the bar.

"I'm glad you've come in."

"Really? Why's that?"

"I can't make it tomorrow."

"Oh?"

"I was going to suggest…"

"There are plenty of other girls I could go with, you know."

"Pardon?"

"I say there are other girls here."

With that, she spun round and made to leave.

"If that's the way you feel, you'd best ask one of them then!"

"Wait, wait. Hold on. Stay here."

He realised that he had sounded rude and abrupt and had surprised himself a little in doing so.

"Give me one good reason why I should."

"What is it you were going to say before I interrupt?"

"I was going to say I can't make it tomorrow, but I can make it a week on Sunday."

"A week on Sunday?"

"Yes."

"You mean, not tomorrow, but the next Sunday? Is that what you mean?"

"Yes. That's what I just said."

"So – in eight days' time? A week on Sunday?"

Judith gave an exasperated sigh and then laughed.

"Yes. How many times do I have to repeat myself?"

"Do you still want to go?"

"Do you?"

"Yes."

"You don't sound too sure."

"It is okay. I am sure."

"Okay. I'll meet you in front of the Baths Hall at seven o'clock."

"A week on Sunday."

The afternoon had taken some very peculiar turns. Perhaps his brother's *'be mean so they stay keen'* theory worked for him, but Gabriel and Tio were very different people. For the time being, sharp dress and good manners would clearly have to be the order of the day.

CHAPTER 10

THE LETTER

Penville, Dominica – 1959

"A letter for you. From England. I have it yesterday, but I know I will see you in the morning, so I give it now."

Lincoln, the Vielle Case postmaster who delivered it into Clara's hand. A letter all the way from Lincolnshire handed to her by Lincoln. She knew that by now half the population of two villages would probably know she had received it, so infrequently had Tio written.

The previous April had marked three years of his absence. Clara had endured three years of speculation that he had taken an English mistress, that he was never coming back, that he had forgotten her completely. Now she should know, as would everyone in Upper Penville, Lower Penville, and Vielle Case and all would have something to talk about – her abject humiliation.

Clara had had three years to prepare for this. She examined the letter, looking perhaps a little battered from its travels. Imagine, she thought, such a thing can come from the hand of someone another world away and be delivered to her own hand. How strange.

She recognised his neat, scripted handwriting on the envelope, something of which the sight had always brought her such joy in the past. Now she would associate it with pain. She did not know what made her so convinced of its contents. She just knew.

They should have married before he left, and she should have tacitly given the nod to him taking a woman in England, so long as she did not have to hear about her and so long as she never had to meet her. Then he would be coming back, just as Gabriel was to return next month, so she understood. She could have settled for second place. Now she would be no place at all.

But if he came back, he would have changed. They all did. Whenever they returned they were always referred to disparagingly as Englishmen, having lost touch with their roots, having strayed too close to the sun and having returned back to the earth, their false airs and graces in tatters. Would she even like him? Would they even have anything in common? He would be full of his talk about how things are done in England, and where he had always thought her cultured and sophisticated, perhaps now he would see her as parochial, maybe just a little less so than others.

The worst of the pain was over before she ventured to open the letter. She should really wait until she returned home at the end of the day, but her resolve may have weakened by then.

She opened the letter. Of the writing, most of which was a blur to her, she could make out the words *'I am very sorry'*. She need read no more. She knew now.

"Bon Jou Titja Celestine."

"Good… morning."

"I have something to discuss with you. Do you have time before school?"

"If it is something very quick Madame Etienne."

"Titja, you know I am always respectful to you. You know I hold you in high regard because I know you are a good titja. You know this."

Clara had braced herself for confrontation. Under the circumstances, she may have welcomed it, but the compliment caught her off guard. For a moment, she thought she might lose her composure.

"Titja, I want to know why you are only teaching Rosemond the story about Henry and his six wives. Why are you not teaching about our history? Do we not have a story? And if we do not tell our own story, who will?"

"I can assure you we have been discussing this very thing, Madame Etienne. We have it in hand. There is… there is no need for concern…"

"Titja, you know I respect you. You know I do not come here to vex you or anything. Titja are you okay? You seem upset. Clara?"

"I'm okay. I'll be fine, thank you."

"Why should we be second in our own home, Titja?"

"You must excuse me now. But I thank you for speaking to me. Please excuse me."

Clara disappeared into the schoolhouse, where she quickly composed herself and prepared for the coming school day.

Clara dreaded going home that day. She had coped well enough during the school day. There was nothing like the bright-eyed optimism of children to infuse life into her. But the very thought of home! How her mother would glory in telling her 'I told you so' or some such words to that effect. It was not to be borne.

Upon arrival at her home in Penville, she decided to sit out on the porch instead of going straight into the house, knowing full well that her mother to be indoors. The crowing would have to wait. Her victory dance would no doubt last for days, months, years. Clara would hear how her mother had never liked Tio, how he had used Clara to advance his standing, just like his brother, how he was overly serious, how it would not harm him to lighten up and drink more.

"I didn't know you pass by so early."

"Yes, Mama. I didn't want to stay there too long today."

Evelyn nodded before sitting down beside her.

"So, a letter from Pierre son?"

No doubt her mother knew about the letter before Clara, such was the grapevine in so small a place.

"Yes, Mama, from Tio."

"Well…"

"Actually, Mama, I will just ask you please not to say anything today. You can tell me what a fool I am tomorrow. You can torture me for the rest of my life and tell me how I will never get married and how no man will ever want me. You have my permission to do that all you want. All I ask…"

She lowered her voice after having reached a crescendo.

"All I ask is: just, not, today. Alright? Not today. Please."

Her mother was silent for a whole minute. Then she spoke.

"So, you think I want to torture my own daughter?"

"I don't know Mama. I don't know what you want. All I know is that I can't listen to anything today."

"Clara, fi. If I could take your hurt away from you and give it to myself. I would do it like that." A single clap of the hands slightly startled Clara.

"And I could tell you that you will always have me, but we both know that is not true because I am an old woman. And because I am old I know some things."

"What do you know, Mama?"

"I know *you*. And I know you are thinking you should have married him and let him take a mistress and now you will be okay."

Clara looked at her mother. How could she possibly know that?

"And I tell you, mwen fi, it is not true. You will never be happy that way because you were not born like that. And neither will he be happy like that, he is not born like that, also. So never mind about I torture you. Make sure you don't torture you."

Clara stared at the ground. She could not truthfully say whether her anguish was over Tio, her own situation or a mixture of both. She would not have been able to function had she not become accustomed to his absence, but the realisation that there would be no redeeming answer to her solitude had come too late in life. There would be no coming back from this. No marriage relatively late in life now.

"What am I going to do, Mama?"

"I will tell you what you are going to do. I have some nice pig snout and salt fish broth I am cooking special for you today. In one hour, we will eat.

"And tomorrow, tomorrow you will go to Vielle Case and teach your children. None of us know how we get here except Papa Dieux. But we here now. We will live here and give thanks for every day. Now go inside and change your clothes and put on something nice."

"Yes, Mama."

Lower Penville
Dominica BWI

Dear Tio.

I received your letter today.

I accepted long ago that after being apart for so long that you would not wish to continue with our engagement. I expected that during such a long stay in England you would probably marry a white woman.

It is true that I am disappointed, but I hope that both of you are very happy in the future.

Yours faithfully
Clara Celestine

11 July 1959

CHAPTER 11

OIL & WATER

Lincolnshire – 1959

Evalyn 'Eva' May straightened the framed Golden Jubilee print of Queen Victoria that stood proudly above the mantelpiece in their semi-detached council house in Ashby, near Scunthorpe. She kneeled down to take hold of pegged rug that lay before the hearth. Getting down to ground level and, more to the point, getting back up, was no easy task, so stiff was her body these days. While she was down, she searched around for anything else she may want to pick up. It may be some time before she would be able to get down there again. A needle that had fallen between the tiles a couple of days ago, perhaps she could reach it. No, she would ask Judith when she came home.

Or then again, perhaps she would not. For her to ask her daughter for something so straightforward, it would require civil discourse. The outlook for that was distinctly gloomy, now that relations with her daughter were at an all-time low since Judith seemed insistent on throwing her life away with her current choice of partner.

If only Judith had known of the opportunities that had been denied Eva because of her sex, she would be less hasty in throwing away her own chances. Judith had been such a clever girl, the only one of her children who had taken any real interest in education. Were girls so petrified of being left on the shelf these days that they opted for just anyone, so long he had a pulse?

There she had been, her own daughter, large as life, with *that* man, right in front of Woolworths earlier that day - for all the world to see! At least Judith had the decency to look embarrassed when the four of them had met. Eva's husband Colin had passed the time of day with him as if the whole situation was the most normal thing in the world. It had been humiliating beyond words!

Who must have seen them in town? Eva had dared not look. Worryingly, she had heard nothing from any of her friends or neighbours. Not even a whisper. That could only mean one thing – she was excluded from the conversation because she and her family were the topic of it.

Struggling for breath, she carried the pegged rug to the rear garden, groaned as she lifted it over the clothes line, then slowly beat out the dust. Her husband Colin was at the bottom of the garden, garden fork in hand, turning over the soil, no doubt deliberately staying out of her way. Surely none of that work really needed doing. Eva was sure he had worked the same patch only a few days earlier.

How different her own life could have been had she married her beloved Herbert and not Colin, had she been able to continue her job as a laboratory assistant in Hull. No, instead she had been forced to give it up after the Great War, and the loss of the opportunity had been to her like the dying of the light.

Herbert was a kind man. He would not have beaten his children should he and Eva have married, unlike this man here. Had Herbert and Eva had children, they may have encountered bullying by other children for being different, but Herbert would have been good to them, kind to them. With her backing, Herbert could have gone on to be something other than a bus conductor, no matter what push-backs he received. He was still receiving many, so she understood from the last time she had spoken to him. He was the only man she had ever truly loved, but she had come to the realisation – as every right thinking adult should – that oil and water do not mix. Herbert's mother was from Ceylon, therefore it was simply impossible that she and Herbert could ever be together.

Judith's five older siblings had grown up under their father's harsh oversight, prompting Eva to insist that she be the one to raise Judith. In doing so, Eva had ensured Judith's protection from her father. That made it all the more mystifying that of all six children, Judith was the one who now appeared most out of control.

If only Judith could find someone like Terry, her niece Jan's husband. Terry and Jan were the only two people in the world with whom she could discuss her daughter. Eva would have given her eye teeth for Judith to encounter someone like him. He was such a blessing, such an asset. How Jan's mother must bless the day Jan met him! But Judith had not fallen for someone like Terry. No, she had fallen for a foreigner. And a coloured one at that!

Colin approached the rear of the house, kicked off his wellington boots and stood in his stocking feet.

"That looked hard work."

"What did?"

"Lifting that rug over the line."

"Is that all you've got to say with everything that's going on right now?"

"What do you want me to say?"

"I don't know. I want you to say that you'll talk to her."

"I'm surprised at you. I would have thought the way you've pined after your Indian bus conductor all your life, you'd be a bit more sympathetic."

So, it was going to be this sort of conversation, thought Eva. They quarrelled only once every so many years, but when they did, feelings ran deep. The intervening period was not so much peace as a prolonged ceasefire.

"Sympathy is not what's required here. Wisdom and good sense are what's required."

"Okay, tell me what you think is wise and sensible."

"I can tell you what's neither. Being with him."

"He's got a name, you know."

"Yes, and what flipping daft name it is too. Whoever heard such a name? Tio!"

"I think Judith said his real name's Ben."

"Oh, so you have discussed it with her, then? Without me."

"Not at length, no. I don't know what your problem is. He seems like a nice enough bloke."

"He might be. But he can be nice at a distance."

"You're the one who's always down at chapel sending money off to Africa and the likes for missionary work. Why do that if you don't like them when they're here?"

"It's not that I don't like them. I'm not that sort of person. It's just that you don't *marry* them. It's not right."

"Who's talking about marriage? Do you know something I don't?"

"Anyone with eyes can tell she's serious. This isn't just going to go away, you know."

"I do know. But who says it should go away? If he's the man she chooses, who's to say that's wrong?"

"It *is* wrong! Everyone knows it's wrong. I just can't for the life of me see why you're the only one who doesn't know it. Hard as you've been on all the rest of them, and yet you're soft as muck with her. Why?"

"I left her to you to bring up. So how she's turned out is down to you, not me. If she's spoilt, well, that's your doing, not mine."

"Terry says there's no way he's an engineer on the works. They wouldn't let someone like that be. He must be lying to her. Pulling the wool over her eyes good and proper."

"I don't know anything about that. All I know is that he seems respectable. He's a hard worker and he seems to like our daughter. And what's it got to do with Terry anyway?"

"I'm glad of his concern. And so should you be, frankly. He sees the big picture here. I'm glad someone does. You don't. That's for sure."

"You say I don't. But maybe I do. Maybe I'm the one who's right."

"Oh, don't talk such nonsense. You know perfectly well what the right and wrongs of this situation are and yet you won't lift a finger to do anything about it."

Colin shook his head disdainfully.

"You're so certain you're right? What if you're not?"

"I am right. And I'll tell you why. Because if they get married and have children, those children will probably end up in a home when the marriage doesn't work – which it won't. They'll not belong here; they'll not belong anywhere."

"Really?"

"Yes, really."

"What about your Herbert then? He's half-caste. Where does he belong?"

"That's different, and you know it. And stop calling him *my* Herbert."

"It's not different, He isn't white."

"I know. That's why I didn't marry him."

There. It had taken three and a half decades in coming, but it had finally been said. And it could not be unsaid.

"Not because you loved me, then? Well, that's nice to know. Oil and water, eh? By the way, which one's which?"

"Colin… look."

Colin, who had previously intended to enter the house decided another stint in the garden may after all not be a bad idea. He sat down on the rear doorstep and pulled on his boots once more.

"Have you ever noticed that things are easier to knock down than they are to build up? I think we've discussed this subject enough, Eva. Don't you?"

PART THREE

England - 1964

CHAPTER 12

BONE STRUCTURE

Lincolnshire – 1964

As Tom Chandler sat upon his bed he pondered for a moment how his life was governed by the diligence of others. He mused on how each day he arose from his bed and before he even opened his eyes, the bed itself, the room's furnishings, the alarm clock that awoke him, the functioning of everything was contingent upon each item, bed, clock, curtains, table, all, having been manufactured correctly. As he traversed his house, he was reliant upon wooden floorboards being tongued and grooved correctly, supported by joists, in turn, borne by load bearing walls, built upon firm foundations. In his bathroom, replete with all the convenience and amenity that indoor plumbing allowed, he splashed cold water from the basin into his face three times, never four. As always, he turned off the tap at roughly fifteen seconds.

As he ate his breakfast he gave thought to how it had been delivered to his table by the farmer, the food processor, the haulier and in turn the retailer. When later he would climb into his car, he would entrust his safety, indeed his very life to the assiduousness and industry of a multitude.

And underpinning absolutely all of these things that enabled him to live such a life was steel. Tom Chandler's job was to ensure that the bone structure of the nation was in rude health.

He lamented how men such as himself were not appreciated in Britain as they were in countries such as Germany. Had he lived there he would have been lauded as a captain of industry and given the status of a professional on par with a doctor or lawyer. Indeed, if he did his job well, the beneficiaries of his labour would remain forever oblivious. In that respect, he was the author of his own misfortune.

Many who knew him assumed he was born into a privileged position in life. He was the son of a coal merchant's labourer who barely had two pennies to rub together. The resources he did manage to muster were used to secure Tom a first-class education, the result of which, when combined with determination and sheer tenacity, was his elevation to the position of Production Manager of Frodingham Ironworks for United Steel Companies Ltd.

Outside the house, of which he was the sole occupant, he lifted the car bonnet of his Rover 2000 and checked his oil and water levels. No need to check tyre pressures, this time, he had performed his weekly check yesterday. Satisfied that everything was in order he returned indoors, rinsed his and dried his hands thoroughly as he had previously before finally setting off to work at the South Ironworks offices, where once again he would play his part in strengthening the nation's bone structure.

Tom Chandler, despite his elevated status, was no great fan of meetings. Unlike many of his peers, he regarded them more as an obstacle to work than an essential part of his role. He was mildly amused how some people changed once around a boardroom table, thespians transformed into a completely different persona once they were given an audience to play to. Only in the period after a meeting did they speak freely and candidly. This was just such a moment as several men reclined around the conference table in a cigar smoke filled room, sipping brandy at the end of a heavy afternoon's session.

"You know, I'm thinking of sporting some impressive sideburns like the chap in that painting there," quipped Jeremy Allenby, one of the boardroom's younger occupants. "Who might that august gentleman be?"

"That, Jeremy, is Rowland Winn, Baron St Oswald," replied William Turner, Executive Chairman of United Steel Industries with mock reverence. "He's the reason we are here right now. Like all the best people, he was a Yorkshireman. He discovered iron ore deposits a couple of miles north-east of here, or perhaps rediscovered is the more accurate word. The Romans discovered it first."

"Really?"

"Yes, indeed. He was very much a man of his time. You'll find with all these philanthropists and visionary types, they want to reinvent the world. Plough their own furrow and all that."

"How so?"

"Social engineering, architecture, you name it."

"So why have I never heard of him?"

"Oh, the fickle finger of fate, I suppose. Hard-nosed economics won the day, you might say."

"I'm not sure I'm following you, sir."

"Come now, we're no longer in the military. There's no need for 'sir'. We're supposed to eschew stuffy formality."

"Forgive me. Force of habit. You mentioned architecture. What architecture are you referring to?"

"The viaduct down on Scotter Road is a prime example. Have you seen it?" asked Tom Chandler.

"I've seen the bridge. Is that a viaduct?"

"As Tom says, if you look closely at it, Jeremy, you can see it's a viaduct. It was buried beneath an embankment in the twenties, I think. Pity, really. It could have been a great spectacle for the town.

"Alas, we're no longer a country of Isambard Kingdom Brunels, but we are at least a country of – well - Jeremy Allenbys and Tom Chandlers."

"I'm not sure I expected to hear my name mentioned in the same sentence as Brunel when I drove into work, this morning," said Jeremy, cheerily.

"Very different era, then. When Britannia ruled the waves. I'm not sure we rule very much at all, these days. The Empire has all but disappeared."

William Turner was reflective.

"I think it probably still exists, barely, but it's been in decline for most of my life, and I'm not exactly a young man. I've always been told that our role is to help to manage that decline in an orderly fashion."

"Surely, what we're doing is the very opposite. This industry is booming, and probably will be for years to come," said Tom.

"Oh, I don't mean steel. People will always want steel. I mean the state of this nation in general. Steel may be on the increase but the sun will soon start setting on the Empire, I'm afraid."

"If you watch the newsreels, read the papers, it seems like we lose at least a couple of colonies each year," Jeremy Allenby lamented.

"Be that as it may, Jeremy. We may be losing the Empire colonies, but we've been gaining its inhabitants. That was mildly amusing at first. I think that raises concerns for the cohesion of the workforce."

"How so?"

"I'm alluding to reports of altercations amongst the men, particularly with some of our foreign employees. It's making the natives restless, if you'll excuse the pun."

"I'm aware of one or two incidents," offered Tom, "I wasn't aware of any sort of epidemic."

"It may not be yet, Tom. I want you amongst others to try and ensure it doesn't become one. These incidents you say have come to your ears - is any group seen as being particularly problematic?"

"Not really. I'd say the Eastern Europeans – Poles, Ukrainians, et cetera, are generally received best by the men. The Asians have a few problems, but by and large, they tend to be quite deferential. Don't like to be seen to rock the boat. The Africans and Caribbean Islanders can sometimes be quite problematic."

"Why?"

"Several reasons. I think that's partly down to the fact that they have a habit of mixing with the local women. That invariably causes strife of one sort or another."

"I don't think it's just that, Tom," added Jeremy, "the locals don't like the idea of these people living in amongst them, which in my opinion is only natural. It's generally better when they stay concentrated in particular areas."

William turner drew hard on his cigar.

"Hmmm, yes. Who would have thought ten years ago these problems would be presenting themselves? I don't know about you, but I thought when they were invited to work here, they'd stay for a year or two, take their money and head straight back to sunnier climes."

"I think we all thought that. Evidently, we were wrong," said Jeremy Allenby.

"And what do the unions think? How do they react?"

"The unions are generally hostile to the idea of a large influx of foreign workers," observed Tom. "Not just the West Indians, I mean anyone they see as coming in and potentially undercutting the labour force."

"Do you think union members are behind this recent spate of altercations?"

"No, not really, I think it just boils down to certain individuals taking a dislike to foreign elements within the workforce. Emotions tend to spill over from time to time."

"Well, the pair of you seem to have an eye for what's going on. Keep me abreast if you think there's anything you think I need to be worried about."

"Of course."

"Another thing upon which we do need to maintain a focus - we've had a string of fatalities and quite severe accidents of late. The numbers are definitely going in the wrong direction. It's bad for morale, it's bad for our bottom line, and it places us on a conflict path with the trade unions. It goes without saying need to do what we can to keep a lid on those figures.

"As we discussed in the meeting, the greatest likelihood is that the Socialists will win the next election. Should that happen, I'll soon be finding myself reporting into Whitehall bureaucrats within Her Majesty's government. I can assure you they'll take a very dim view of high fatality levels, so we need to keep these incidents to a minimum."

Turner stood, signifying the adjournment of the day's deliberations, before offering one final thought.

"Gentlemen, when I say *we*, I mean you, of course. I'm leaving these matters in your very capable hands."

CHAPTER 13

A TIPPING POINT

At the Mourillon household on Cottage Beck Road, there was a knock on the back door. The back door? That suggested informality, and therefore must be family or friends. Certainly not the man from the Pru. He would have come to the front.

It was Judith's cousin, Jan.

"Hiya. I thought I'd pop in to have a look at your new bedroom furniture. You mind if I have a look?"

"Of course, come in. How did you get here? Is Terry not with you?"

"He's in the car."

The early years of Judith's life had been marked by the affectionate oversight of her cousin, older by seven years. Having someone of Jan's age available to advise her through some of the difficult phases of growing up had been of infinite value to Judith.

At first, the arrival of Terry in Jan's life made it seem as if Jan being part of a couple meant twice the affection. At first.

As time progressed, however, Jan somehow seemed to disappear in the relationship and Jan and Terry became Terry and Jan. As so frequently happens, his opinions became her opinions, his worldview her worldview, and, crucially, his dislikes became her dislikes.

Then a tipping point.

It was the briefest of conversations with Terry during a chance meeting on a bus Judith had taken to Ashby, a town which was joined at the hip with Scunthorpe, where she had lived at the time. It happened three days after her first encounter with Tio. Evidently, Terry had caught wind of the proposed date with Tio at the Baths Hall when Judith had postponed to the following Sunday from the evening originally proposed.

"I hear you're going on a date with that black chap," Terry had said, quiet and concerned in equal measure.

Judith had replied effusively and had started to tell Terry all about Tio. Terry had simply replied:

"I think that would be quite unwise."

He was neither animated, nor angry, nor anything of the sort. Just calm, neutral, matter of fact, as if saying two plus two equals four or $e=mc^2$. The imprudence of a date with a man such as Tio was simply a given. He did not need to expand on why he thought the date unwise. He and his family were known for their trenchant views on immigrants. Judith had heard those views expressed on many an occasion.

It was a tipping point for Judith, also. Her cousin's then fiancée changed in her eyes from being a rock of constancy to someone obstinate and pig-headed, from a decent, principled man to someone she now viewed as supercilious and perhaps a little too presumptuous.

Had it just been that one statement he had uttered, she would perhaps have thought herself as being unfair to him. Shortly after the frequency of Terry and Jan's visits to Judith's parents' house saw a sudden increase. Hushed 'family crisis' meetings were invariably scheduled when

Judith's absence would be assured when she would be working at a nearby sweetshop.

Jan was mindful that she was taking a gamble with the relationship between herself and Judith. It did not pay off. Rather than 'seeing sense' Judith had pulled in the opposite direction, leaving the closed door meetings from which Judith was excluded appearing very much as a personal betrayal. Like it or not, the battle lines had seemingly been drawn.

And now, here was Jan, appearing once again within Judith's life, prompting her to wonder if Jan and Terry were seeking to make yet another unwelcome intervention. On the other hand, maybe this evening's visit perhaps some sort of rapprochement, perhaps a split in the once impregnable alliance between Jan and Terry.

For her part, Jan found it equally hard to comprehend the change that had taken place. True, she had spoken at length to Judith's parents about her concerns, about their concerns, but Jan insisted that it was only because Judith had shut her out of her life and demoted her from the place of importance. One minute they were sharing the most important experiences of their lives, then, seemingly all of a sudden, Jan was out in the cold.

Now this man held that place of importance, what chance was there for her to get to know him, now that Terry would not even countenance the idea of Tio's existence? Jan was now subject to suspicious glances, and her cousin looked at her accusingly as if she was a terrible person?

All Jan wanted, she insisted, was a chance to get used to the idea of Tio. She once explained this to Judith, who then relayed her concerns as best she could onto Tio. His response was characteristically blunt – why should he worry about the thoughts of people who, as far as he could see, showed him no respect?

The rot truly set in when Jan and Terry refused the invitation to attend Judith and Tio's wedding, six weeks after the death of her Aunt Eva, Judith's mother. The decision not to attend the marriage in Holy Souls Church on Frodingham Road, less than two miles away from their home was in very stark contrast to the attendance of some of Tio's relatives from thousands of miles away. From that point onwards, she was not sure that her relationship with Judith would ever be the same again.

Wars, Jan observed, were always started by men. If women ruled the world there would be far less of them, or perhaps none at all, or they would be different types of war, anyway.

So, they were divided. And because Jan was half of a couple, whatever Terry's thoughts were regarding Tio were attributed to her also.

Apart from Jan and Terry, opposition to Judith and Tio was split down generational lines. Judith's friends tended to think her new date exotic, definitely a good dresser, probably a good dancer, even though they had yet to see him dance, and likely someone who may not treat her well in the long run. But who cared? It was only a date. After all, this was the rock and roll generation.

The older generation, however, viewed things very differently. A war had just been won to fend off the enemy from the gate, why now this Trojan horse? Yet more proof, many said, that Britain had won the war, but was inexplicably losing the peace.

"Invite Terry in. No use sitting out there on a cold evening like this."

"He says he needs to stay in the car, keep it running. He doesn't want to turn it off in case it won't start again."

Tio arose from the table.

"I'll go get him."

"No, no. Really, it's alright. I'd prefer if you didn't. He'll be fine out there for a few minutes. He's already said so. Just leave him."

Silence prevailed. Tio returned to the table.

"Aren't the boys growing? Especially Andre. Gorgeous, isn't he? Look at those long eyelashes!"

Jan stroked the toddler's head with genuine affection. What age was he now? Four? If things continued in their present state, Andre would grow up barely aware of Jan's existence.

Judith had studied Jan intently as she spoke to Tio. Suddenly everything became clear. Her face was a little flushed, her eyes, slightly reddened. She and Terry had argued. He had stayed without. She had come within. Perhaps the impregnable alliance was breaking. Perhaps she would get her cousin back, her friend back.

Upstairs the two women studied the furniture, Judith regaled her cousin with blow-by-blow details of how Tio had driven a hard bargain by virtue of having paid cash instead of purchasing on the never-never.

Jan's young cousin was clearly all grown up now. Here she and her husband were, he only had a modest job on the works, and yet they seemed to be buying the very best of everything, perhaps not straight away, but they were doing well. She had always thought Judith would flounder without her material and emotional support. Quite evidently, that was not the case.

But still, but still. Jan had heard how these men did not treat their women well, and from what she had seen of Tio, she was by no means sure it was not true. Yes, she and Terry had had their own issues, but that was different. Terry had predicted that the marriage would not last a year. And yet five years later here they were, still going. Who knew what went on behind closed doors, though?

She wanted to like Tio – but these doubts!

Jan had arrived just as Judith was about to serve tea, so they returned downstairs to allow Judith to continue.

"Would you like something to eat, Jan? We can split it another couple of ways, easily."

"No, it's okay. Really. I'll pop outside the door and have a ciggy if you don't mind. Don't want to smoke while you're eating."

"Okay, you can leave the door open if you want so we can talk. Are you sure Terry won't come in?"

"No, don't worry about him. He's okay."

After finishing the cigarette, Jan joined the family at the table, occasionally glancing at the boys. Judith told her about their plans to move somewhere further from the steelworks. Not long ago Jan would have been horrified by the idea, but here her cousin was, with ideas for the future and seemingly a different way of doing things. Who was to say it would not work out for them? At least they seemed to have an appetite for life.

No doubt when she spoke to Terry, he would once agin instil all manner of doubt, but right now she was enjoying the fact that it looked as if her relationship with Judith may actually be restored, or at least be restorable.

As for Tio, he was an enigma to her. Certainly, he could be an awkward so-and-so, but she and her husband had not attended his wedding. They had opposed it in the first place, and yet so far as she could see, he seemed perfectly alright with her, and prepared to be alright with Terry if he would only step through the door. Would Terry be the same, she wondered, if he had been treated as Tio had?

As all these thoughts ran back and forth through her mind, her husband sat in his car with the engine running for the full forty-five minute duration. No doubt he would not be in a good mood once she returned. No doubt they would argue. But that was his choice. He could have simply entered the house.

Judith joined her outside as she was leaving. Jan lit another cigarette. The two women embraced, happy to be together again.

"Did I just see Tio eat the bones of that chicken?"

"Yes," Judith laughed, "it's a Dominican thing apparently."

"I don't think I've ever seen that before."

"Neither had I until I met Tio."

Jan stared at the ground for a moment.

"You know we love you, don't you?"

"I know you do, Jan because you're here now."

"Well, Terry's only down the road there. He's here too."

"But he's not, though, is he?"

"I don't understand, not what?"

"He's not here. Not really. Look Jan, I'm glad you're here. I'm glad you've come today, and I'd like you to be part of my kids' lives."

"I'd like that." She drew hard on the cigarette. "Are you happy Judith?"

"Am I happy?" She paused. "I don't know, I'm happy enough. I'm not saying life's perfect, any more than anyone else's life is, but we'll be okay, I think."

"Tio. He seems a nice bloke when you get to know him. I'm sorry if we… I'm sorry if I misjudged him back then."

"Well, you didn't know him. There's chance to now. I just want the two of us to be alright – you know. Like we used to be. You know what men are like, it'll probably take years before they get on. It might never happen. We can't wait for that or we may end up waiting forever."

"We will be."

Jan walked the short distance to the car knowing that continuation of the argument with her husband was a betting certainty. She suspected that her own doubts would set back in regarding Judith and Tio, fuelled by Terry's input, of course. But at least she and her cousin were now talking.

When Jan and Terry had married, many of the things that marked her as an individual she had entrusted to his safekeeping under the assumption that she wanted, he did also. Then, over a period of time, his likes, dislikes, prejudices and foibles squeezed many of the things - and some of the people - she held most dear out of her life.

Now a tipping point.

She would not let that happen again.

CHAPTER 14

SPEAK ENGLISH!

Tim Barnes, known to his friends as Ted, drew up on his motorcycle, the one true love of his life, turned off the engine and lit up a cigarette atop one of Lincolnshire's few hills. It was a small hill, but he was king of it. Out here in the countryside, he need not be concerned about noise – he could rev his engine to his heart's content without worrying about upsetting his unspeaking, taciturn father. Some of his friends had more modern, faster bikes, but none received the loving attention bestowed on his 1958 BSA 'Beezer' B33 with its impressive 500cc capacity single cylinder engine. Upon this marvel of British engineering not a single spot of rust was permitted to reside.

He wore a small open-face motorcycle helmet, clear goggles, thick leather jacket, boots and small gloves. He may not be Marlon Brando in The Wild One or James Dean in Rebel, but he was confident he looked better than those specimens he saw most days riding their scooters back and forth at shift changeover back at the steelworks. Ted Barnes would never have dreamt of using the love of his life for the short mile-long commute to the ironworks.

He had thundered down the long, straight Ermine Street, the ancient Roman road that ran from Lincoln towards the Humber. There he could open the throttle and let the world seemingly fly past in a blur, after which he veered off eastward and took the quiet country road towards the Lincolnshire Wolds, one of the few parts of the county that did not lack feature. He had cruised along its roads through picturesque scenery and undulating hills, knowing not to drive too fast around these country lanes because of the danger of farm vehicles suddenly appearing around blind corners. He was as much concerned about what a collision may do to his beloved Beezer as about any possible danger to his person.

He wound about and in and out, oblivious of any local connection to Tennyson, far more mindful of the nearby motor cycle racing circuit. There was no racing event today. That meant he could enjoy the pleasures of the open road in solitude without other motorcyclists trying to befriend or even speed past him.

Those who thought him shallow - almost every person he had ever known - knew little what great pleasure he drew from the countryside on a day such as today. Nor would he ever tell them. For Ted, days like today were to be enjoyed, not spoken about.

These were prosperous times for him, chiefly due to several years' avoidance of anything remotely resembling adult responsibility. Not only that but the greyness and austerity of the fifties were now drifting into memory. He had money in his pocket, but nowhere else. No reserves with which to get married or start a family due to spending too much time out drinking and sponsoring his unnecessarily complicated love life.

His longsuffering mother, ever the proxy for unpleasant messages, had recently informed him of his father's insistence that his rent-free days in their small two bedroomed house on Trent Street in Scunthorpe would likely be over soon. All the more reason, he thought, to enjoy the moment. He cranked up and revved his engine of his Beezer, then set off down the country lane at a modest pace, the wind in his face once more.

Later, upon return to his place of residence, he lovingly wiped down his motorbike, before covering it with a tarpaulin, weighted down at the bottom with several bricks. He returned inside the house and prepared himself for the afternoon shift.

"Oi, you! Speak English!"

The group of four labourers, who until then had been engrossed in an animated conversation in Bengali found themselves subject to Ted Barnes' glare.

"Yeah, you. You're in England now. No more of that. Speak English or nothing at all. Alright?"

The four, now completely silent, met his stare for a moment.

"Alright?" pressed Barnes.

"Okay. No problem," said one of the labourers.

"That's right, mate. There'll be no problem so long as you and your mates understand how things are."

Some fleeting, barely audible words were exchanged between the four, which Barnes was unable to hear. It seemed that they had decided to diffuse the tension by leaving the 'snap cabin' prematurely. Barnes, satisfied with this outcome, leaned back in his chair and placed his hands behind his head, master of all he surveyed.

As the labourers made their way back to the blast furnaces, Barnes' dominion over the space was rudely interrupted by the arrival of his Welsh charge-hand, Wyn Owen, accompanied by what he could only assume was one of the two new starters due to arrive that day.

"Blister! Thought I'd find you in here."

"Yeah, yeah. I've only just sat down here. I've just had to give them lot a flea in their ear about not speaking the Queen's English."

"Really? You thinking of taking it up any time soon?"

"Very funny, Rev. Bit rich coming from a Taff. They really ought to dig that Offa's Dyke a bit deeper you know."

"I'm impressed that you even know what Offa's Dyke is, Blister. And there was me thinking you were thick as two short planks. Ted, this is Philip; Philip, this is Ted or Blister if you prefer. We call him Blister because he tends to appear when the work's done. Actually, you'd best call him Ted. He might punch you if you call him Blister."

Philip allowed himself a nervous laugh before offering his hand to Barnes.

"Ted."

Ted Barnes did not respond. Philip looked to Wyn for reassurance.

"Rev?"

"It's what the men call me on account of me being a churchgoing man."

"Ah."

"I go to church too," protested Barnes, "sometimes. It's just that last time I went, someone was splashing water on me head. Oswald Hotel's my church these days. Minister there quite regular, I do."

"On the subject of your 'ministering skills', Blister, we have another new bloke starting up today. He's coming over from the Seraphim Plant."

"Sounds like a barrel of laughs. Who is he?"

"Theo Murray. Coloured bloke."

"Huh! Makes me laugh, them lot. They all seem to have the same surname."

"Same surname as your old friend Everton, yes. Possibly because he's his younger brother."

Wyn Owen allowed a moment for the information to sink in.

"You see young Philip," continued Wyn, "our large workshy friend here had his nose broken by the brother of the man who's coming to join us."

"I was sucker punched."

"Don't make me laugh! He actually warned you not to call him that name thirty seconds before he hit you. It's your daft fault if you go picking fights with Sonny Liston lookalikes."

"Aye, the bastard didn't even lose his job either. If that had been anyone else, he'd have been sacked. It just shows that it's the white man who's discriminated against in this country."

"The reason he didn't lose his job was because at least two witnesses told the foreman exactly what happened. They told him that you'd asked for it and that he'd warned you about calling him a monkey. Several times. Evidently, that was good enough. Or maybe the foreman just didn't like you. Either way, the bloke kept his job."

"Well, at least he's having the decency to return to the place of his birth soon. I'll give him credit for that."

"Where does he come from, this bloke?" asked Philip.

"Africa," said Ted.

"West Indies." Wyn corrected.

"Same thing."

"Ignore the idiot. I'm clearly casting pearls before swine here."

"Charming!" Ted feigned offence.

"Well, you just can't give it a rest, can you, Blister? Always got to push it over the edge. Now I'm telling you - when the new bloke comes tomorrow, I don't want your usual… I don't want you… just behave yourself. Okay?"

"Calm down, for crying out loud, man."

"I *will* calm down. I'll calm down when you stop deliberately winding people up. There are enough enemies in this place with management. We'd all like to live peaceful lives."

"What are you on about? I've never even met the man. He's not even started on this shift and already he's creating havoc."

"I'm just warning you, that's all. We treat people fairly on this shift. I don't care how they go on on other shifts, but we do things right here."

"Aye, well warn away! This is a free country when last I heard. It's unbelievable, you soon won't be able to say anything in this country."

Despite his bluster, Ted Barnes held his Welsh colleague in higher regard than any other individual on earth. Few people had ever really thought him sufficiently worth bothering with to correct him before he had worked with Wyn on C Shift.

Ted occasionally took comfort and assurance that someone possessed clearly defined standards of right and wrong. That said, Ted had little or no intention of adhering to those standards, but at least they gave him a reference point. He may occasionally mock Wyn for his beliefs, but he would probably have been mortified if those beliefs and convictions had appeared to falter in any way. Happily, for Ted, there was no sign of that happening.

Through Wyn, he had received more guidance - usually in the form of chastisement - than he had ever received from his own father, who had barely done more than grunt at him from behind his newspaper for the past decade or so.

Wyn, revived by the intake of sugary tea, continued the induction of his new charge, warning him of the extreme dangers of their working environment.

"So, you're the foreman, Wyn?" asked Philip innocently.

"Foreman? You must be joking. I think I've blotted my copybook too often to ever become a foreman. No, young Philip, I'm just the charge hand."

"Our illustrious foreman," began Ted, his interest evidently piqued, "is a gentleman called George. That's his surname, not his Christian name. Mr. John George Esquire used to be our shop steward couple of years ago and was, without doubt, the laziest, most bolshy, argumentative man you will ever meet in your life. An absolute thorn in the side to the bosses, so they did what they always do with men like that - they promoted him."

"By that token," Wyn cut in, "Blister ought to be made up to production manager any day now."

Philip managed to stifle a laugh, which, had he done so, would not have been conducive to good relations with his large vocal workmate.

"Poacher turned gamekeeper," continued Ted, unperturbed. "He knows every hiding spot and every electrical substation where you can put your feet up. And the reason why he knows them is because he used to spend half his shifts in them pretending he was doing union business when he was actually asleep. Sold us down the river completely, he did, just like all of them. They're all in it for themselves."

"Thank you, Ted, for that potted history of industrial relations. Have you anything else to add?"

Wyn did not necessarily disagree with Ted, but listening to a polemic about laziness and self-interest from him was a little too rich for his palate at this time of the afternoon.

"It's true what I said."

"Well, be that as it may, none of this need concern our educated young friend here. All he needs to know is not to trust George or any of the bosses for that matter."

"Educated, eh? Educated how?"

Philip reddened and shuffled awkwardly.

"I've been studying at the technical college. Metallurgy."

"Oh aye?" Ted's fickle amity was in danger of swinging away from the newcomer. "This bloke could end up being our boss. Watch him. He could be a management spy."

"I don't think there's any real danger of that. The bit about being anyone's boss, I mean. To be honest, I would like to have got a job in the labs, or even the drawing office. But those jobs are a bit oversubscribed at the moment, and I don't have my full qualifications from the college yet. I think they just took one look at me and thought that because I'm big, I'm bound to be strong, which I'm not really."

"Well, lad, one thing's for sure. You don't need qualifications to handle a shovel and lump a few bricks around. Just a strong back and brute force and ignorance," said Wyn.

"So, when you've done all your studying, what qualification will you have?" asked Ted.

"City & Guilds. I'd like to study further if I can. Maybe even one day do a degree… they're talking about being able to study for degrees from your own home now."

"From home?" Ted seemed amazed, "I can just see that – test tubes and chemicals on the kitchen table. I've never heard anything so bloody daft in my life. People like us don't go to university."

"Ignore him, young Philip. It's a good thing you're doing."

"It's getting ideas above his station, that's what it is. It's like me mam says: you can't run with the hare and hunt with the hounds. Think on that, lad."

Wyn sighed. He had chastised Ted several times to no effect, what good would repeating himself do?

"Yes, well with that pearl of wisdom, we'd best go outside and I'll show you where you'll be working. Come on, lad, this way."

CHAPTER 15

KEEP OUT

At the end of a tiring shift on the steelworks, Tio Mourillon trudged homeward up the Cottage Beck Road. The winter wind blew eastward as if to carry him home, but less helpfully carrying along some of the acrid smells from Appleby Frodingham.

Combined with the fumes of ancient works buses and tired looking cars, the mildly toxic cocktail stung his throat. He thought back to Dominica, the time he and his brothers ventured up to Trois Pitons to the volcanic Boiling Lake. It was not boiling as such, more lukewarm and as such was a great treat for the young Mourillons, on the one occasion they ever visited it. They were given a simple message to remember – warm water good, fumes bad. If their senses alerted them to a proliferation of any volcanic gases, they were to come away immediately.

Tio Mourillon had spent the first quarter century of his life breathing clean ocean air.

'This cannot be good, for my family to grow up breathing such air,' thought Tio, 'I am no expert, but I know that such things are not good for their health.'

As if to emphasise the thought even further, a man in his sixties walked falteringly towards him while having a coughing fit.

"Are you okay?" Tio enquired.

Bent over, the man struggled for breath before replying.

"Thanks… thanks, I'm okay, pal. I should really cut down on the Woodbines. I'll be okay. You go on your way, but thanks anyway."

Tio left the man and his smoker's cough and went on his way.

"What on earth is that smell outside? Is it from the works?" asked Judith the instant Tio entered the house.

"It is sulphur from the steelworks. You must have smelled it before."

"I have. Never as bad as this and never in winter."

"I think something leaked from the by-products plant at the coke ovens also. That is why the smell is worse today. It will be cleared up by the morning."

"Oh. Let's hope it does. Your dinner's in the oven."

Tio retrieved his meal and proceeded to devour it.

"Jan came round this afternoon. She doesn't think we're eating properly."

Tio gave Judith a quizzical look.

"She says we should be giving the kids proper food like pies and chips and mince, apparently."

"That's proper food?"

"So she says. Says we shouldn't be eating all this veg that you grow in the back garden. She says the war and rationing are over. She says it's not the modern way of doing things."

"The woman is off her rocker."

"And Mrs. Hastings has been complaining about Andre again."

"Again? What is wrong with the woman? He is just making the noises that any kid makes. He is not loud most of the time."

"Well, she says it's disturbing her and she's thinking of complaining to the council."

Tio shook his head.

"We need to move out of here."

"Out of where? This house? This town?"

"Out of this town, like we discuss the other day. I liked it when we first move here, but we need somewhere better. Somewhere like where you used to live."

"I thought you'd given up on that idea. Is this because of Mrs. Hastings?"

"No, she does not bother me. But we need to move to somewhere in the country."

"I only moved from a small village ten years ago. I don't really want to go back to somewhere like that."

"Why?"

"Because there are more things to do here. You've got shops on your doorstep, it's close to work…"

"That is the point. It is too close to work. You can smell how close it is to work."

"But this is a nice house. Andre and Gershom were both born in this house."

"Colette was born in the hospital. So we have to live there? When we were young we could swim every day in the rivers or the sea. We could go out for hours. It is good for children to grow up in such a way."

"It's not the same here, Tio. You couldn't possibly let kids swim in rivers here. For once thing, they're dirty. For another, they'd probably drown in the strong currents."

"Okay, but I'm just saying, it is still better for children to grow up playing in the open."

"And we don't know whether there's anything available. Where I grew up, houses are mostly just for farm workers."

"So, we will have to go to the estate agent and see if they have anything."

Judith, still unconvinced, was reasonably hopeful that the idea would be stillborn once the practicalities of the matter came to light.

"I am going to see Gabriel and Everton," said Tio after consuming his meal.

"At this time of the night? Won't you be tired in the morning?"

"They will both be leaving soon. I want to see them before they go."

Tio put on his donkey jacket and walked the mile or so to his brothers' house, all the time pondering he and his family's options.

"Tio!" Everton boomed as Tio entered the rear door of the two up two down terrace rented by the senior – and now junior - Mourillon brothers, "Emile, pour your brother a black and tan."

Like all Dominicans, Tio thought himself a formidable domino player. He much preferred the game to cards. Cards tended to involve higher stakes. Higher stakes sometimes led to cheating, and cheating to fighting. Besides, he was never much of a gambler.

Once the black and tan – a mixture of Guinness and Newcastle Brown Ale – was poured, Tio joined the Domino table. Duke Ellington sounded out from the stereogram. Six men, seven including Tio, crowded the dining room and adjoining small kitchen, half of whom were smoking, all of whom were drinking.

"What's this about you thinking of moving to the country, Tio?" enquired Everton.

"He's leaving the country?" chirped Emile.

"No, he's thinking of moving *to* the country."

"You leaving your little brother here alone, Tio?" Gabriel boomed.

"How do you know about this?" Tio was visibly irate.

"No need to be vexed, boy," Everton soothed, "your wife tell me. How else would I know?"

"Did she tell you we are only thinking about it?"

"She say that, yes. But I know you. I know you get that lickle idea in your head and it grows like a seed."

Gabriel towered over the domino table as if to impose familial authority.

"Boy, the English country is no place for a black man. I am not even sure it is a place for a white man if he not from the country."

"Why?" asked Tio, suddenly aware of being outnumbered.

"Because the people do not want anyone who is not from there."

"But we are all from the country. We all even grow up without shoes and Portsmouth people there call us goats. You will both be going to the country when you get home. You won't be going to Portsmouth or Roseau."

Gabriel sucked his teeth.

"It is not the same, boy. Where we will go, we have *family*. We will have land. We will build up new house from the ground. Every house here a hundred years old."

"Boy, I understand why you want to live away from town. If I stay here, I would want to go from town also. But they right when they say the country is not a good place to go here," Everton, generally the voice of moderation, opined.

"See, Tio," continued Gabriel, "you remember when we catch the bus to the seaside and we stop in the country. You remember when we go inside the shop and some foolish woman start screaming."

Everyone in the room was laughing now. Tio's grand plan was evidently failing scrutiny. The Mourillon family had thus far weighed it in the scales and found it severely wanting. To venture further away from the town, would be to forsake an oasis of familiarity, a refuge within which strength and protection were to be found in numbers.

Tio's irritability about the subject was not as divorced from the conversation topic as he tried to have himself believe. True, they were indeed from the country, and yet when they arrived in Britain, like the vast majority of West Indians, the brothers had undeniably gravitated towards an industrial town. After all, most of the jobs they sought were in urban areas. Whenever, on occasion, they had ventured out into the country, it had proved very much to be strange terrain.

Maybe it was because people who lived in rural areas had often done so for generations. The responses of older locals varied from mild bemusement to flat out hostility. Younger country folk were slightly better, but even those who confessed a love of calypso, the blues and soul music reverted to casual racial epithets whenever it suited them. All in all, much of the English countryside carried a distinct feel of a no-go area to Caribbean islanders.

"Judith is from the country. She father come from there also."

"It is not the same for you here, boy," replied Gabriel, "you go from this town. You know what it say on all the signs?"

Tio knew well enough what was written upon them but did not want to concede.

"It say 'keep out'. It say 'no trespass'. It say, 'come over this fence, I will shoot you with my big gun'."

"Where does it say that?"

"Okay, maybe it does not say that, but it might as well."

John Two, Gabriel's long-time friend and workmate perked up.

"Back in me dad's era, there were a load of blokes who went onto the Duke of Devonshire's land in Derbyshire up one of the hills up there. Kinder Scout or somewhere that way on. Anyway, they set the gamekeepers and police on them, put some in jail for a while."

"And that is how they treat *white* men, boy."

"He already say that is years and years ago when they go around in horse and cart," said Tio.

"Hey, you cheeky sod! I'm not that old. I said nowt about horses and carts."

Gabriel placed a consoling hand on his John Two's shoulder.

"Maybe you just look like an old man, my friend. I'm ten years older than you and I look ten years younger."

More loud alcohol-driven laughter and banter just fuelled Tio's frustration, the thread of the conversation all but lost. Despite seeming to be in a minority of one, it only served to make him more determined. He needed to get to the bottom of how things worked here in England.

Tio decided it was wise to try and discuss the idea no further. Better to throw his concentration into the art of dominoes. After a satisfying two hours at the table, he made to leave.

Everton joined him outside.

"You okay, Tio?"

"Yes. I am okay. It is going to be very strange when you and Gabriel go home. Are you looking forward to being at home?"

Everton sucked his teeth as he leaned over the short fence overlooking the neighbour's garden.

"I am not sure, boy. Yes and no. It will be very strange. We will see."

"You will be like a stranger back in our own country."

"I know. Do you think you will ever go back there?"

Tio shrugged.

"Do you want me to say anything to Lipson about your land?"

His land in Dominica. He had all but forgotten it. For now, he was content that Lipson was taking good care of it. That would have to be sufficient.

"No, Lipson is taking care. That is fine. I don't know if I will ever go back. I just don't know."

"I think you will not go back."

"No?"

"No. You will not go back."

"Has Judith say something to you?"

"Of course she talk to me. She tell me she cannot talk to you."

Tio was about to protest, but Everton placed a hand on his arm.

"Nah be getting vexed, boy. She just say it will be too hot for her there. And she will know nobody. And the children too young. She is right."

Tio was in too great a tiredness and alcohol induced haze to protest. Far better to think things through when his mind was clear, which was not now. He and Everton bade each other au revoir before Tio made his way home.

Home – so much meaning could reside within a single word. When someone mentioned the word 'home', where did he think of? Did he think of Fon Bèlè, Penville, and the Atlantic Ocean with Marie Galante in the distance, or Cottage Beck Road where the sky sometimes glowed in the reflection of the dross from the furnaces being poured out?

Surely, he was kidding himself in even asking the question. Just as eight years ago, the decision had already been made. For better or for worse, he was staying in England.

He needed time to think things through fully. As things stood, he was being overwhelmed by a grey cold that seeped through the soles of his shoes, bit through his clothes, permeated his life.

If he was to stay, he would need the green warmth of home to banish the grey. If he was to stay, he had best find somewhere he could truly call home, not merely a roof over his head.

CHAPTER 16

TAYLOR & NEPHEW

Clive Taylor took a moment to examine himself in the rear-view mirror of his newly purchased Triumph Spitfire sports car. He had made a point of parking on the road in front of Taylor & Nephew - Estate Agents, Surveyors, and Auctioneers. His uncle, by contrast, parked his more utilitarian Humber Hawk in the designated parking space behind the premises. What, after all, was the point of having a shiny new sports car if no-one could see it? Where on earth was the fun in that?

His tie straightened, cream suit jacket brushed down, he alighted his vehicle and strode jauntily across the road and into the office.

"Afternoon ladies. Linda, you're looking the picture of loveliness as always. You too, Cynthia, of course."

"Thank you, sir," said Linda, "flattery will get you everywhere."

"Yes, thank you, sir. Always nice to be an afterthought."

Cynthia's response was as acerbic as ever. Linda, unlike her colleague, made little pretence to feign activity, giving her compact almost undivided attention.

"Well, aren't either of you going to ask me why I'm looking like the cat that's got the cream?"

"Go on then, do tell," replied Cynthia.

"I actually managed to get a Yorkshireman to part with his money. Seriously."

"The Mortal Ash Hill detached?"

"The very same."

"Very good, sir. Well done."

"Hang on, what's all this 'sir' stuff? I'm not my uncle. He's sir, I'm Clive."

Cynthia shook her head.

"Doesn't feel right calling you Clive, sir. Perhaps Cliff. Makes you sound rugged, like a film star or maybe a pop star."

"And do you think I look like a film star or a pop star?"

"Would you like us to answer honestly or as employees?"

"I think you just did answer. Oh well, clearly my Hollywood career will have to wait."

He sauntered over to the office and headed to his in-box, and clasped a thin wad of correspondence.

"So, what's been happening in my absence? Any appointments?"

"Just one. A Mr. Murray, or something like that, he's the gentleman Alan spoke to the other day. He wants to look into purchasing the property in Roxby. He said he'd like to come in to see you this morning."

"This morning? What time?"

"Twenty minutes' time, actually. We didn't expect you to be coming in so late."

Clive glanced at his watch and then at his reflection in the window and quickly composed himself as if about to play a stage role.

Mr. Mourillon plus spouse had visited a few days previous but had been dealt with by Alan Dove, a colleague who had been standing in for Clive Taylor. Already property owners, the Mourillons had an uncharacteristically firm idea of what they required – something in an outlying village within cycling distance to the steelworks. No doubt in the course of time he would acquire motorised transport, perhaps one of those awful scooters, assuming he would learn to drive of course. Clive had learned to be pragmatic about customers such as these. They certainly were not the type of customers he had ever imagined he would be dancing attendance upon, but the booming steelworks was giving rise to an increasing number of foremen and middle managers seeking to buy properties. That could only be good news for Taylor & Nephew of which he was the nephew.

They had been driven by Alan Dove to look at a few bungalows in other local villages such as Scotter, a few miles to the south, but none had been deemed suitable.

Murray indeed, thought Clive Taylor. Mr. Mourillon must be French. That would make a nice change.

"Excuse me. I'm here to see Mr. Taylor"

"Ah… Sorry, where are my manners? A very good afternoon to you, sir. I am he. How may I be of assistance?"

"Benoit Mourillon. I spoke to someone here about the bungalows for sale in Roxby."

"Mourillon eh? French?"

"I'm from Dominica in the West Indies."

Tio watched Taylor's expression, waiting for a flicker of recognition of his homeland. None came.

"Of course, I see."

It was quite apparent he did not. Tio did not mind.

It occurred to Taylor that an Englishman been shaking his hand at this very moment, he would not have felt at quite such a disadvantage. A glance would have told him where in the social spectrum he stood, his likely income, the most appropriate area within which the man was likely to feel comfortable. Yes, that was important, the client really must feel comfortable in the neighbourhood within which he would likely spend the rest of his life.

The man before him, however, was a wild card. Yes, he was well dressed, but, from what Taylor had seen of the West Indians around town, even the ruffians tended to dress well. He had a soft lilting accent, but where did that place him socially? Something could no doubt be inferred from the fact that he was seeking to buy property, or at least he thought it could. The not insubstantial success of Clive Taylor's career had been built upon being able to read people. Here, before him, stood a man whom he had no idea how to read.

"So, you're interested in the new builds. You do understand you would have to buy from plan?"

"I'd have to…?"

"Buy from plan. The houses, or at least some of them, aren't yet built. The only way you can tell what they'll be like is by seeing the blueprint, the draftsman's technical drawing. I expect the houses will actually be completed sometime next year."

"Oh, I see."

"Linda, would you fetch the blueprints for the Roxby properties? This way sir."

He led Tio into the office.

"You know Roxby at all, Mr. Mourillon?"

Tio was clearly impressed by the fact that this polished, erudite man could actually pronounce his surname correctly.

"My wife grew up there. She left when she was twelve."

Clive Taylor's eyebrows raised.

"Yes, lovely village. Much sought after these days. There really isn't a better area. I'd quite like it if there were many more for sale there, to be honest, but alas."

"Are the bungalows detached or semi-detached?"

Linda entered the office with the plans. As Taylor unfurled them upon his desk, Tio felt a momentary surge of pride. What could be better than to view plans for his family's future in such a way? Finally, he was getting somewhere in the world. Finally, he was at the level he wanted to be at, talking meaningfully with educated, professional people. What could be better?

"Well, as you can see from the blueprint, it's just the garages that are attached so we refer to that as link-detached."

Tio shot at him a suspicious look. No doubt this was the sort of creative terminology for which he had heard estate agents were renowned – or put another way, infamous.

"What are you talking about? Something is either detached or linked."

Taylor, slightly taken aback by the Tio's directness, smiled.

"No, Mr. Mourillon, I can assure you, it's a legitimate term used to describe properties such as this."

Tio studied the plan intently.

"There isn't much room down the side of the property."

"No, but it's a small trade-off for the fact that there's plenty of land to the front and rear. It's a decent size, and the location, close to the church, is first class."

Tio admired Taylor's assured competence. He knew what he was talking about, and his confidence in his subject matter assured Tio what was potentially the most important transaction of his life was indeed in safe hands.

"As you can see, each of the properties has three bedrooms, quite large gardens. A school and church close-by, so very suitable for a young family. Do you have any children?"

"Two boys, one girl. Another on the way."

"Well, the close proximity of the school and church will be ideal then."

"I assume you work on the steelworks, Mr. Mourillon?"

"Yes, I'm a Lubrication Engineer," Tio said proudly.

"Excellent," replied Clive Taylor, none the wiser.

They discussed the price - £3,250 or thereabouts depending on specification. Tio already had a property from which he would probably have £650 after legal and estate agent's fees.

"So, you'll need a mortgage of approximately…"

"Two thousand, six hundred. And that means I'll need to be earning twenty-five pounds a week."

"That's… correct," murmured Taylor as he finished scribbling figures on a small notebook.

"Yes, I can afford that."

"Very good then. I suppose the next thing to do is for me to contact the builder and see if we can arrange a meeting."

Tio arranged to come to the office midweek to determine the timing of the meeting with the builder. Satisfied that all was in order, he said his farewells and left.

Taylor shuffled pensively into the reception area.

"Your face!" laughed Linda.

"Excuse me?"

"Well, you looked really surprised when he worked those figures out really quickly."

"Yes, I suppose he did."

A momentary awkward silence hung in the air.

"And are we going to sell it to him, then? I thought perhaps we may not want to."

Clive Taylor bridled at the question. He silently chided himself for having opened the door to such familiarity, eschewing his uncle's advice on such matters to be friendly by all means, but always to maintain a level of formality for the sake of professionalism.

"No, no," Clive Taylor did not raise his eyes, "his money is as good as anyone else's. He just needs to consider whether or not he'll be… comfortable there, that's all."

With that, he made his way upstairs to his private office.

"Well?" asked Cynthia.

"Well, what?"

"You know perfectly well what. You've put him in a bad mood now."

"He seemed in a perfectly good mood to me. He was definitely in one when he first came in."

"He *was* in a good mood then, but not anymore, thanks to you and your questions."

Linda couldn't conceal a slight grin as she was gently upbraided by her senior colleague.

Managing Taylor Jr. as a rule, was done by a combination of feminine charm, feigning avid interest in any given topic of conversation, and, when all else failed, playing the obtuse card and helplessly asking him to guide them through the complexities of the business, despite knowing its day-to-day workings far better than him.

"All I can say is that it's good job you're his favourite. For now."

"I'm sure I don't know what you mean."

"Before the end of this day, every joke he cracks is hilarious, every item he wants fetching is a pleasure, every observation he makes is fascinating. Agreed?"

"Agreed," replied Linda casually., "no change there, then."

CHAPTER 17

PRIMORDIAL

"Lads, we've another new starter joining us today," announced Wyn, "Everyone, this is Theo Murray. Theo, this is Philip, another new starter, as of yesterday, this is Ted, Brian, Mick and Tommy."

Tio nodded to some, shook hands with others.

"Theo's joining us from the Seraphim Plant, so no doubt you may have seen him around."

"Depends what shift it was," offered Ted to muted laughter.

"Got something valuable to contribute, Blister?" asked Wyn. "We're all ears. Are you going to give us all the benefit of your manifold wisdom?"

"Bloody hell, thought I was in church then. No, Rev, just adding a little joviality to the day's proceedings. But I'll say my three Hail Marys later if that's okay."

"That's very kind of you. Now…"

"No, no. Theo is very welcome on this shift. We're a broad minded and very welcoming bunch, we are. We'll talk to anyone."

"So will I," said Tio.

"Murray, eh? You don't look very Scottish. How comes your name is Murray?"

Dominica, Guadeloupe, Martinique or England. Tio knew that this was the same dance in any land. A new man enters a group and one will stick out his chest, take a bold stance and say 'Here I am, I am king of this hill. Pay tribute to me, and acknowledge that I am king'.

"It is Mourillon. It is a French name."

"Murray-on. What's Murray on about?"

More laughter.

"So, Theo Murray," continued Ted, "what part of the world do you come from?"

"Why do you care? You cannot see it from the windows of the Oswald Hotel, so you would not know it."

Surprised laughter burst out, even from those who had been egging Ted on.

"He's got you figured out, Blister," and "fair play to him." were the sounds to which the men were accompanied as they made their way back to their places of work.

As they made their way towards the cast house, Philip came alongside Tio.

"Afternoon. I'm Philip."

"Yes, I know."

"I only started myself today. I'm only here for a year at the most. Get a bit of money, you know, until I can study to get some better qualifications and get a job in the drawing office or the labs."

"I started here eight years ago. I thought I was going to be here for two years at the most. But here I am."

"What happened?"

"My wife happened. My children happened."

"And your wife, is she from here, or is she from, well, where you're from?"

Tio looked his young co-worker over.

"You ask a lot of questions."

"Sorry. I don't mean anything by them. It's just… you're the first person from your part of the world that I've ever met. Anyway, if you don't ask questions, how do you ever learn anything?"

Tio smiled.

"Dominica. It's in the Caribbean. And my wife is from round here."

"Ah, okay. I'll look that up in the atlas when I get to the library."

"Don't mix it up with the Dominican Republic. That is another country."

"Okay, thanks. To be honest, I've no idea where the Dominican Republic is, either."

"So, you are a student?"

"Yes. I'm doing metallurgy up at the technical college. I'm hoping that leads to a degree if I'm lucky."

"I don't think it is luck. I think it is hard work and study."

"Yeah, I suppose you're right there."

"I wish I had the chance to study like you. I only had an elementary education."

"Okay. Is that all that was available where you're from?"

"No, there are people who go further in education. I just wasn't one of them."

"Most people think I'm bit of a swot. I'm afraid I'm not very with it."

"A swot?"

"Er, someone who studies too much, rather than being interested in girls, cars and motorbikes and all that stuff."

"Listen, boy, these people will call you swot now. In five years' time, they will call you boss."

"Ha! I doubt it. It's a nice thought, though. I'm not sure they would take any notice of me even if I was their boss."

"You won't always be young and you won't always be the new boy."

"No, don't suppose I will. Well, nice talking to you, Theo. I think you're working front-side. I won't be doing that until next week. Perhaps see you later."

Before he got too far, Tio called him back.

"Philip. This man, Ted. Be careful of him. He will try and push you around because you are new. Because you are a big bloke he will want to make you look bad. Make sure you stand up to him."

"Yeah, you're right about that. He gave me a hard time earlier on, actually. Several times. And even though I'm big, I'm not…, well I'm not tough or strong or anything. I noticed you seemed to get the better of him pretty quickly, though."

"I've known plenty like him in the past."

"In a funny sort of way, I admire him, I suppose."

"That big lump? Why would you admire someone like that?"

"I don't know, because of his confidence maybe. Because he seems good at his job from what I can tell. Because he seems to know a lot about politics and what's going on in the world."

Tio shook his head.

"That is not confidence, boy. People who are confident don't shout their mouth off like him. That's people with no confidence."

"I'm not sure you're right there, Theo. He looks pretty confident to me."

"And trust me, he does not know much about what is going on in this world. He only knows about a few pubs and drinking places where he takes his women."

"Perhaps he can send one of them my way. I've never had a proper girlfriend or anything."

"Well, I can't help you there."

"Thanks for the advice anyway."

Most of the young people Tio had encountered up to now on the steelworks had left school at fifteen and gloried that their school days were over. Tio sighed at the very thought. If he had had the opportunity to study until the age of fifteen, he would have held a pen in his hand instead of a shovel.

It seemed that everyone wanted something they lacked or thought they lacked. He had always wanted greater educational opportunity; Philip had that, but wanted more confidence, which somehow he was convinced Ted had in abundance; Wyn apparently wanted a peaceful life or at least a cohesive crew, but there was no likelihood of that happening anytime soon; Ted - what Ted wanted did not bear thinking about.

Wyn took it upon himself to induct Tio and Philip into their new working environment. He talked the two newcomers through the ironmaking process using blast furnaces. He focused on the aspects that they would need to pay attention to – those being the less skilled manual and invariably dirty jobs such as helping the bricklayers whenever they relined the ladles with refractory bricks, clearing blockages, clearing spillages, clearing the runners.

Their job was to ensure this huge industrial beast remained fed via the charging elevators, and whenever it needed to dispense slag it could do so freely, and of course, most important of all tapping – periodically running off the molten iron content from the furnace.

"This town grew here because of the local iron ore a hundred years ago, but it's not good enough to use on its own now. Has to be mixed with imported foreign ore."

"Bit like the workforce down here – it's a bit of a mixture - Ted's from Yorkshire, I'm from the Welsh valleys. I know it's not exactly the far reaches of the earth like Theo here, but this is a town of incomers."

"I don't think Ted likes me. He made me feel a bit nervous when he was talking about me being some sort of spy."

"Oh, don't be worrying about any of that, young Philip. Ted says at least two hundred stupid things every single day. Sixty seconds later he's probably forgotten what he said. So, don't you go reminding him. If he knows something bothers you, he'll use it to wind you up every hour of the working day."

"How did he get his nickname? Is he a bit lazy or something?"

"No, lad." Wyn laughed, "he's actually quite a good worker. He likes stringing out his breaks, yes, but he's quite a strong chap. Just mouthy."

"So why do you call him Blister?"

"He used to work down in the melting shop. So, you know that we reline the ladles here and that we sometimes do them when they're still pretty hot and everything?"

Philip did not know but thought it best to nod.

"Well, he goes in one of the ladles down there while there are still a few flames coming from it. You have to enter those things with wooden clogs and thick fireproof trousers. You have to keep moving your feet so your wooden clogs don't catch fire, and you have to walk around like John Wayne so your hot trousers don't burn you.

"Of course, Ted being Ted, he decides he's not going to do the John Wayne walk. And he wouldn't listen to the older men telling him not to stay in there for more than five minutes at a time. So, of course, his legs got quite badly burnt. Got lots of blisters on them. Hence the name."

Philip pondered Wyn's words as if listening to a sage dispensing the cumulative wisdom that had been handed down throughout many generations.

"I know you're a student and everything, but the only studying you need to be doing at this moment is royalty. These are the four queens. Victoria, Anne, Mary and Bess."

The three men craned their necks to take in the four huge towering behemoths above.

"Why have they named them after queens?" asked Tio.

"No idea, Theo. Absolutely none. Come on, time we went front-side. They'll be tapping soon. It's quite a sight when you see it the first time."

Having to shout over the roar and hiss of the furnaces, Wyn led his charges into the cast-house to a vantage point overlooking the runner - a small sand-bound trench less than two feet deep, through which the molten iron would flow. Several of the old hands had gathered to watch. It was evidently still a spectacle even to those who must have seen it many times.

"So that's the lance we use to puncture a hole into the crucible, the bottom of the furnace. They use an electric lance these days. We used hammer and bar back in the old days. Hard, dangerous job. Very dangerous."

"Anyone ever hurt doing all this?" asked Philip.

"People are getting hurt all the time. Sometimes killed. Why do you think I'm showing you around and not leaving it to someone like Ted or one of the others? I'm doing my best to make sure that neither of you is among them.

"Here we go, look, they're through. You'll see the molten iron come out now. You have to be careful not to get too close. One, because of the heat. Two, because it sometimes can be a bit unpredictable and spit at you, especially if it comes into contact with cold metal. Catch it in your face and you could lose your eyesight or worse. It's happened more than once."

"What happens if they don't tap the furnace, or if they don't tap it in time?" asked Tio.

"Good question, Theo. Let's put it this way – iron has a nasty habit of breaking out in places you don't want it to. That's why the men always have to be on their toes if you get my meaning."

Once tapped, the molten iron crept slowly and inexorably down the run, illuminating the surrounding gloom of the cast house.

"Important this, isn't it?" Philip gestured pensively to their surroundings.

"How do you mean?"

"I mean, it's not just anything we're doing here, is it? It matters. Watching that was a bit… a bit primordial really, isn't it?"

"I wouldn't know, young Philip. You'll have to tell me what that word means."

"Like something from the beginning of time."

"Aye, I suppose so. It's taking something raw and unrefined, putting it under heat and pressure, getting rid of the waste, and you're left with something that's been refined in the fire. Now, there's a thought to leave you with."

CHAPTER 18

FOUNDATIONS

For Tio Mourillon, today was a good day, a productive one, given that he had just completed his final night shift and had yet to go to bed. Earlier in the morning, he had completed the purchase the land for the property in Roxby, to which he now found himself walking. Five hundred pounds of his hard-earned money, and worth every penny. He was finally beginning to feel as if he was getting somewhere. He already owned – or at least mortgaged – his house on Cottage Beck Road, but it fell short of the place he could truly make his own, a place upon which he could stamp his identity. The new place would be different. In Dominica, only a man of substance and standing would be able to afford to purchase such a good sized property.

Today his route took him from Lysaght's steelworks, across the country, through the open cast mines area where Rowland Winn had rediscovered iron ore a century ago, through an area called Bagmoor, past a wooded area, and finally through to the village itself. He had been told this area possessed some of the area's more interesting scenery.

During the previous night shift, he'd discussed the very same subject with Wyn.

"Look, Theo, however long you're planning to stay in this country, try and make sure you see some of the nicer parts of it."

"What do you mean?"

"I suppose what I'm trying to say is that not everywhere is as grim as here. Once you get out in the country, there are some beautiful spots here on these islands."

"Such as?"

"Well, the Welsh valleys, for instance, where I'm from. You can go south east a bit, to the Wolds. That's Tennyson country."

Brian chipped in.

"What are you talking about, Wyn? If he wants to see decent countryside, he needs to go north of the Humber. Way north. God's own country, Yorkshire. Centuries old cottages, dry stone walls, mountains, hills, crystal clear rivers and streams. Now that's countryside. Not like this neck o' the woods."

"I have heard about some of these places," said Tio, "but it takes a long time to get there if you do not have a car."

"Fair enough, that's true," conceded Wyn, "but there's always somewhere you can go locally. Near where you're thinking of moving, for example. You perhaps ought to take a walk in that direction. See the countryside. There's a stately home not too far from Roxby. If you catch the works bus to Lysaghts, you can visit it on your way to the village."

"You mean like a museum?"

"Perhaps a bit like one. You can go around the rooms of the house and see the paintings and statues and everything and see the grounds. I'm sure you'd find it very interesting. Loads of history in places like that."

Tio shook his head.

"That is your history, not mine. Lots of dead Englishmen who did not treat people like me well. I would not find it interesting."

"Ah, here we go again," Ted was now riled. "taking a pop at us again. I'm getting sick of this, you know."

"Blister, no-one's talking to you. Theo and I are having a perfectly amicable conversation. We don't need any drama, thank you very much."

Ted snorted behind his newspaper and said no more.

"Okay Theo, forget about the stately home if that's not what interests you. But I promise you'll like the grounds."

"How long a walk is it?"

"An hour, maybe. Give it a try. I promise you'll like it."

He had been walking for one or two miles, his journey had taken him past Normanby Park and over the roads that led through the iron ore quarries. Contentment soon started giving way to worry at not entirely knowing where he was going.

Help came in the form of a mines policeman had pulled alongside him in a Land Rover, asked him if he knew where he was going.

"I want to get to Roxby. Can you tell me which way is it?"

"You're heading in the right direction. What takes you there?"

"I'm having a house built there."

"A house built?"

The policeman, somewhere in his late thirties, but looking much older, made little attempt to hide his incredulity.

"I'd best be nice to you then, seeing as you must be rolling in the money and all. See that road up the hill over there. Go right up it and it will take you to the top of the village. Keep your eye out for the gamekeeper, though, he's a funny bugger. Keeps threatening people walking their dogs that he'll shoot them – the dogs that is. I'll be blown if I know what he'll do with you? Probably mount your head over his fireplace or something."

Tio laughed, thanked the man and continued his journey, cheered by the fact he now knew the way.

A mile later, he veered off to the left of the road, heading north and was now in a picturesque area of hilly meadowland overlooking the ore mines. Lack of sleep finally caught up with him. There was no-one to be seen for over a mile, maybe two, in any direction. He could perhaps have a quick nap, just long enough to regain his strength. Half an hour perhaps.

The sun was shining, the sky cloudless. A skylark hovering above performed its frantic aria. There was no reason anyone would need to come here, he may as well just rest. And rest he did, for nearly three hours.

He awoke to the skylark once more. As he arose, he knew from the position of the sun in the not quite so cloudless sky it was nearing midday. It was such a secluded spot, so picturesque. When the sun shone in this country it could be truly beautiful. A different beauty altogether from his homeland, less raw, more subdued, but beautiful nonetheless.

The poems that he had been taught by heart from the age of five upwards – he could see why people wrote them now, not that he could recall any. Something about roaming over valleys and hills and encountering flowers. The beauty of creation, Father Leutens had impressed upon him, could be understood by all, no matter what their language.

There was so much he could barely remember – the never silent, evergreen, seldom tamed Dominican wilderness; even the language of his father, Patois - he no longer had cause or opportunity to ever use it. When would he ever need to use the patois term for machete or plantain in Lincolnshire? His children would grow up never speaking a word of it.

He missed the sea, its sights, sounds, smells, everything about it. Trips to the grey sea in England were annual affairs, by train or bus. It was nothing like the blood warm sea back in Dominica. In his youth, he had gloried in the vast expanse of the Atlantic, been humbled by its raw power. It was an ever-present amenity, a place where one could indulge in a 'sea bath' at the end of a gruelling day, just lie back and float until the water infused life into a weary body. That was all gone now.

So much of the very substance of life was profoundly different to before. For one to increase the other must decrease. Extreme green had given way to green and pleasant, teeming humidity to the temperate. The country and everything that had made it seem alien to him, and him alien to it had changed. He who was once far off was now brought near.

Life had changed. He was here now, not there. Nor would he ever return.

"Oi, you! What are you doing here?"

Startled, Tio turned around to see a stockily-built gamekeeper with a ruddy complexion, a shotgun resting over his right arm and a deerstalker hat that made him look far older than his mid-thirties.

"You do know you're breaking the law here by trespassing? You do know that, don't you?"

"Yes. So what?"

The gamekeeper was a little taken aback, seemingly weighing up the nature of the man before him. Tio certainly did not look like any poacher he had ever seen.

"What are you doing here?"

There was little point other than telling the truth.

"I'm taking a shortcut to the village."

"Really? And how did you know this was a shortcut?"

"Someone down the bottom told me this was the quickest way."

"Did he now? I think I can guess who that was. I bet he told you to steer clear of me, didn't he?"

"Yes, he did. He said you were a miserable sod, too."

This seemed to amuse the gamekeeper, who wore the insult as a badge of honour.

Tio, tiring of the exaggerated standoff, made to continue his journey. The man would probably wave his gun at him, maybe make some noise, but nothing more. He had encountered such people back in Dominica. They carried machetes rather than shotguns. The English had a good expression for these types – all mouth and no trousers.

To his surprise the man made no attempt to hinder his progress. Next moment he was walking alongside Tio.

"So, what brings you to this neck of the woods?"

"A house. It's being built. I'm going to see the builder."

"Hmmm, that must be the plot just down from the church."

"To be honest, I don't know where it is. All I know is that it's somewhere on the longest street."

"Some use you are, setting out to see someone and not knowing where you're going. It's fortunate I know the way then, isn't it?"

"It's a village. I have been to plenty places in the past and not known where to go. I will knock on someone door and ask directions."

The gamekeeper pondered this for a moment.

"Yeah, I somehow don't think that's a very good idea. I'll drop my gun off at the lodge and take you there."

"Oh, okay. Thank you."

The gamekeeper, who introduced himself as Jed made a short diversion to drop off his gun, no doubt thinking that it would be unwise to be seen carrying it in what turned out to be a be an extremely sedate but quite picturesque village. Roxby consisted of five streets, four of which were named after the points of the compass, the fifth having no name and therefore going by its adopted name middle street.

Roxby was an ancient farming village dating back to Roman times. It was less than a mile from what could loosely be described as a cliff, elevated from the Humber estuary.

It was not that Roxby never changed, it was more that it only ever did so gradually, which for many was what gave it its appeal. Its population was seeing its first increase since Victorian times, when there had been a sudden decline due to farm labourers opting for better paid new jobs in the iron ore mines and later the iron and steel industry. Its past inhabitants had comprised a permanent core of blacksmiths, wheelwrights, cobblers and stonemasons, augmented seasonally by itinerant farm labourers.

The streets were dotted with various farm buildings, tied cottages, a Victorian school, two vicarages, a Primitive Methodist chapel, a Norman church, but absolutely nothing in the way of pubs or shops. Adjacent to each tied cottage was more land than necessary for each tenant to grow crops or to make some nod towards floral décor. This, thought Tio, will be perfect.

Springing up within some of these expanses were a few newly built large ostentatious modern houses. No doubt the locals thought them monstrosities, unwelcome intrusions of modernity, or perhaps they welcomed an infusion of life into the sedate, of new into the old.

The village's most abiding characteristic was its quietness. The only sign of life today was that the children were attending school, but even they were closeted inside at present.

Tio's destination was somewhere on North Street, somewhere near the church apparently. It should not be hard to find.

"He's not much of a talker," said Jed of the builder, "he's… actually, I'll let you see for yourself."

"What?"

"It's just that you seem like someone who knows his own mind. I'll let you make your own mind up without any interference from me."

"Fair enough."

Slightly bewildered, Tio assumed he would find out what lie behind Jed's cryptic comments soon enough. Once Jed was confident Tio knew where he was going, he went on his way.

A newly built detached house closest to the church was in the last stages of completion. Tio paused to admire it –

pristine, modern, perfectly formed. If his house was to look anything like this one, what could be better for a man such as himself to live in a place like this?

In the adjacent plot in which the foundations were being dug, two men were conversing, one large, with thin dark, slicked back hair, another barely beyond a youth, sporting a basin haircut. The plot on which they stood must surely be Tio's.

Tio approached the larger man and held out his hand.

"Good afternoon. Mr. Cooper…"

"Careful!" said Cooper sharply, almost a shout, "you've just knocked my marker out."

He moved swiftly to Tio's rear and replaced a peg to which a string was attached.

"Oh, sorry. I didn't see that."

Cooper tutted and secured the peg. Tio once again offered his hand.

"I'm Mr. Mourillon. Did the estate agent, Mr. Taylor, tell you I was coming?"

Cooper did not reciprocate. Tio, feeling more than a little foolish, lowered his outstretched hand.

"He did not. What is it that I can do for you?"

"I'm the new buyer."

"Are you now? It's a bit early to say you're the new buyer, isn't it? Why would you think you're the buyer when you haven't even spoken to me yet?"

"What? That's why I'm here. I've come all the way from town to talk to you."

"And why's that?"

"Mr. Taylor, the estate agent, told me to come and see you. He said you would be expecting me."

"Well, I'm sorry but I don't know anything about that."

Tio was confused and speechless for a moment. Surely Cooper must have been informed that he was the buyer of the next property to be built. Perhaps he was annoyed because Tio was late because of stopping for a rest.

"What are you talking about you don't know? He told me he had spoken to you. Are you saying he did not speak to you?"

"You'll have to speak to Mr. Taylor."

"About what? I've already spoken to him. That's why I'm here to speak to you. What is the matter with you, man?"

"Well, *man*, what's the matter with me is that I have nothing more to say to you. Talk to Mr. Taylor."

With that, Cooper barged past Tio and started loading tools into his truck. Tio thought to say something. Nothing came. Bewildered and embarrassed, he shuffled away, further discussion pointless.

Jed, who had apparently watched the whole thing from a distance, was waiting near the church, apparently unsurprised by what he had witnessed.

"I see that went well."

"You saw that?"

"Yeah, I saw it. I knew it was going to happen, didn't you?"

"Know what? No, of course I didn't know."

"I knew you were coming. I think half the village knew you were coming."

"You knew…?"

"Come on. We'll go back to the lodge and grab a cuppa, then I'll give you a lift back into town. One thing you should have learned about this country by now is that everything looks better after a cuppa."

They walked back in silence, Tio shaking his head as he mentally replayed the conversation, trying to make sense of it. A chorus of barking caged beagles met them at the gamekeeping lodge, no doubt used for hunting.

Once within the lodge's Spartan kitchen, the two men sat down at the table. Tio could have been forgiven for thinking it had not been cleaned for a great many months, if not years.

Considering Jed's reputation for awkwardness, it was perplexing that he was thus far proving to be an ally. Perhaps he enjoyed their shared status as outsiders. Whatever his motivation, right now allies were in short supply.

"I think you may have a bit of a problem if you're looking to buy there."

"Why?"

Jed heaved off his muddy boots, then took a loud slurp of his barely drinkable tea.

"Because he doesn't seem to want to sell to you."

"Why?"

Jed raised his eyebrows, surprised that Tio even asked the question.

"Because you're a coloured bloke, of course."

"Of course? Why is it of course?"

Jed chose to ignore Tio's question, simply coming up with one of his own.

"Why is it you want to move here?"

"My wife grew up in this village."

"I know that. Why is it so important for you to move here as opposed to anywhere else?"

"Because it seems like a good place. We want to move here and build a life for ourselves. And I've decided this is the place where we going to do it."

"it's just… I can't believe you've travelled half way around the world just to end up in this sleepy backwater. Mind you, saying that, I never supposed I'd end up here, either. I thought I'd be sitting somewhere else. Thought I'd have a chest full of medals, sat in a pub telling tales of derring-do. Did I mention there's no pub in this village?"

"I already knew that. That does not matter to me."

"It's strange. This is a place I'd like to get away from. And here's you, trying to come here."

Tio seemed too preoccupied with recent events to pay much heed to Jed's musings.

"Before I went to see the builder, you were going to say something about him. What was it?"

"It doesn't matter. Forget it."

"It must have mattered enough for you to mention it in the first place. What was it?"

"It's probably not what you think. If you're thinking that I was going to say something bad about him about him, I'm not. It's the opposite. I've heard quite a few people speak quite well about him. Say he's a good builder. Treats people fair. That sort of thing."

This was not what Tio wanted to hear. The last thing he wanted to be told about the man who had been so rude and disrespectful to him was what a marvellous person he was. He treated people fair? That could only be true if 'people' excluded Tio. Where was the fairness in his treatment? Perhaps Jed was not such an ally after all. Perhaps Tio should just have caught the bus back into town.

"Look," Jed continued, "I'm not particularly in the know with all this. As you not so subtly pointed out earlier on, I'm not exactly Mr. Popularity in these parts myself. I don't really get to hear all the rumours, but I wouldn't be too surprised if there's more to what's gone on today than it first appears. That's all."

"I don't know anything about that. I am not a detective. I just go by how he was with me. I had good reason to go and see him. I spoke to the man in a decent way and the man treated me with disrespect."

Jed nodded and tried no more to press the point. He disappeared outside in his stocking feet, returning moments later carrying something.

"Here's something for you and the little lady."

He heaved a brace of rabbits onto the kitchen table.

"You know how to skin them and everything?"

"Of course I know how to skin them. I lived in the country until I was twenty-five. Anyway, it's okay, you don't have to do this."

"I know I don't have to do it. I must want to, otherwise, I wouldn't be doing it. Go on, it's a gift from me to you. Take them."

"Thank you. Are you sure?"

Jed laughed.

"You really are hard work, aren't you? Look, just take the bloody rabbits."

"Thank you."

"You must be a country person. A townie wouldn't have any idea what to do with them. They probably think things like this are born neatly chopped up in a butcher's."

"Come on, let's be on our way. Your missus will be thinking Tom Cooper has buried you in the footings of that house."

CHAPTER 19

SOFTER THAN OIL

Linda knocked lightly on the office door before entering, tea in one hand papers in the other. She did not normally knock, but the day previous she had been chided by Mr. Taylor Snr. about several things, most significant of which was the necessity of formality and professionalism within working relationships.

Linda, of course, had heeded the edict that greater workplace formality was now the order of the day. Formality was asked for, formality would be given.

"Will that be all, sir?"

Clive Taylor, glanced up towards her, somewhat startled by her brusque manner. He suspected that the gentle word he had asked his uncle to have with everyone had in fact been a sledgehammer to crack a walnut.

"Thank you, Linda." He tried his best to keep his tone soft and friendly. She was having none of it.

"Mr. Murray called in earlier. He wanted to see you, but I told him you wouldn't be in until the late morning."

"Look, Linda…"

"Will that be all, sir?"

"Yes, yes."

He knew what to expect from the visit. He had had a fractious conversation with Tom Cooper a couple of days ago. Cooper was one of those individuals who tended to shout down the phone at the best of times. At one point Clive Taylor had to hold the earpiece away from his ear.

Soon enough, Tio arrived looking visibly agitated.

"Come in, Mr. Mourillon. How can I help you?"

"How can you help me? You can tell me why the builder was so ignorant. He wouldn't talk for more than a few seconds. I made a special journey on my day off to go and see him."

"Okay, Mr. Mourillon. Please sit down. Let's see if we can get to the bottom of this. What exactly did he say?"

"He said I needed to talk to you."

"Did he expand on that at all?"

"The man barely say a word. He was damned ignorant if you ask me."

Taylor reclined in his chair and twiddled with his fountain pen.

"I'm going to say something and I'd like you to hear me out. Now, before I say anything, I don't want you to infer any ill will or malign intent on anyone's behalf, particularly on behalf of Mr. Cooper. You understand?"

"No."

"Look, there's no point in beating round the bush. Here it is. Mr. Cooper doesn't want to sell to you."

"He doesn't… What are you talking about? Why?"

"Well, not to sound indelicate, because you're a person of the coloured persuasion, so to speak."

Tio struggled for a moment to process the information. He was well acquainted with the mind-set of those, sometimes even his workmates, who said half-jokingly that him moving next-door would lower the value of their property. Some were joking, some were not. But surely there were laws that forbade this sort of thing. Or at least he thought there were. He would have to involve a solicitor, but doing so would increase his budget and timescale. Where would it all end?

"He can't do that."

"I'm afraid he can. He can sell to whomever he wants. Conversely, he can withhold sale."

"I don't understand. What exactly is his objection?"

"Mr. Cooper believes if he sells to you, he won't be able to sell the remaining properties. In fairness to him, I don't think it's an entirely unreasonable position, although I fully understand it can't be pleasant for you to hear."

In fairness to Tom Cooper! Everyone apparently wanted to be fair to that man. Did fairness to Tio not matter?

"I'll talk to my solicitor about this. I'm not having this."

"You solicitor? You already have one?"

"Mr. Tennant on Priory Street. We're using him to sell our house."

"Ah yes, of course. James."

Taylor paused, giving the matter great thought.

"Mr. Mourillon, I think we have to be pragmatic about this matter. Much as we would be overjoyed to sell you this property, it would appear that we've encountered an insurmountable obstacle.

"My fear is that you may construe a motive from Mr. Cooper's actions that really isn't there. I wouldn't normally let on the nature of a confidential conversation but in view of the circumstances, I think it's only fair to divulge at least a little, if for no other reason than to put your mind at rest.

"We discussed the matter at some length. We really did. Mr. Cooper isn't seeking to upset or offend you in any way. He's aware of the fact you have very young children and naturally wonders how tolerable it will be for them being amongst – well - those who aren't of a similar background. You must surely have considered that yourself?"

As Clive Taylor spoke, a feeling, low and familiar stirred in Tio's stomach. Tio was sure he was in the right, and yet the outcome of this conversation would place him firmly in the wrong. Here, again, he was met with an enemy that never confronted him in the open battlefield, but only ever fought a guerrilla campaign. This conversation may well end with Tio signing some document that would damn his chances forever. Keep things simple, he told himself, agree to nothing, sign nothing.

"Look, I've already started to sell my house…"

"Don't you think that's a little premature, Mr. Mourillon? I think you're in danger of exposing yourself to some considerable financial risk."

"What do you mean?"

"Property purchases such as this have a number of components linked together. It's called a chain, as you'd imagine. The point being that you don't initiate an individual part of the chain without the other parts being in place and ready to go."

Last week, Tio had enjoyed Taylor's use of professional speak. Today his language was completely impenetrable.

"If what you are saying is that I shouldn't have started talking to a solicitor, how could I know all this was going to happen?"

"But that's my point, Mr. Mourillon. You don't set the process in motion until you know everything's agreed. Clearly, that was not the case here."

"Because that man is refusing to sell to me!"

Tio realised his voice was raised far more than he had intended. He was struggling to keep a lid on his frustration.

"Mr. Mourillon, I do hope you realise I'm trying to help here."

"I do realise that. Look, sorry, I know you're not the one to blame for all this thing. I just…"

"Thank you. I do understand your frustration. I'm afraid it's just one of those very difficult situations that arise from time to time in the business of moving to a new house."

"I need to think about this."

"Of course. You're always welcome to come and discuss it with us. We'll help in any way we can."

"Thank you. I appreciate it."

"You're very welcome Mr. Mourillon. I suggest you discuss this with James…, sorry, with Mr. Tennant. He'll no doubt be able to cast some light on how you stand legally."

"Thank you."

"You really don't need to keep thanking me, Mr. Mourillon. Goodbye for now."

Had his brothers been on hand to discuss the matter, he was sure they would have disparaged him. *'Why on earth are you moving away from where you have the support of other West Indians, from where you can be a support to Emile, your brother? You are moving to somewhere where you will be away from family and alone. Look, guess what has happened? You are alone. Why are you surprised at that?'*

On the one had there was an undeniable logic to what Clive Taylor was saying. And yet, and yet. There was an undertone, a voice, no more than a whisper: that Tio and those like him were inherently less, below par, somehow wanting. Or was that completely in his imagination?

In Dominica, whenever his father was about to slaughter a goat or a pig, he would soothe the animal with soft words, spoken in velvet tones. Today Clive Taylor's words had been softer than oil, but Tio suspected they concealed a drawn sword. Gentle words with ill intent could be the most potent of weapons.

And this sword was double-edged. First the insult, the disrespect. Second, and perhaps worse, was the logic that he should embrace the insult. After all, everyone was concerned for his welfare, for his children, for the greater good of all, for the cohesion of the community. What Clive Taylor was advocating, or at least conveying on behalf of others, was simply conventional wisdom, no more, no less. And what is wisdom if not the accumulation of collective experience, knowledge, and good judgment?

Surely it was presumptuous, even self-indulgent of Tio to fly in the face of those who knew – well – better than him.

Tio felt a long way from home, and his hopes of having a home away from home were rapidly diminishing.

He must seek legal advice. Yes, his solicitor would surely be able to cast some light on this.

TIO

I find days like these very tiring. Maybe it will sound strange to you, but I feel ashamed. Then I say to myself 'you have nothing to feel ashamed about' but it does not stop me feeling that way.

You have to understand, when a hundred people say that you are wrong, you sometimes think you must be wrong, even though your head says 'you are right' and your heart tells you 'listen to what your head is saying, you are right', you still think you must be wrong.

I have been told for many years that every man who ever insulted me or treated me with disrespect is really a good person. I have been called five hundred names, but I have never met a prejudiced person. Perhaps if you ever see one, you can point them out to me. They must be very rare.

You know, it takes a very strong person to stand their ground all the time. I do not know if I am such a strong person. Right now, I am just a tired one.

My children will not have to go through these things. They were born in England. They will be educated. They will not be made to feel like a piece of dirt when they want to do basic things. Life will be different for them. It will be better for them. I will teach them to be proud of who they are.

But first, they need a place in this world.

CHAPTER 20

YOU'RE A GUEST

Dominica, West Indies – 1938

At the Vielle Case Government School, head teacher Mr. Sorhaindo cleared his throat. Total silence prevailed in the classroom of Vielle Case Government School. Twenty-four uniformed bare-footed children, having deposited their slates on their desks, stood in a line at the front of the classroom, hands outstretched.

Those having journeyed from Penville had bathed in the Balthazar River several minutes before arrival and as always were thoroughly clean. Those from Vielle Case and the immediately surrounding areas knew well enough the necessity of cleanliness and the consequences of failing the inspection. Fortunately, today all passed this stage of the test.

Now hair inspection.

"Joel Seaman. I will expect to see your hair shorn by the beginning of next week. Please relay this message to your mother."

Then teeth.

"Very good. Children, form a semi-circle. Today, the renowned poet Mr. William Wordsworth. I hope for all your sakes you have memorised as required."

"Lipson Mourillon, begin."

> *"A barking sound the shepherd heard*
> *A shout is a fox or…"*

"Milton Baptiste, bring me Discipline!"

Milton Baptiste promptly arrived with a long hardwood cane. Lipson Mourillon positioned himself over one of the front desks. The cane was then dispatched onto the offending child's buttocks. Lipson then returned to the semi-circle.

"Benoit Mourillon, begin."

> *"A barking sound the shepherd hears,*
> *A cry of a dog or fox,*

"*As of* a dog or fox. Continue."

> *"He halts, and searches with his eyes*
> *Among the scattered rocks,*
> *And now at distance can discern*
> *A stirring in a brake of fern,*
> *And instantly a dog is seen,*
> *Glancing through that covert green."*

"Benoit Mourillon, well done."

The remaining verses were then read one by several other slightly fearful pupils.

"Class, what is this poem about? Raise hands. Claude Baptiste. Yes?"

"About a wolf that attacks the sheep?"

"Incorrect. No-one mentioned any wolf. Emanuel Alexis?"

"It is about a shepherd and he hears a dog, and he follows the dog, and he goes to the rocks, and he finds a traveller who is the dog master, and the traveller is dead."

"Emanuel Alexis, correct. Yes indeed, the unfortunate tourist of Helvellyn. A young man who died who ventured into unfamiliar terrain attended – and possibly even consumed - by his faithful companion a whole three months after his untimely demise. Children, return to your desks."

The children shuffled back to their desks but remained stood, Lipson Mourillon shuffling a little more gingerly than the rest.

"So, children, if any of you are thinking of an imprudent climbing expedition on Morne Aux Diables, please take note. This traveller ventured further than wisdom or his abilities permitted. Not only should you remember the poem, but I counsel you to remember this cautionary tale of the unfortunate tourist of Helvellyn.

"You should go only where you belong."

The young Tio raised a faltering hand.

"Tio Mourillon. Speak."

"But sir, where do we belong?"

"You belong in this classroom learning wisdom and prudence, of course."

Tio did his best not to be seen to furrow his brow, lest Discipline pay him a visit.

"Class, be seated."

1964 – TENNANT & TENNANT, SOLICITORS

LINCOLNSHIRE, ENGLAND

The secretary at Tennant & Tennant Solicitors shot Tio a disdainful look, then sternly announced that it was not protocol for the solicitor to do impromptu meetings, so there was no point in him waiting. Tio was having none of it, convinced that if he argued for long enough, made sufficient of a scene, he could achieve his outcome by sheer force of will and tenacity. If that meant this supercilious woman's feelings becoming collateral damage in the process, so be it.

A whispered word from a clerk to the secretary and all was changed.

"He will see you now, Mr. Mourillon. Go right through."

Tennant, a portly man in his mid-fifties ushered Tio into his office. The entire rear wall of his smoke-filled office was bedecked with uniform hard backed legal volumes, prompting Tio to wonder if they were there for effect. Did anyone ever read them? The dust suggested not.

Tennant wore a three-piece suit that had seen better days. Had Tio encountered someone of such unkempt, dishevelled appearance back home in Dominica, he would have thought it indicative of their lack of status. Not so, here in England. Only serious, professional people could afford to appear so scruffy and still maintain credibility. It was a badge of honour, a sign of confidence that they had mastered their field sufficiently for them to indulge in true British eccentricity.

Tennant left Tio under no illusion at all that he thought it an impertinence that Tio had hired him in the first place.

Even in their relatively amicable conversations – and this conversation was not going to be amicable – he sensed that this man thought the world not to be spinning quite correctly on its axis. Yes, he may be paying Tennant's bill, but the correct order of things was that some deference should be accorded. And this goat of a man from Penville would not defer.

Did Mr. Mourillon from Cottage Beck Road not realise that there was an order of things here? Where Tio sat in that order was unclear, but it certainly was not at the top, nor anywhere near.

Tio, for his part, had never been any good at hiding his dislike of a person. It made for some very difficult conversations from time to time, and this was likely to be just such a conversation.

"Ah, Mr. Mourillon. Please sit down. I've just come off the phone with Clive Taylor."

"You've…?"

"He's apprised me of the situation vis-à-vis the bungalow you were hoping to buy in Roxby."

Tio was by no means happy that Tennant had foreknowledge of his visit. Tio was behind the curve in a matter of which he should have been very much ahead of it. He had always prided himself on his ability to think and act quickly, but doing so required early possession of the facts – and right there he was in possession of very few of them.

"*Were*? I still *am* going to buy it."

"No, it would seem you're not, Mr. Mourillon, not if Mr. Cooper refuses to sell it to you. I'm sure he has his reasons."

"Hang on, I am paying you to advise me, not agree with him. I know what his reasons are and they are not good reasons."

"Be that as it may. It makes no material difference to the facts. And may I point out that I'm not necessarily agreeing with him. But I *am* advising you, Mr. Mourillon. I'm advising you that in this case there's very little you can do."

Tennant took several puffs of his pipe, much to Tio's now very visible annoyance.

"If he doesn't want to sell to you, there's no provision within the law to make him do so. I'm sorry if that's a matter of inconvenience for you, but there it is."

As James Arthur Tennant spoke, Tio quietly seethed. The words dripped with contempt, bordering on open hostility. This was no time to be side-tracked by such things, he determined, the extent to which he liked or disliked Tio was of no consequence. The fact that he could not or would not further Tio's cause was of every consequence.

"Look here, Mr. Mourillon, I simply don't see why you're making all this fuss. If you can't buy this property you'll simply have to find an alternative one where no-one raises any objections, perhaps somewhere with a greater number of people similar to yourself. I really don't see the problem in that."

"It is not for him or you to dictate to me where I can live. I will live wherever I can afford to live, and I can afford to live here."

"It would appear that you're labouring under a misapprehension about the strength of your position, Mr. Mourillon. What seems to elude you is that you're a guest here in this country. If I were a guest in someone's house, I'd hardly think it appropriate to go into their dining room and start rearranging the furniture or ordering the householders around, be that Mr. Cooper or anyone else for that matter. Mr. Cooper is taking a perfectly reasonable stance. And my considered opinion is that you'd do well to cut your losses - such as they are – and seek to live somewhere… more… suitable."

"Suitable?"

"Yes."

"Who gets to decide what is suitable for me? Is it written in the law? I think your law protects me also. But even though I come to you to advise me, because you have gone to school to learn about the law, you want to ignore it. And now you talk to me about furniture and all that rubbish."

As Tio spoke, he leaned forward and prodded Tennant's desk to emphasise each point. Instinct told him not to fall into the trap of raising his voice too high. To do so would be to fulfil whatever archetype to which Tennant had doubtless already assigned him. No, he would stick to the facts and not deviate.

"Listen," Tio continued, "I do not care *what* your opinion is about where I should live. If I want your advice on that, I will ask for it."

"I do *not* appreciate your tone, Mr. Mourillon. It's not the way things are done here. And regarding Mr. Taylor…"

"Who said anything about Taylor? It's Cooper I'm talking about."

"Yes. Yes. Of course. Mr. Cooper…"

"Save your breath. And another thing, you are finished as my solicitor. You are fired."

Tennant laughed in a moment of sheer incredulity.

"Fired? You really do appear to have delusions of grandeur. You have no idea the way things are done…"

"So you keep saying. I think '*you are fired*' means the same in any country."

"Very well, you'll have my bill in the morning."

"You can send whatever you want. I am not paying it. You have not done your job."

"We'll see about that! Good day to you, Mr. Mourillon. Please close the door on your way out."

CHAPTER 21

WHAT NOW?

A pregnant silence reigned over the besieged Mourillon household as they considered their dilemma. Tio had been far too consumed with his own thoughts to convey all of the previous day's happenings to Judith, leaving her with all of the backlash and frustration, but no real grasp of the essential details.

"Tio, can you please take those *things* out the kitchen? They're attracting flies." She said, gesturing towards the rabbits.

He arose from his chair, took the brace of rabbits, wrapped them in newspaper and took them to the brick outbuilding, returning to his seat without saying a word.

For what seemed like the hundredth time he shook his head whilst staring into the distance, again replaying the previous day's conversations in his mind.

After some coaxing, he finally he began to recount the previous day's goings on, including a blow-by-blow account of his sparring match with Mr. Tennant.

"Tell them to stuff it, then. We don't want their rotten house!"

Tio gazed into the distance, unresponsive, shaking his head.

"But we do." He said after what must have been a full minute.

"We do what?"

"We do want their rotten house."

Silence reigned. More head shaking.

"We're not having it," said Tio as if his encounters with Tennant and Cooper had only just happened, "we're not going to let this man Cooper and Tennant and every Dick, Tom and Harry tell us what to do."

"Yes, but what are we going to do about it? They know the law better than we do. That's what they're paid for. They've got all sorts of legal qualifications and experience in building and selling houses."

"Listen, they don't know better than me or you. They don't know more than us. They aren't better than us."

"I'm not saying they are better than us. They just know better. They're bound to…"

"They *don't* know better!"

"I don't know why you're getting so angry at me. I'm affected by this just as much as you. The children are affected by this. The baby's affected by this if I keep on worrying this way. The whole family is affected."

"Why is this about you? Of course, the whole family is affected. Who do you think I am fighting for?"

What Judith hated about their many arguments of late was their inevitability. She could see them coming, they both could and yet somehow neither could manage to stop it from happening. It was like walking along a path, seeing a large hole ahead and yet still falling into it.

In the first few years of marriage, she had convinced herself that it was a passing phase, an aberration. How quickly what she hoped would be the exception had become the rule. But even a rule did not have to mean it was inevitable, perhaps, this time, an argument could be avoided.

"I bumped into Elaine Bristow yesterday on the market. She asked me 'Are you still coming to Roxby, then?' You could tell all the time she was hoping I'd say no. Flipping cheek!"

Tio did not reply, absorbed in his own thoughts.

"So, what are we going to do?" asked Judith.

"I'm going to see the MP."

"Mallalieu? How can he help?"

"Of course he can help. He'll know how to deal with them. He'll know what I can do. What are you asking all these stupid questions for, woman?"

"I'm just trying to find out what's going on. We're in this great big mess that affects us both and you're barely telling me what's going on. I know it's hard on you, but I hate this whole damned mess."

"You think I like the way these people are?"

"No, I just said it is hard for you too. You just heard me say it. They were the last words that came from my mouth!"

"Why are you starting an argument at a time like this?"

"I'm starting an argument?"

"Yes, you are."

"Oh, it's pointless trying to talk to you. I wish I'd never…"

"You wish what? Go on, say it!"

"What I was going to say I wish I'd never suggested going back to Roxby."

Silence once again hung in the air, heavy and resentful. Upon each misunderstanding further misunderstanding, with each angry exchange yet more anger.

Tio laced up his boots and headed out of the house without speaking.

Ten minutes later he returned at the back door and found his wife expending her nervous energy at the ironing board.

"I am sorry." He said, without looking at her.

"I'm sorry, too. I suppose it's just the worry of this whole thing. It's a good idea to go see Mallalieu. Go see what he has to say."

Tio very rarely if ever apologised. The fact that he did so now spoke volumes to Judith as to how deeply worried about this situation he was.

CHAPTER 22

SPELLING OFF

With Gabriel and Everton now settled back in Dominica, life would be different for the English branch of the Mourillon diaspora. The older brothers had earned sufficient to fund whatever projects they hoped to sponsor, they had travelled the world, or at least some of it, and had experienced life in another country. They had also acquired at least some ways of doing things that would prove useful back in their homeland.

Dominica was in the early stages of establishing itself as an independent nation, and Tio's brothers were now able to be an integral part of that process. Remaining in England would offer them no such opportunity.

Tio, for the time being, was going nowhere.

"Theo, can you slow down? You're walking too fast."

"Philip, you are a young man. You should be able to walk faster. You have too much weight on you, boy."

Tio paused for no longer than five seconds to allow his younger workmate to catch up. He was becoming accustomed to Tio's directness.

"Big bones. That's what my mother says. That's the reason I weigh so much."

"It's not your bones. It's the fat you have on top of them."

"I do like my food. I won't deny it. What's the food like where you come from? Is it better than here?"

"Everywhere the food is better than here, boy. Everywhere."

"Okay, go on then. I'm interested. Why is it better?"

"Well, first of all, it has some taste. Nothing has any taste here. Second, everything there is fresh and healthy. Third, everywhere is close to the sea, so there are all types of fish. Fourth, you can grow your own food."

"Ah well, you can do that here. My uncle has an allotment. He grows potatoes, green beans, carrots."

"No, boy. You can grow every type of fruit and vegetable there. And the price you pay for a few bananas here, you can buy a whole bunch for that same money there."

"I think I'd like to go there. Sounds lovely. Do you miss it?"

There it was. The question Tio had now banished from his mind. Did he miss his home? He missed security, belonging, extended family, support - all the things that came with home.

"I miss some things. Life is here now."

"But I hear your brothers are going back soon. Have you never thought of it?"

"What's the matter? Are you trying to get rid of me, boy?"

"No, not at all. I'm not sure I can say the same for Ted. I think he'd like to buy you a ticket if he could, but that's Ted."

"I am only joking with you. I have thought of going back there, but it would be hard for my wife with the heat. And she would be a stranger there, also."

"I bet you'll miss your brothers being here, though."

"Of course I will miss them. My oldest brother, Gabriel, is the reason I came to here in the first place. But they have families back home. They have spent enough time here."

"It's just that... well, the way you describe it, it makes me wonder why you came over in the first place. I don't mean that in an offensive way or anything. But it does make me wonder."

"Why does anyone do anything, boy? Money."

Ted Barnes emerged from within the cast house and made a beeline towards Tio and Philip, the two newcomers to the crew.

"You two! Me and Tommy need a break. Come inside and spell us off for half an hour."

Philip readied himself to move indoors as instructed.

"Stay where you are, boy."

"But he said..."

"Never mind what he said. Stay where you are."

Ted now looked visibly agitated.

"I've just asked you to spell us off. Now get your arses in there!"

Tio moved to position himself squarely in front of Ted Barnes.

"Listen, mate. You are not my boss. If Wyn Owen or John George come and give us instruction, we will do as they say. But you? You can say what you want. We are staying here."

Philip grew visibly nervous as he watched the two men face each other, sensing at any moment they may come to blows. Ted blinked first. Perhaps the memory of his experience with Tio's brother, Everton, sowed a seed of doubt.

"So, it's going to be like that between you and me, is it?"

Tio did not reply.

"Well, don't think I'm going to forget this in a hurry. You just watch your back, mate. Just watch your back."

Ted continued mouthing threats and curses as he made his way back into the cast house.

"I think you've upset him, Theo."

"He will get over it."

"I don't think he will. I thought he was going to punch you."

"You need to learn how to read men like him, boy."

"I think I read him well enough to know he'll be gunning for the two of us, now. He won't just be upset with you. He'll be upset with me, too."

"He will get over it."

"You keep saying that. Funnily enough, I'm not feeling very reassured."

A figure emerged from the cast house, not bulky enough to be Ted Barnes.

"Oh, great. Here comes Wyn, now. This shift keeps getting better and better."

Philip rose to his feet once more, readying himself to speak to Wyn.

"It's not you I want to speak to, lad. It's Theo. Ted tells me you're not prepared to spell him and Tommy off. Is that right?"

"No."

"No? So, he's lying?"

"He's not telling you the full truth, no."

"Let's not go round the houses, here. What's your side of the story?"

"I told him not to give me orders. He is just a worker, same as me, same as Philip. I told him if there is instruction, that it has to come from you or from the foreman."

"I don't always have time to come and hold your hand for every part of the shift."

"In that case, he just has to come and say that you sent your instruction. That is all he need to do. Not to come and order me around like the order comes from him."

"Wouldn't it just be easier if we worked together and helped each other out, instead of being like this with each other."

"Listen, Wyn. I have no issue with you. But I do not like that man."

"Aye, well he's not your biggest fan, either."

"I don't care what he thinks about me. He is a fool. His opinion about anything in this world does not matter. But he will not tell me what to do unless he is a charge-hand or a foreman. If you think he is so great, then ask the managers to promote him. But I think you and the managers also know he is a fool."

Wyn drew breath to respond, but desisted.

"You tell me what you want us to do and I will do it, Wyn. But not him. Not that man."

"I'd like the two of you to go spell Ted and Tommy off."

"Okay, that's fine. We will do it. Come, Philip. Let's go inside."

CHAPTER 23

MALLALIEU

Edward 'Lance' Mallalieu, as he approached his sixtieth year, had enjoyed over a decade and a half of tenure in the Brigg and Scunthorpe parliamentary seat. His constituency was a solid Labour stronghold, given its strong working class underpinning. Mallalieu had made the transition from a Liberal in the pre-war years to an Atlee Labour man post-war. He enjoyed his first success under his new colours in the 1948 Labour victory and managed to retain his seat despite a change of government and several consecutive Labour defeats.

Oxford educated and a trained barrister, he boasted a full head of wavy hair that was once blonde but now silver. His appearance was polished, his manner erudite, still possessing sufficient of the common touch to be able to comfortably converse with his constituents. He knew them and they knew him sufficiently well to re-elect him several times.

At a party-political level, he was the definitive safe pair of hands. The word in Westminster was that his star was very much in the ascendancy. Should Labour win the coming election, he may well be heading for great things. He was, however, perhaps too good a constituency MP for his own good for him ever to make serious inroads into the higher echelons of government. Testament to this was an ever-busy surgery, much to Tio's frustration today. It had been a solid week before Tio had been able to see him, a week of high anxiety and frayed nerves.

He greeted Tio with a firm handshake, looking him full in the eye.

"Please sit down, Mr. Mourillon. What can I do for you?"

Tio embarked upon a detailed monologue, explaining his predicament at length when outlining the events of the past two weeks. Mallalieu listened intently and patiently for over five minutes before finally speaking.

"You say that the first time you met Cooper was when you went out to see him on the building site?"

"Yes, I'd never seen the man before that."

"I'd have to say, given what you've told me today, that I don't share Clive Taylor's optimism that Mr. Cooper's motives are entirely honourable. I think he's being disingenuous there."

"He's…?"

"He's not telling the truth."

Tio wondered why he did not just say that in the first place.

"Perhaps I ought to qualify what I just said. At least *one* of them is being less than truthful. Which one or ones? I don't know. You don't know. And we may never know. That doesn't matter really. The pertinent fact is that that they're stonewalling you."

"I know, but what can I…"

"Mr. Mourillon, I have one question for you. Have you bought the plot of land?"

"The land? Yes, I have, but what use is the land if he won't build…"

"That's what I was hoping you were going to say. Given that that's the case, I think you'll find you're in quite a lot stronger position than you perhaps thought you were."

"I am? How am I in a strong position?"

"For the simple reason that should you choose to, you can refuse to allow Mr. Cooper on the land. You can turn him off it, should you so wish."

"I can? Are you sure?"

Lance Mallalieu smiled and savoured the Tio's surprised expression for a moment or two.

"Yes, indeed you can. And yes, I am sure. I'm assuming you have all the necessary paperwork – land registry, et cetera?"

"Not with me, but yes, I can prove I own the land."

"Excellent."

It only occurred to Tio at this moment the extent to which the past two weeks seemed to have been one piece of bad news after another. Try as he may, nothing had stemmed the downward tide. Until now.

"What if he sues me or something?"

"It's by no means beyond the realms of possibility that he could threaten some form of legal recourse. In my experience, builders work to short timescales and tight margins. That's clearly the case with Mr. Cooper, given what you've told me about his 'concerns' for want of a better term. I would venture to say that the very last thing he'll want is to enter into some kind of protracted litigation, trust me on that."

Mallalieu sat back in his seat, clasping his hands together, looking altogether satisfied.

"No, Mr. Cooper won't do any of that. He'll build your house. He has very little choice."

Tio released out a huge sigh. No doubt he could have lived had he not been able to buy this house. After all, people get attached to all manner of things all the time. They learn through necessity how to cope if they do not get them. But having this house built mattered. Quite why it mattered so much, he was by no means sure, but it did.

"I can see you're pleased with what I'm telling you, Mr. Mourillon."

"Tio. Please. Call me Tio. Pleased?" he laughed, "yes, I think you can say I'm pleased."

"And you say you have a property for sale?"

"Yes, someone already wants to buy it. I've been worried we'll be without a home."

"No, no, trust me, it doesn't work like that, or not if it's done correctly. No, you won't have to move out until you're ready to move in. You'll be quite safe in that respect."

Tio laughed again for no particular reason. It was just good to laugh. It seemed a long time since he had done so.

"I have to take my next appointment now, I'm afraid, Mr. Mourillon… I beg your pardon, Tio, but here's my card. My phone number is on there should you need to call regarding anything else."

"Call? Why would I waste money on the telephone, when I can just come here and see you in person?"

Lance Mallalieu smiled.

"Yes. I suppose there is that. Goodbye, Mr. Mourillon. Or should I say au revoir?"

CHAPTER 24

TAJ MAHAL

Vielle Case, Dominica – 24TH May 1938

Head teacher Clive Sorhaindo cast an imperious eye over his assembled pupils.

"Today is a very special day. Can anyone tell me why?"

"Because it is Tuesday 24th of May."

"Oliver Seaman, that is correct, but would you like to tell the class a little more?"

"It is Empire Day."

"Correct! Class, take out your slates. Write down the watchwords of Empire Day."

Mr. Sorhaindo scribbled four lines on the board.

"Number one, responsibility. Number two, duty. Number three, sympathy. Number four, self-sacrifice."

"Children, this is the 'Union Jack'. Today is Empire Day. This day has come around once more, over the course of this day you will hear all about its history.

Head teacher Sorhaindo paced back and forth in front of an attentive class, raising his voice to emphasise each point.

"Now children, citizens of the empire should:

One: Love and Fear God

Two: Honour the King

Three: Obey the laws

Four: Prepare to advance the highest interests of the Empire in peace and war

Five: Cherish patriotism.

"There are fifteen points in the list of duties of a good citizen of the Empire. We will consider these five this morning and the remaining ten this afternoon."

"Children, remember - the King is your king. This flag is your flag. Be seated."

Lincolnshire, 1964

There was an unspoken but well established way of doing things on C Shift. A newcomer started at the bottom of the crew's social pecking order. The team weighed him in the scales, and so long as they were not found severely wanting they may eventually deign to accept him.

Any Englishman worth his salt would know that that was the order of things. But that was an Englishman. A foreigner – well, what would they know?

Today was Brian's turn – one of the quieter members of the crew – to quiz Tio.

"So, Theo, how long have you been in this country?"

"Eight years."

"Do you need some special papers or stamp on your passport so you can stay here?"

Tio briefly considered ignoring the question completely. As far as he was concerned, his status was nobody else's business, least of all any of his nosey workmates.

"No."

It was coming, any time now.

"I'm not being funny or anything, but if it were down to me I'd make sure all jobs are filled by British workers before allowing anyone in. I mean… it's okay you being here and everything, but we don't want any more coming in. There's only so much room in this place."

Tio had lost count of the times that an initially amicable conversation was a precursor to someone bestowing upon him all their manifold wisdom on race, politics and world affairs. Normally he tried to close such conversations down, but times such as this he was captive.

"Pity you didn't think of that when you went into everyone else's country then, isn't it?"

"What do you mean?"

"I mean that the English went all around the world and put yourselves in the top spot in their countries. I think you never asked them if they had too many people there or if they wanted you to come over. You just went there and took the best of everything."

By now Ted was looking increasingly agitated.

"Yeah, but that was different, wasn't it?"

"Different? How?"

"We went over there to bring civilisation."

"Don't make me laugh."

"We did. Your lot were eating each other and all that type of thing. We went out as missionaries to help them. Isn't that true Rev?"

"Don't bring me into it. In my opinion, you'd all be best leaving this whole subject alone. It'll end in tears, I promise you."

"Mine and Brian's point is that we went out to all those places to civilise them. It's a well-known fact."

"You need to go down to the library and read some books, Blister. There was a church in Africa hundreds of years before there was one here. You never heard of the Coptic church?"

"No, never heard of it."

"Precisely."

"Look, Theo, everyone knows the British Empire went all over the world and built all these uncivilised countries up.

Including yours. Some of the greatest buildings in the world are there because we British went out there and built them."

"Name one."

Ted appeared to be momentarily at a loss.

"Well… I don't know. The Taj Mahal."

"The Taj Mahal was built by the Indians, not the British, you daft sod.", piped in Brian, irritated that his conversation had been hijacked.

Ted was unperturbed.

"Okay, okay. I got that one wrong. I never claimed to be clever as Prof or Rev. I still say that it's a well-known fact that we went into countries like Theo's and civilised them. I don't see how anyone can argue with that."

Tio let out a mirthless laugh.

"So, according to you, all these people went out to all these countries to help them. Is that right?"

"Aye."

"Alright, I have a question for you: if they helped all these countries - America, Kenya, India, and all these places in the Empire – how comes nearly all of them want to fight a war to throw you out?"

"Because they're bloody ungrateful, that's why! Same as you. And if that's the way you feel about this country, why don't you bugger off back to where you come from?"

The laughter and joviality of a few moments ago had by now evaporated. Some in the room nodded in agreement. Others sighed and moaned at the grim inevitability of the two men clashing and moved away to enjoy the rest of their break in peace.

"Tell me, Theo," pressed Ted, "what are you doing here if this is such a terrible country?"

"I will tell you what I'm doing here. I am paying my taxes, I am going to work, I am supporting my family, I am paying for the roof over my head, I am obeying the laws. In fact, I'm probably doing more than someone like you. Don't come asking me your rubbish, when all you ever do is live off your parents and go down the bloody pub, mate."

"Okay, okay," interjected Wyn, "I think this is getting out of hand. At this rate, I'm going to put a ban on talking politics."

"Don't look at me!" protested Ted as he rose to leave the room, "talk to Martin Luther there."

Ted's departure was followed by his usual entourage of two or three workmates, leaving only Wyn and Tio.

"I think he meant to say Martin Luther King."

Tio remained silent.

"I think you went too far there, Theo. You can't talk like that in this country."

"Really? Tell me why."

"Because… you just can't. People will ask exactly what Ted asked. 'What are you doing here, then?' I felt like saying it myself. You must like it here at least a bit or you wouldn't be here."

"I can't understand you, Wyn. I would have thought with you being Welsh with all your history between your two countries, you would understand."

"Well, that's a whole other thing, Theo. Our conflicts are ancient conflicts. They go back over thousands of years. Conflicts and disagreements change, they go under the surface, I suppose."

"Look, if people from England go to Wales or Dominica or any country in the world, do they stay quiet and have no opinion? Do they say 'we can't say this, we can't say that' in case the people there do not like it?

"No. They say what they want. They tell them what language they can speak, they tell them how they can live. They tell them if they can vote. They stay with other English and do not mix. Do you see me do any of that?"

"But it's not the same thing, Theo…"

"Why not? Why is there one rule for you and a different rule for me?"

"I don't know about all that, Theo. I'm a steelworker, not a United Nations diplomat."

"But right is right and wrong is wrong."

"I dare say it is. But how does that help you? Even if you were one hundred per cent right in what you say, and Ted one hundred per cent wrong, how does that help you? You've still got to work with these chaps. You've still got to get through this shift, then the one after that, and the one after that. You've got to exercise some wisdom, Theo."

"Yes, maybe you are right. Maybe I do. But if you think I am here to bow down to a fool like him, if he thinks he can decide whether I pass some loyalty test. The only test is in his head."

"Theo, look…"

"Before you say anything else, my name is not Theo. It is Tio."

Wyn appeared mildly stunned.

"So… we've been calling you the wrong name all this time?"

"Yes."

"I thought it was just your accent. Why didn't you say something?"

"Because sometimes it's just a waste of time, Wyn. Do you think I open my mouth every time someone says something wrong or something stupid? I live with stupidity and ignorance every day since I come in this country and say nothing."

Wyn remained silent and thoughtful for a moment.

"Let me put it this way. I think you'll understand what I'm getting at here. If I were to invite you to my house, even if there were things you seriously disagreed with, knowing you as I do, I don't think you would just say whatever was on your mind in my house, would you?"

Here was Tenant's voice again, this time delivered through the voice of the closest thing Tio had to a friend on C Shift.

"No, I wouldn't," said Tio.

"Well, there you go."

"Wyn, I like you. You seem as if you are a good man. But I am not coming to your house. I am building my own house."

"Tio," Wyn smiled and shook his head, "I can't believe I've been calling you the wrong name all this time. I'd like you to write your home address down for me."

"Why is that?"

"Because if the day ever comes that I'm facing the hangman's noose, I'll be writing to you to come and plead my cause for me. Come on, let's get out there and make some iron."

CHAPTER 25

INFLUENTIAL PEOPLE

"Ah, Mr. Mourillon, I was hoping I would see you. Please come in. Sit down. What can I do for you?"

Clive Taylor, as ever, exuded affability and confidence.

"Actually, before you answer, I did happen to speak to James Tennant the other day. Although he couldn't divulge the details of your conversation due to client confidentiality, I do understand that it was… fractious."

"Mr. Tennant is no longer my solicitor."

"So I understand."

"Mr. Madeley is representing me now."

"Ah. I was completely unaware of that."

"There's no reason why you should know."

"Yes, but you know how things are – small town and all that."

Tio did know. He had not forgotten how last time he had sat in this office it was he who had been behind the curve, had lacked the necessary information, and how doing so had disadvantaged him considerably. This time, he determined, would be different.

"Anyway, the reason I'm here is to tell you to inform the builder we are going ahead."

"You're…? How?"

"Because the plot of land is mine. I've bought it."

"Yes, I know you've bought it. I'm sure if it comes to that, you can sell it back and you'll, of course, be fully recompensed. I can't promise you won't lose something on the legal fees, but…"

"I have bought the land, so I can turn the builder off it if I want."

Taylor appeared shocked, but not entirely surprised. He must have known all along the strength of Tio's position. He could have told Tio what Lance Mallalieu had told him, but had clearly chosen not to. No, instead Clive Taylor had constructed an altogether different narrative and tried to make love to Tio's ears.

"I must confess to being a little taken aback by this choice of action. May I ask what has brought it about?"

"I've spoken to Mallalieu, the MP, and I got some advice from Mr. Madeley."

"Ah."

Tio watched Taylor's expression closely as he spoke. This was the first time he had seen anything resembling a crack in his otherwise polished manner. Seeing this man's self-assurance punctured gave Tio a perverse sense of satisfaction.

After a moment or two, Taylor reclined in his chair.

"Hmmm. Do you mind waiting here for a short while? I need to make a phone call in the other office."

Taylor disappeared into Taylor Senior's office and closed the door behind him. The 'short while' he had promised turned out not to be very short at all. Taylor eventually emerged and sat back down at his desk appearing visibly agitated, remaining silent for a full thirty seconds.

"How well do you know Roxby, Mr. Mourillon? I know your wife hails from there. My question is: how well do you know the village?"

"Not very well. I know it is a bit of a dead village according to my wife, but I have been there once. It seems like a nice place."

"Dead village indeed," said Taylor wryly, "what I can tell you for certain is this – there are some very influential people in the village who can make your lives... uncomfortable."

"You what? Is that a threat?"

"I'm simply being candid. You seem to a man who appreciates straight talk, so I feel it's my duty to be as open and honest with you as possible."

"So, these powerful people, what are they to me? They won't invite me to their bridge card club or into their houses? So what? Who says I would even go in their houses if they wanted me to? What are they going to do?"

"I dare say you may feel that way. Does your wife? Will she be able to cope with being ostracised? And your children. Do you want them to grow up somewhere where they have nothing in common with their children their age?"

"Last time I spoke to you, you say to me 'my door is always open, come any time', you are my best friend who ever walked the earth. This time, you talk to me, you care about my wife and my children. But you still want to make sure I don't buy the house.

"My wife will be fine. And kids are just kids. They'll play with other children with no problem. Children are not worried unless grown-ups teach them such things.

"So, let me tell you this." Tio prodded the desk as he spoke, "*I can do what I want on my land!*"

Taylor remained silent, his lips pursed.

"Tell Mr. Cooper we are going ahead. If he has any objection at all, I will order him off my land."

Clive Taylor was a man who liked to know for sure that when he spoke, whatever he said was correct. Right there, right then, there was nothing he could do to gainsay Tio. Things were not supposed to turn out this way. How on earth had this happened?

He would have to live to fight another day. He determined to call Cooper later that afternoon, by which time he hoped to have gathered his thoughts and calmed down, which would not be for quite some time.

CHAPTER 26

TOM COOPER

There was a knock at the door of the Mourillon household at 7.15 pm in the mid-August evening.

"Are you expecting anyone?" asked Judith.

"No. Can you see who it is?"

Tio would be up very early in the morning for the morning shift. Hopefully, whoever it was would not be staying too long. He would need to be in bed in a couple of hours.

"It's no-one we know. It's a big dark haired chap and I assume that's his wife."

Tio jumped up to the window and glanced towards the door.

"It's Cooper, the builder."

"Oh. Do you think he's come for an argument?"

"I don't know."

It seemed unlikely that a man like Tom Cooper would have brought his wife to their house if his intention was for there to be any kind of a scene. Little could be ascertained from what he could see of them through the net curtains, but somehow Tio doubted he need be concerned about any escalation into physical violence.

He straightened his shirt and went over to the door, closing the lounge door behind him.

Judith could hear the low boom of deep voices, by no means raised, for approximately a minute.

The lounge door opened and in came Mr. and Mrs. Cooper.

"Oh. Excuse me, let me just clear these toys and things out of the way. I'm sorry, we weren't expecting anyone."

"My wife Judith. This is Tom Cooper and his wife Vera."

"Hello. A bit like the comedian, then. Come in, please have a seat."

She looked for signs of Tom Cooper being agitated. He was clearly not happy, but he seemed more upset than angry.

"Would you and your wife like a cup of tea? Judith put the kettle on."

Both politely refused. This was a very different Tom Cooper to the abrupt individual Tio had encountered in Roxby.

"Can I just say something for a minute or two, please? If it doesn't sound too forward I'd just like to say my piece and – well - you can have your say after that."

He looked around the room as if asking everyone's permission. Tio nodded cautiously.

"I'm really unhappy about something. Something's not right, so I'm here to set the record straight."

Tio cursed his own folly. He had let them into his home and was about to hear a tirade. Had he known this was Cooper's intention, he would have kept him at the door.

"I would never refuse to sell to you because of you being a coloured bloke. I'm just not made that way. It goes against everything I believe in. I like coloured people, I do."

"You could have fooled me, mate. You were bloody ignorant when I came to see you."

"Aye. I dare say I must have appeared that way."

"Appeared? There's no *appeared* about it."

Tom Cooper sighed.

"There's a story behind that day, actually. Things aren't exactly as they must have looked."

"Oh aye, here we go. That's exactly what the estate agent said. 'Things aren't like they look!' It's alright you saying that, but you're all happy to make my life miserable in the meantime."

"No, Mr. Murray. I'm not happy to make your life hard at all. In fact, I'm very sorry if I have helped to make your life any harder at all. But what you've been told about me refusing to sell to you just isn't true. It's the estate agent who's been driving this, not me."

"How do I know if I can believe you? You say it's him. He says it's you. How do you expect me to know which one of you is telling the truth?"

"I understand your position, I really do. I doubt that I would know who to believe if I were in your shoes. But I'm a good Catholic man. And the things that are being said about me aren't true. I've only just realised that I'm being blamed for all this and I came straight over as soon as I understood that you and your wife have been given completely the wrong impression."

"So you say."

"Tio, Tio," interjected Judith, "I do think he's being sincere. Why else would they both have come?"

Tio widened his eyes towards his wife in silent rebuke. This was far better left to him to handle.

"On the day you came over," said Cooper, "young Mr. Taylor had already been round that morning. He told me that under no circumstances were I to discuss the building of Plot 2a with you."

"Why?"

"For the same reasons as you've already been told, but he was the one going on about being able to sell other properties, not me. Apparently one of Clive Taylor's friends lives in the village so I assume they've been talking together. I think it may also be one of his friend's daughters as well, I'm not sure."

"It seems very strange to me that you suddenly have this change of heart when you get the message that I can order you off my land."

Judith knew only too well how Tio could often lack grace when accepting apologies. She had found that out long ago and consequently had stopped ever apologising to him. It was if he had to progress through a tunnel of entrenched obstinacy until he felt that his point was fully made and victory won. Once he had completed that process he could be far more generous spirited, but mid-tunnel he was immovable.

"You've bought the land already? To be honest, I didn't even know that. To say I'm the builder, I seem to be the last one to get to know anything. Well, you can disbelieve me if you want, but I came here to tell you that I'll build your house for you, Mr. Murray."

"Good!"

"I think my husband means thank you." Judith chimed in.

"Thank him for what? He's only doing what he has to do."

"Come on, Tom. I think we've taken enough of these good people's time. I'm sure they have things they'd like to be getting on with."

It was the first-time Vera Cooper had spoken. She was not the type of woman Tio would have expected to have been married to someone like Tom Cooper, or at least the Tom Cooper he had been led to believe existed. He expected to see either a trophy wife or a bullied shrew, but the Coopers seemed to be more of an equal partnership than he would ever have expected.

"Mr. Murray. I *am* sorry for the way I was that day. I know I came across bad and I can't blame you for still being angry about being messed around and passed from pillar to post the way you have.

"I can't do anything about the all that, it's in the past. All I can do is make things as right as I can now, so even though I've been the one who has been made to look like the villain in all this, I still came around as soon as I found out what was going on to look you in the eye and put things right.

"I'm offering my hand to you, Mr. Murray."

Tio wanted to remind Tom Cooper that he had once offered *his* hand twice to no avail. He wanted to tell him just how much anxiety had been caused to Tio and his family. He wanted to tell him that his name was *not* Murray for crying out loud!

Instead, he shook Tom Cooper's large, calloused hand.

As Tom and Vera Cooper returned to the Bedford truck parked on the road outside the Mourillon residence, Vera placed her hand upon Tom's.

"You know, I think that's the most words I've ever heard out of your mouth in one go since I've known you. I was actually quite proud of you."

"Aye, well I meant it."

"I know you did, love. I know you did."

CHAPTER 27

ISOLATED

Lincolnshire, 1964

Tio's argument with Ted marked a watershed moment. From that point onward, he found himself increasingly isolated, much to Ted's visible satisfaction. Many thought it only a matter of time before the two men would come to blows. There was talk of odds being taken as to who would win. Fortunately for all, neither the bets nor the physical conflict materialised.

Tio's day-to-day routine changed. He now found himself ostracised during tea breaks. Apart from Wyn and occasionally Philip, none of the remaining crew members would speak. In the cast house, discourse was minimal.

This had not escaped the notice of John George, who had only recently received an edict from Tom Chandler that problems of this sort, particularly with foreign elements, should be nipped in the bud.

"Wyn, can I have a word with you for a moment?"

"Certainly, John. How can I help?"

"The new chaps. How are they getting on? Should we be keeping them?"

"Okay, in their own ways. Philip is a clever lad, as you know. Not very strong, though. He struggles a bit with the more physical side of things."

"That's the one the men call Prof?"

"Yes, it is."

"Well, perhaps we can look at him trying his hand as a fitter's monkey or perhaps an electrician's. See if he has the aptitude for it."

"I'll mention that to him."

"Yes, do that. What about the coloured bloke?"

"Well, I'd be a liar if I said there hadn't been a problem or two."

"Problems? In what way?"

"He and Ted don't get on, but that's nothing unusual."

"Is he a good worker?"

"He is. Pretty strong, not afraid of hard work. Quite bright, too."

"Well, there's your reason for him not getting on with Ted. Ted likes the ones with nothing between their ears. Do you want me to get rid of him? The new bloke, I mean."

"No, there's no need for that. He'll no doubt settle in time."

"I hope he does, Wyn. I hope he does. I don't want anything blowing up in our faces."

As John George strode away, he turned to offer a final thought.

"So, don't forget, Wyn. You're the one who vouched for him as being okay. Okay?"

Wyn smiled wryly at John George's neat little sidestep, and the fact that he had not seen it coming.

From an early age, Tio Mourillon had found himself prone to replaying conversations over and over in his head. Truth told, he knew it was not the healthiest of habits, but the knowledge made him no less prone to occasional bouts of navel contemplation.

The problem with mundane and generally unrewarding work in a physically hostile environment was that time dragged. Men needed distraction of one sort or another to alleviate the endless monotony. Usually, that came in the form of company, comradeship and conversation, but the problem was that all three were in short supply of late. Philip was usually paired up with other members of the crew, and there was no rush of volunteers to fill his place.

Nevertheless, Tio knew his isolation could not last forever. Sooner or later someone else would be cast in the role as villain. For now, he occupied that position. Best to apply himself for the time being to whatever he was asked to do and let the furore run out of steam, as these things inevitably did.

Brian, Tio's co-worker, caught his attention in the late hours of an afternoon shift.

"Murray, the brickies need some mortar for a couple of hundred refractory bricks."

Tio was not oblivious to the fact he had been demoted from Theo to Murray.

"Is the instruction from Wyn?"

"No, I dreamt it up myself. Are you going to do it? Or do I need to go back to the foreman and tell him you refused?"

"I will do it. Keep your hair on, mate."

"I'm not your mate. And as far as I can see, you don't seem to have any."

After Brian had left, Tio did his best to undertake his newly received instructions. He made his way to the section where the ladles were being relined and started gathering a few tools together in preparation.

Again, a multitude of thoughts swirled round in his head. Perhaps he should have bitten his tongue and never have taken the bait from Ted, just smiled, done the wise thing, the expedient thing.

On the other hand, had he ever initiated the conversation? He had been an unwilling participant. He had simply stated his point of view, as would any Dominican, had they been present. Why should he kowtow to a man like Ted Barnes, or any of his ilk? He had witnessed men like Oswald Lawless doing that very thing, laughing along at demeaning jokes at his own expense, repeating them even. Worst of all, Oswald would speak harshly to other West Indians to curry favour from his tormentors.

On the other hand, maybe Tio was being too hard on Oswald Lawless. Perhaps the Bajan was just doing what he saw as necessary to survive. Who knew? Maybe Tio would find himself having to adapt in a similar manner.

No, what was he even thinking? Such a man lacked self-respect. They did not know who they were. Did they not know that they were as good as any of these men who thought it their birth right to talk to Tio and his countrymen with such disdain?

"Oi, you! Leave that hose alone. I'll be using it in a few minutes."

The voice and the accent were vaguely familiar to Tio. Scottish, with a heavy accent, possibly Glaswegian.

Tio motioned to ignore the command. He had used this hose to mix mortar many times. There was no special requirement for him to cede it to anyone else, no matter how assertively the order was given.

"I'll say it only once more. Leave the hose alone. You do understand English, don't you?"

Tio recognised the owner of the voice. It was Iain McKay, one of Shane Phillips' acolytes. One of those who had cheered, who had aided and abetted Phillips when he attacked the Nigerian several years ago.

"I have as much right to use this hose as you, so don't tell me what to do with this bloody hose."

Tio bent down and started to gather the hose. Then the briefest of sounds behind him. Then a huge thud. Then darkness.

Move!

A torrent of unruly thoughts competed for his attention. Whatever sounds he could make out beyond the extreme whistling in his ears shouted that he was still in the cast house. Had seconds, minutes or hours passed?

Move! Open your eyes!

Tio tried to get up. His body would not obey him.

Move! You may be hit again!

He managed to open at least one of his eyes momentarily. No-one was in his immediate vicinity. Incredibly, McKay was using the hose ten, fifteen yards away as if nothing had happened. He occasionally glanced in Tio's direction. Seemingly satisfied that there was no danger of Tio being able to retaliate, he continued working.

Chances were minimal of Tio being able to hurt anyone but himself. By now, he had somehow managed to crawl onto all fours. Eventually, he could stand, but the moment he was upright, he nearly collapsed in a heap again.

The cast house was as dangerous place as any in the world for a person not to have their full wits about them. He had to get out, and soon. This was the worst of times to be friendless. What he would have given for someone to guide him out.

Somehow, he had managed to clamber out of the building. The cold night air met his face, but only served to make his dizziness worse. The night air struck the moisture on the left side of his forehead. He must be bleeding. His left eye was all but closed.

Then, he was back on all fours, this time vomiting. Then, somehow, he was upright again. The sound of a car horn, followed by the voice of a cursing driver. The more he regained his senses, the more intense the pain in his head, and possibly everywhere else. He had to find his way home.

An hour later, he was on the doorstep of his house. How he got there he could barely recollect. Thankfully, now, he was in a place of safety.

"Whatever are you knocking like… Oh my goodness! What have you done?"

"I don't know."

"What do you mean, you don't know? You've got blood all over you. Have you been fighting."

"Somebody hit me with a shovel."

"Who? Who would do something like that? Let me have a look at your head. Why didn't you go to the medical centre on site?"

Dazed and confused, he was still in a state of shock. He found it impossible to sit still.

"He could have killed you. You need stitches in that wound. You need to get that looked at."

A duster was the nearest thing to hand. No time for niceties.

"I can't understand why you didn't hit him back."

"What?"

"Why didn't you hit him back?"

Why had Tio not hit him back? Unconsciousness was an obvious reason, but right now the answer completely evaded him.

Why had he not hit the man back? Yes, that was what he must do.

Thirty minutes later, Tio was back in the cast house. By now he could see clearly out of his right eye and partially out of his left. The pain showed no sign of subsiding, but single minded determination saw him through to this moment.

Iain McKay was working in the very same spot as before. Someone gestured to him that Tio had returned. He looked Tio up and down.

"So, you've come back for your hose, have you? Your wee friends came around looking for you. I told them the last time I saw you, you were lying around on the job, doing nothing."

Tio said nothing. He instinctively scanned to immediate area for anything McKay might try to use as a weapon. Nothing was within easy reach. It was now or never.

The next thing Tio knew, McKay was lying prostrate on the cast house floor. He did not appear as if he would be getting up for the time being. Somehow Tio had put him there. He may also have shouted at him, he may not. And yet, in all the concussion-induced confusion, Tio could recall a fleeting expression on McKay's face as if to say, *'this is not what I expected, how on earth has this happened?'*

As Tio staggered away, two of McKay's workmates rushed to their friend's assistance. Tio thought it unfortunate that there had been witnesses to the altercation. There would certainly be consequences.

I am not sorry, thought Tio. He was not sorry at all.

Wyn sat alongside Tio in the Frodingham medical centre shortly before midnight. Wyn and Philip had helped their unsteady workmate over the quarter mile or so distance, during which time Tio had mentioned roughly a dozen times that he was not sorry for what he had done.

He may not have been sorry, but he certainly looked in a sorry state. By the time the blood had been washed away, the stitches sewn, the wound dressed, Tio resembled something close to a human being once more.

"So, what happened?"

"I fell. I tripped over a brick."

"Must have been some brick. Iain McKay also fell?"

"He must have done."

"Fortunately for you, look, that's what he says, too. And you're not sorry you fell, apparently?"

"No."

"Okay, let me ask you this. Do you think you will be tripping over any more bricks and falling in the near future?"

"I don't know. It was not me who started the fall."

Wyn sighed.

"We can't keep having this sort of thing going on, Tio. Even if it's not you starting these things, management are gunning for people involved in things like this. And if it reaches their ears, it won't be the likes of McKay getting the sack, it will be you. I know it's not fair, but that's the way things are here, and they're not going to change any time soon. You do understand that, don't you?"

Tio made some gesture of acknowledgement, whether a nod or a shake of the head was unclear, but Wyn chose not to labour the matter.

Wyn shook his head pensively.

"What?" asked Tio

"You know, we work in one of the grimmest, most inhospitable industries in the country. And the only way most chaps manage to keep turning up every day is by being able to have a laugh from time to time."

Tio shot Wyn a quizzical look.

"So I should see the funny side of when someone nearly kills me?"

Wyn could easily have capitalised on Tio's admission, but chose to ignore it.

"No, Theo, that's not what I'm saying at all. I suppose what I'm saying is one way or another we've got to get past all this arguing and fighting. No-one like the way things are right now. I think it's driving everyone barmy, including me."

Tio shrugged. It was a tall order if anyone expected joviality from him anytime soon. Survival was his priority for now.

"Come on. Let's get you home."

PART FOUR

England - 2010

CHAPTER 28

HALL OF FAME

Lincolnshire – 2010

On a rainy August Sunday morning, Judith Mourillon pondered her busy schedule for the day ahead. She unlocked and opened the door leading into the foyer adjoining the century old Methodist chapel and the more modern flat roofed extension, used formerly as a Sunday school, but now a general village resource for occasional art exhibitions and quiz nights. She entered the chapel, shifting a small table into place upon which she placed a white tablecloth in preparation for communion upon which she placed the non-alcoholic communion wine and the pieces of bread-bun she had bought from Tesco two days previous.

The central heating was timed to come on at eight in the morning, then off at ten, leaving just the radiator valves to open in preparation for the nine-thirty start. Today, she would be welcoming the new circuit minister to the chapel. He would no doubt have his own thoughts about today's format. Likely, though, he would lean on her experience and ask her what seemed most appropriate. She would suggest a 'hymn sandwich' meeting.

They would enter the vestry, where she would pray for the minister, at which point they would enter the chapel, in which there would be no more than five people. They would start with a call to worship, a prayer of adoration, a hymn, the offering would be taken and blessed, another hymn, a brief sermon, a hymn prayers of intercession, the final hymn, then grace – and there it was - a hymn sandwich.

Later, when it was finished, she walked the few hundred yards down South, Middle, and North Street, returning home and then readying herself for the visit to Scunthorpe Hospital that afternoon. She prepared herself a meal of vegetable soup, which she ate upon the living room table, adjacent to the dresser upon which stood the hall of fame.

It was never really meant to be the hall of fame. It just evolved that way. First the photo of Andre after his passing out parade at Dishforth Police Training School one year before his death on duty in 1979 in a car accident. Then the graduation photos of Gershom, Colette, and Suzanne. Suzanne, although she was the youngest, had been the first to graduate, eight years before her death late in 1992. Now, with the grandchildren having started university, Tio and Judith were either in need of a bigger dresser or smaller photos.

After she had finished the soup, she checked through a few photos of the garden - the front mostly, taken with the express purpose of reassuring Tio that all was being carefully tended as he lay ill in hospital. It was in full bloom and looking at its glorious best.

Over the many years Tio and his family had lived there, the garden had been his signature talent and his passion, having heeded his father's words to tend that for which he was responsible. He was no longer in the Caribbean where his ancestors had once had no choice but to make their home, but now in Europe, where he had made his.

The front garden was bounded by a hawthorn hedge, which Tio and his father-in-law skilfully laid and layered to an even height of three feet. Years ago, an area had been measured out, the soil prepared, stones removed, then rolled with a heavy iron roller then raked again in preparation for receiving the lawn seed. Between the hedge and lawn, a deep border within a semi-circular recess sat centrally, and within which an almond tree was given pride of place, standing above the deep red of hardy fuchsias.

In the front right-hand corner, closest the street a prunus cherry tree, upon which Jed, the gamekeeper embarked upon a clandestine night-time mission to fix a *'Vote Conservative'* poster one night in the run up to one election during the early 2000s, source of much amusement to everyone in the village except Tio, and eventually even him.

Adjacent the lawn, a yellow flowering potentilla bush grew, standing above dahlias of bright red, deep purples and yellows, running alongside what was once a gravel drive, which was later block paved.

Every year blue lobelia, white alyssum alternated at the lawn edge, behind which sat orange marigolds, backing onto the potentilla hedge.

A five-foot hawthorn hedge bounded the rear garden, which backed onto a field. The rear garden no longer functioned as it did for many years as a vegetable plot. Time had necessitated a transition to something more decorative, more leisurely, so the rows of potatoes had become the rear lawn and a large trellis sectioned off the area previously populated by root vegetables, soft fruit growing up bamboo canes and covered with green netting for protection from birds. Now in its place were roses and flowering and evergreen shrubs sat between chequered paving slabs.

The coal bunker had been knocked down many years ago to give way to one of three patios, the onions gave way to a summer house, behind which sat a greenhouse some way back. Towards the end of the rear garden a sturdy garden shed, misshapen by the sheer weight of content from car boot sales such as tools, mowers, trimmers, drills, fertilisers. The shed, the garden, the summer house were all imprinted with the signature of a man whose interpretation of horticultural beauty was different to the more uniform English take on things. It was more chaotic, more resourceful in its use of anything and everything available to him as if Roxby and its locality were a desert island.

The current state of all things horticultural was captured for posterity in the photos Judith had had developed for Tio's inspection, now that he was unable to see his garden for himself as he lay in hospital.

He was there under examination, due to his inability to eat anything for a good two weeks prior to his admission, no longer able to eat even the light meals and subsequently liquid meals that Judith had prepared.

Today, for Tio, a special treat. His granddaughter had dropped by for a few minutes, full of the brightness and optimism so prevalent in the very young. Not that he remembered it being prevalent in him at that age. He perhaps did, but lately it was such a struggle doing anything other than reflecting on the past and dwelling on the negative.

She breezed into the place with some of her college friends. Her friends had stayed out of the way out of either shyness or respect. He could see them chatting together, pulling each other's legs, laughing, mimicking some celebrity well known to them, but unknown to him.

How very different to when he first arrived in England, to when he met his Judith's parents and her mother and so many others could seemingly see nothing but the colour of his skin. And yet the three girls, a cosmopolitan trio, seemed utterly oblivious to anything beyond what was evidently so hilarious on their smartphones. Actually, what seemed many lifetimes ago, he did remember laughing like that once, with his brothers and occasionally their friends. Perhaps he was being too hard on himself, he was bright and optimistic once.

Optimism was in short supply for Tio today. The medical staff – the specialists, duty doctors, nurses and others seemed not to be getting to the bottom of whatever was stopping him eating. Had it not been for the fact he was being intravenously fed, he would be – he would be in a very much worse state.

The oncologist, Mr. Khan, had casually dropped a bombshell that both Judith and Tio were struggling to come to terms with. He had made a passing of mention that perhaps his inability to keep down any solids – or, for that matter, any orally ingested liquids now – was perhaps due to 'the cancer'. When had it become *the* cancer? Previously the cancer had been precancerous cells, which, they had been assured, was a very different thing altogether. Now it was *the* cancer. Just like that.

Judith had raised concerns with the duty staff, who had reacted with a combination of concern and defensiveness, and the basis of her complaint had seemed, too complicated, too nuanced, too easy to bat away. Both Judith and Tio found the whole matter profoundly wearing, and it had left a very bitter taste in their mouths. It was not that they did not care, it was that they did not seem to care enough.

Those who did care, however, made life distinctly bearable on a day-to-day basis. Today he was being attended upon by a nurse Hollis, who had made a point of coming to chat to him at the beginning of each of her shifts.

"Mr. Mourillon, you'll never guess what. Morning, by the way."

"Good morning. How are you?"

"I'm fine thanks. No Mrs. Mourillon today?"

"She will be in a bit later. She is at church."

"Ah, okay. Well, don't you want to know what I was going to tell you?"

"Oh yes. Sorry. What were you going to tell me?"

"One of your old friends from the steelworks is in the next ward. He says he's coming over to see you in a few minutes."

That could be anyone. He would need something more specific.

"What did he look like?"

"Big bloke. Fair hair. The bit that's not grey. Talks a lot."

"Ah, that will be Ted Barnes."

"Oh, okay. I thought his notes said Tim Barnes. His daughter sometimes serves me in T.J. Hughes."

"I think that is his real name. But we always called him Ted. Like my name is Benoit, but everyone always calls me Tio."

"Really? When did that start?"

"Oh, when I was tiny. In Dominica in the West Indies."

"Oh, I have some friends who went on holiday in the Dominican Republic."

"No, that is a different place nearer to America. Dominica is in the Eastern Caribbean."

"That's really interesting. I'd love to talk to you about there. Did I ever tell you I got married in the Caribbean?"

"No. You never told me."

"Yes. In Barbados. We had a lovely wedding on the beach, lovely honeymoon. My mum and dad were there but he didn't want his family to be. I'm glad. They've got plenty of money, but they're not every nice people."

Tio nodded.

"So, there you go, Mr. Mourillon. We have something in common. You were born over there and I was married there. See you later."

Ten minutes later a booming voice woke Tio with a start.

"If I'd realised they'd let anyone in here, I wouldn't have come."

It was Ted Barnes. Tio smiled.

"How are you? You okay?"

"Ah, fair to middling. I think they ought to rename this place the British Steel Reunion Club. Throw a stick in any direction and you'll hit a steelworker. Can't move for them in this place."

"What are you in here for this time?"

"Nothing wrong with me. I'm as fit as a fiddle. I just like the food here, and looking at the nurses. What about you?"

"I think I am fine too."

Tio gave Ted a probing glance. He had something on his mind. Knowing Ted, it would not be long before he unburdened himself of it.

"Can't breathe, can't smoke, can't drink. Can't stand up straight. Can't go to the bloody toilet without going to the bloody toilet if you get my meaning."

Ted paused for a brief uncharacteristic few seconds. It was not good to see him like this. Ted was loud, Ted was ignorant, Ted was insufferable, but he was never like this.

"What's the point of a big strong bloke with no strength?"

The question hung in the air.

Perhaps these are the things one only sees at the end of their life, thought Tio.

"Well, at least we get to this age. Plenty never get here."

"Aye, true. We've lived through some history. Speaking of which, you see some Indian company is buying up the Scunthorpe plant?"

"Of course I've seen it. It is on the local news all the time."

"Don't know about you, but I'm just glad it's been bought up and not closed. I don't care who buys it, so long as they're good for the town. You never know, they might have a load of new customers."

"Could be. I don't think the place will close. They cut it down. They do everything they asked. It is in good shape."

"If it closes down it'll just about be the death of this town. There'll be no jobs, hardly. And the jobs that do exist are taken up by bloody Poles and Lithuanians and suchlike."

"Oh, here we go. Why do you have to start all that nonsense again?"

"What nonsense?"

"Why are you always against immigrants and foreigners?"

"Ah, come down off your high horse, Theo. Anyway, they don't like your lot, you know."

"Who?"

"The Poles."

"Well, if that's true, that is their problem. I don't see why there is always someone to be against. Someone on the outside. I remember when the people to be against was me, so I will not join in with it."

"Calm down. The last thing either of us needs is getting wound up right now."

A brooding pause brought about by a stab of pain silenced Tio for a few seconds.

"Anyway," continued Ted, "I'm just saying things were a lot better in the past. I tell you what, this country would be a lot better if things went back to how things were then."

"What rubbish!"

"It's not rubbish. It's true."

"You just want things to go back to when people like you were high, and people like me were low. Why can't you lot just make the best of things as they are now without blaming somebody all of the time?"

"You lot? You'd really come down on me if I said that."

"You did. About a minute ago."

"Did I?" Ted laughed, "Yeah, sounds like me. This conversation reminds me of the way Wyn always used to straighten me out. I don't mind telling you, I shed a few tears when that man died. Far more than I ever did at my own dad's, miserable old sod. Went right over to Neath near Port Talbot to his funeral."

"You should not talk about your father like that."

"Why not? He was miserable."

"It doesn't matter. He was your father."

The fact that Ted had so little energy to argue concerned Tio far more than anything he might say.

"How long ago is it now since Wyn die?"

"It was in eighty-six. He was big in singing circles there before he died."

"I was in the West Indies. I took my family there."

"Did they like it? In Dominica?"

"They loved it. Wait… what did you say?"

Ted grinned.

"I said did your kids like it there?"

"No. Not that. Did I just hear you say Dominica?"

"Aye. Well that's where you're from, isn't it?"

Tio was speechless. Ted could no longer restrain himself and burst into fits of laughter.

"This joke's been over forty years in the making. Wyn told me I was to drop it into the conversation and then watch your face when I did it. He wanted to be present when I did it, though. It was worth the wait!"

Laughing brought Tio another surge of pain.

"You both planned that?"

"I was either to say 'Dominica' or to come out with some patois that you'd taught him. I was going to try, but I can't remember all of it."

"He teach you some patois? I don't remember teaching him. What did he teach you?"

"Ball fin…"

"Bal fini, violon en sak."

"Yeah, I think that was it. What does it mean?"

"It means the ball – the party is over. The fiddler has packed up."

"Aye," said Ted, "pretty much sums things up for us, then."

CHAPTER 29

BIG MOUTH

Lincolnshire, 1964

Four days after the fracas with Iain McKay, Tio returned to C Shift. The swelling above his left eye had gone down significantly. The bruising had darkened, but would be gone soon.

The crew members were not entirely sure how to receive Tio. Knowledge of his having dispatched someone of Iain McKay's notoriety, however, seemed to lessen their appetite to appear at odds with him. Besides, another matter much closer to their heart was bothering them this morning – money.

Ted, as ever, was most vocal on the matter.

"I'd like to know why C Shift is getting less overtime than every other shift on the blast furnaces."

John George's many years as a shop steward, followed by his latest incarnation as foreman left him well equipped to win these verbal sparring matches.

"Barnes, you know the reason perfectly well. You get offered the same opportunity to do overtime as every other shift, But C Shift members don't take up the offer nine times out of ten."

"But the only overtime offered to us is to do double shifts, and double shifts for us means doing the full sixteen hours.

If other shifts do doubles, they get to go home early on their second shift."

"Yes. That's down to the discretion of the foreman."

"In other words, you."

"Exactly."

"So why can't you come to an arrangement where we can go home early on a double shift?"

"Because I'm going by the rules of the United Steels Company Limited. Other foremen can bend the rules a little, but it's their arses on the line if something goes wrong. I'm not putting mine on the aforesaid line. Not for you, not for anyone."

"But things are more likely to go wrong if we're here for sixteen hours. People are more likely to make mistakes if they're knackered all the time."

"Well, the answer's simple, Barnes. Don't do the overtime, then."

"Well that's bloody charming, that is. Wyn, say something, will you?"

"What do you want me to say? He's made it clear what his decision is."

"Is that how you're going to leave it? I thought you were one of the clever ones on this shift. At this rate, we'll hardly get any overtime at all. Poor relations, C Shift. That's bloody well us."

"Well, needless to say, Barnes, my heart bleeds for you. In fact, think if you look closely, you'll see the beginning of a tear. Or maybe it's just indigestion, I'm not sure."

"What about you, Scrapper Murray? Never seen you shy away from an argument. Aren't you going to contribute to this conversation?"

Tio had no intention of replying to Ted until John George decided to rile him.

"Ah, yes, Scrapper Murray indeed. Good to see you back on the shift after your fall. Nice shiner there. You'll get the opportunity to explain it later on this morning. I'll be calling round in a couple of hours to accompany you to the offices. To talk about your 'fall'."

John George wore an expression of quiet satisfaction as his words were digested.

"So, you say the reason why we cannot go home early on a double shift is because it is the rules?"

"Yes, Murray. That is correct. We have to adhere to the rules. You may not like to hear that, but…"

"But when you want us to do our job and to keep your production target, you like us to bend the rules plenty then."

"Such as?"

"Like tying the safety switches back. Like working sometimes on our own on front-side when we should always be two, like…"

"Yes, yes. I get your point. But that's completely different."

"Why is it different?"

"Because it is, that's why."

"That is not an argument."

"Look, Murray, if you ask me, you're lucky to even have a job. Personally, I doubt you will after today, we'll have to see. But don't push your luck!"

Tio was adamant.

"No. No, you are in the wrong here. If we have to go by the rules, we have to go by all of them. If you want us to do things properly, we will do everything properly."

"So, you're going to work to rule? Is that what you're saying?"

"No, I'm not talking about working to rule. You said we have to do things by the rules. I am agreeing with you. We will do things by the rules."

John George scanned the room.

"Is that how you all feel?"

For several seconds, no-one spoke. Tio's mind raced as to what he would have to do for his next job, given that this one would end today.

"It is," said Wyn, "if the rules are what's stopping us leaving early on a double shift, then we'll start looking at the other rules as well."

John George's neck began turning red.

"Okay, you can knock off early if you do a double shift. Does that make you happy?"

A subdued cheer went up across the room.

"Enjoy it while you can, Murray. I can't see any of this affecting you."

John George was as good as his word. Two hours later, shortly before 10.00 am, he accompanied Tio to the Frodingham works offices. For a moment, Tio's chief concern was in his being the one person present considerably dirtier than everyone else. That soon subsided.

As the hearing began, Tony Booth, the man readying himself to speak, did not give Tio a reassuring feeling that this was going to go well.

"Mr. Mourill… if you don't mind, it's easier if I just call you Mr. Murray. I know that's not your real name, but it's easier for everyone if I don't spend fifteen seconds making a fool of myself, every time I address you. Is that okay?"

Tio shrugged.

"Mr. Chandler from the Frodingham Ironworks has asked to sit in on this. Quite why, I'm not sure. It's a bit unusual, but I've acceded to his request. I'm not sure I had a choice, but…"

"Yes, yes, yes. Very well. Let's just get on with this, shall we? And the only reason you acceded was because he outranks you, so you didn't have much choice."

Jeremy Allenby clearly wanted proceedings over and done with as quickly as possible without tangential matters taking up further time.

"We've already heard Mr. McKay's side of the story and we've had his written statement," continued Booth, "we've read yours, and I must admit the details are pretty sparse. We'd like to get your side of the story before passing… before making any sort of decision."

"It is simple. I was doing my job. I needed to use a hosepipe that is there for everyone to use. This man start shouting that I have to leave it alone. I don't take any notice of him because I need to do my job, so I pick it up. Next thing I know the man hit me as hard as he can with a shovel. He could have killed me."

"So you say. But he didn't, did he?"

"He didn't what?"

"He didn't kill you. You were well enough to go off site, which you did without the permission of your foreman. You said that you spoke to your wife, then went back to work and struck him."

"I don't deny I hit him. If I did not hit him he would be trying it again with me and everyone else."

Tony Booth shuffled in his chair. He wore an expression one of restlessness and irritability.

"Yes, but my point is that there was a much greater degree of premeditation in your actions than in his. I can understand why he did what he did. He'd asked everyone to leave an item he needed for a while. He lost his temper when you deliberately ignored him. You, on the other hand, went off the site – for all we know to go fetch back up or support or something. You say you just spoke to your wife."

"So, he hits me with his shovel, I have a big bump on my head, and I'm more to blame than him? What is going on here? I thought this was supposed to be a fair hearing."

In the corner of his eye, Tio could see Tom Chandler, who appeared to be listening intently, rubbing his ear profusely from time to time. Some sort of tick, no doubt. He found it extremely distracting.

"So, he hits me with his shovel, I have a big bump on my head, and I'm more to blame than him? What is going on here? I thought this was supposed to be a fair hearing."

"Are you suggesting it's not fair, Mr. Murray? That would be a serious allegation if you say such a thing, and something that would be viewed very dimly. I would be more careful with your choice of words if I were you."

"What you just said is that he is less to blame than me."

"And that's our opinion. And…"

"Actually, Tony," Jeremy Allenby cut in, "it would help things greatly if you waited until we've expressed our view before you convey our collective thoughts."

"Very well. That's my opinion. You accept that you went off site and you came back on site with the intention of resuming the fight?"

"I don't accept it the way you put it."

"How would you put it, then?"

"I went off because I hardly know where I was. I spoke to my wife and she asked me why I don't hit him back. So, I came back and see him again. And I hit him."

"Yes, well. It would seem that you've told us as much as we need to know. In the interests of fairness, is there anything else you'd like to add to help your case at all?"

Tio allowed himself a wry laugh.

"No."

"Would you mind going outside the door for a few minutes to allow us time to discuss our final decision?"

Tio left the room and sat out in the corridor several yards out of earshot.

Tony Booth shook his head.

"It aggravates me that we've got to give both of them the sack."

"Which one would you prefer not to see fired, Tony?"

Tom Chandler was not subordinate to Jeremy Allenby, but his input to proceedings was very much at Allenby's discretion. This was his show. He saw no harm in Tom quizzing Tony Booth, though, it would be interesting and possibly revealing to hear what would come from the inevitable conflict.

"I've made my position perfectly clear, I think Murray is more at fault because what he did was premeditated. I don't like his attitude either. Seems to me that he's got a bloody great big chip on his shoulder."

"Ah, now you see, I find it very interesting that you use that particular phrase with regards to Mr. Mourillon, Tony."

"I'm not sure I understand what you're getting at."

"Aren't you? You see I'm a great believer in the precise use of language. Do you know the exact meaning of the phrase you've just chosen to use?"

Tony Booth looked searchingly to Jeremy Allenby, half in expectation of some sort of intervention. None came.

"I took the time to look it up. It means someone who bears a sense of resentment based on a real or perceived injustice. I'd be interested to know who you think Mr. Mourillon resents, bearing in mind he has no history of initiating altercations, unlike Mr. McKay, whose list is lengthy, to say the least. I'm just interested to know why that phrase comes so readily to hand regarding Mr. Mourillon. That's all."

"Look, I've given my honest opinion here and, excuse me for saying so, I can't help but feel my words are being – well, if not twisted – certainly turned into something I didn't mean. You're a very clever chap, Mr. Chandler. I'm sure you can tie a secondary modern educated man like me in knots. I just say things as I see them and I do so honestly."

Jeremy Allenby was keen to bring things to a conclusion.

"Okay, let's not turn this into an all afternoon affair. I think we're where we expected to be at the outset. They'll both have to go, it's as simple as that. Can we call him back in? Let's get this over and done with."

Tio re-entered the room and took his seat facing the three men. Jeremy Allenby spoke.

"Okay, Mr. Mourillon, I've listened to contributions from Mr. Booth and Mr. Chandler and it's really quite straightforward. The sanction for fighting is instant dismissal. Had you retaliated immediately you may have gained a reprieve, but with the level of premeditation involved... well, there's really very little to say about it. We'll give you a week's notice. I've no doubt you'll think this unfair right at this moment, but given time to reflect, I think you'll see that you left us with very little choice."

Tio did not linger. He would leave worrying about paying the mortgage and bills until tomorrow. Right now, he was too angry.

Much as he wanted to get away from the building immediately, there was a necessity to wait a further five minutes to allow a secretary to process some documentation.

Finally able to leave, he exited the building. He paused, unsure whether he should immediately return home or return to the ironworks. To his rear, sudden rapid footsteps.

"Mr. Mourillon?"

It was Tom Chandler.

"I'd like to speak to you for a moment."

Tio said nothing as Tom Chandler caught his breath.

"I have a suggestion. I'm hoping you might find it agreeable."

Tio stared blankly at him.

"Sorry, but I don't know who you are. I know you were in there, but that's all."

"Of course. I'm Tom Chandler. I'm the production manager of Frodingham Ironworks."

They shook hands. This was exalted company indeed.

"I have my own thoughts about what just happened, and I think it better for everyone if I keep them to myself. Anyway, to get to the point, I'd like you to come and work for me permanently. They're within their rights to terminate your employment. I'm within mine to rehire you. If you were to accept, you would be a permanent employee on the South Ironworks."

Tom Chandler allowed a moment for Tio to digest what he had said.

"I do, however, want to emphasise that there really can't be any sort of repetition of the incident with Mr. McKay. Is that understood?"

Tio nodded.

"Very good. We have a vacancy for a position on C shift."

"I have been working as a temp on C Shift."

"Good. Well, you'll hopefully not have too many bedding in problems then. There are some good men on there and some – well, let's just say less good ones. I'll expect you to get on with all of them, Mr. Mourillon."

Tio was disoriented. Just as his anger was reaching its apex, this man came out of nowhere to throw cold water over it.

Tio nodded and mumbled his assent, then turned to continue his journey.

"Where are you going, Mr. Mourillon?"

"I'm going home."

"No, you must complete the remainder of your shift and complete the remaining shift pattern."

Tio, no less perplexed, took heed. He bade Tom Chandler the briefest of thanks and set off toward his workplace.

The remainder of the shift was mercifully quiet, which was a relief. Mindful of Tom Chandler's warning not to get into any conflict, he was careful to keep his head down. Who knew? Perhaps this could become the new normal.

Only at the end of the shift did his heart sink when finding most the crew members gathered, apparently waiting for him. This was the last thing he needed. Had Tom Chandler not distinctly instructed him not to get into any further arguments only two hours ago?

The reassuring sight of Wyn emerging through the makeshift assembly assuaged his heightened sense of alarm.

"Tio, we're thinking of getting together for a swift pint up at the Queens. Being as you're apparently one of our crew, I've been asked to ask you if you'll join us."

"It is okay thanks, Wyn. Anyway, I don't drink much."

"Neither do I, to be honest, but we thought on occasion of what went off earlier today we ought to – well - celebrate a little."

"Earlier today?"

"The overtime thing. It's going to make a big difference to some of us. Well, to all of us, really. Come on, you need only stay fifteen minutes if you're busy. The Queens is only round the corner from your house. We just thought it would be good for everyone's morale. I'm sure even you'd agree it could do with a bit of a boost."

Wyn was right. Being in a state of conflict and forever having to be on your guard was exhausting. And as he had said, it need not necessarily take long.

In the bar of the Queens Hotel, every man chipped in a shilling to cover their pint. They were all strangely on procession, no-one had started drinking yet. Wyn then raised his voice.

"Come on, Blister. You've had plenty to say for yourself just lately. I think it should be you to raise the toast."

Ted then semi-reluctantly stepped away from the bar, pint glass in hand.

"Aye, I suppose he's right there. Well, we've had our disagreements, as you all know, but that doesn't mean I can't give credit where credit's due. And any enemy of John George is a friend of mine. In fact…"

"Just get on with the toast, Blister. Some of us would like to go home sometime today."

"Okay, okay. Here goes – to Theo's big mouth."

The men jovially echoed the toast to the accompaniment of smiles, handshakes and the occasional pat on Tio's back.

Minutes later, as he pondered the encounter when making his way home, what struck Tio most of all was that the many of his workmates seemed more relieved in the thaw in relations than he did.

A moment ago, he was the villain. Now, apparently, he was the man of the moment. He had sought neither. He had just been Tio.

CHAPTER 30

OLD WARRIOR

On a balmy late September afternoon, Terence Taylor had decided to sit out the intended round of golf with his friends at Woodhall Spa, south east of Lincoln. Sixty-one years of age, he wore thick rimmed spectacles a deep navy blue blazer, white shirt and the maroon satin tie of RAF Squadron 617 at Scampton near Lincoln, upon which sat motifs of a dam with three lightning strikes.

An encounter with a group of motorcyclists at the Lincolnshire coast earlier in the day had ruined any possibility of an enjoyable afternoon. It had affected him profoundly and left him trying his best to make sense of what had happened.

He had accosted a teenager on the seafront promenade for throwing litter on the ground, only to find he was suddenly surrounded by a group of leather jacketed youths. He was not physically harmed as such, but he had been pushed and jostled and the incident had left him shaken. Years ago, he would have been able to have physically imposed himself and put up a staunch defence, but recurring back problems had long since diminished his physical prowess and, correspondingly, his confidence.

Clive, his nephew and junior partner in the business, approached the outdoor table on the club house patio at which he was sat. More of a surrogate son than a nephew, Clive was the man to whom he hoped he would be able to hand over the reins of the business, given the untimely death of his own son shortly after the war. Clive had a penchant for sports cars and all things ostentatious, but that did not detract from the promising start he had made running the Scunthorpe office, where he had so far shown himself industrious and prone to take the initiative.

"Clive, you not doing a round?"

"No, Uncle. They'll be a good four hours. I can't say I feel like listening to four hours of election talk – impending socialist Armageddon, the end of civilisation as we know it, et cetera."

"I can't believe you're spending your Sunday afternoon with a bunch of old codgers like me. I'm sure you have plenty better to do."

"Oh, you know me, Uncle, if there was such a thing as a diploma in glad-handing, I would imagine I'd get flying colours. Got to oil the wheels of commerce, as the saying goes. Besides, there's plenty of life in the old dog yet."

"Hmmm, well this old dog felt pretty toothless this morning, I can tell you that. It was awful. It's at times like that that you wish you were thirty years younger."

"I'm sure."

"I just don't understand what's happening these days, Clive. Those kids – teenagers they call them now – there was no such thing as teenagers in my day. They had no respect. I wouldn't have *dared* to speak to an adult like they spoke to me, let alone touch them."

"Did you report it to the police?"

"No, what good would that have done? They have better things to do. Perhaps if I'd been harmed to any great extent. I just felt so powerless – and daft, to be honest. But, I'm perfectly alright, which I suppose is the main thing. You just don't expect that sort of behaviour.

"You know, I used to laugh at people who used to say we won the war but lost the peace, but I honestly think they're right. Seems like the barbarians are at the gate at times. You can't help but ask yourself: 'Is this what we fought the war for?'"

Clive remained attentive amidst the head shaking.

"I can only imagine what it must have been like, Uncle. Bloody hooligans."

"Anyway, enough about all that. How's business?"

"Good. As you know, there's a proposal for lots of new council housing to the south of the town for the steelworkers, which doesn't help us, but we're experiencing quite a lot wanting to buy properties in the surrounding villages. Not exactly nouveau riche, more aspiring types really, foremen from the steelworks, that sort of thing."

"And where are they looking to buy?"

"Anywhere, everywhere. Out of sight and hearing from the works if they can."

"Aye, you can't blame them for that."

"No indeed. It can be a bit problematic if they try and buy where they're not best suited. It can create a bit of social upheaval."

"How so?"

"Oh, the usual things – neighbours objecting, things like that."

"Well. It doesn't sound like anything you can't handle."

"I'm confident I can, sir."

"Your mother – I know she's your mother and all – but she's a pompous, silly woman. I say that even though she's my own sister. To be honest I think you've done well to turn out the way you have. That's why I placed you in that office. I wanted to see you prove yourself with some of the rough and ready types. Cut your teeth, so to speak. From what I've seen so far, you seem to be coping admirably."

"Thank you, Uncle. That means a lot to me."

"You're very welcome, son. You know what my hopes are for you regarding the business."

"Of course."

"It won't mean anything to you now at your time of life, but when you get to my age, you realise how important it is to have something to pass on with your name on it, otherwise no-one will know you even existed.

"Your name – go up to the end of the Broadway here and see all those poor sods who never made it back from the raids we flew over Germany and Italy listed on the monument. Their names are etched there in marble, but they're remembered for doing a good thing."

"I'm not entirely sure I understand what you're trying to tell me, Uncle."

"Aye. I dare say I am going around the houses a bit. I'm saying the Taylor & Nephew name can't be seen to be damaged in any way. No matter what you or I may think about having darkies living here on our doorstep, we can't afford to be the ones fighting against them. It could hurt our name forever. It perhaps wouldn't hurt some businesses, but it will ours. We can't afford that sort of thing. Make it go away, Clive."

"Oh, that. How did that come to your ears?"

"Of course I heard about it. Do you think I don't know what's going on in my own business?"

Clive Taylor smiled wryly.

"Understood, Uncle. Point taken, I'll have a word with Tom Cooper. Make sure he changes his stance."

"Clive," said Terence as his nephew prepared to leave, "I'm not so green as I am cabbage looking, you know."

"I'm not even sure what that means, Uncle."

"I mean it's a changing world, son. I'm not at all sure it's changing for the better, but I do know it's changing. I can't give those youths a clip round the ear like I would once have been able to. Sometimes you have to do things differently to the way they were done before, Clive, if you get my meaning."

"I'm sure those boys deserved 'a clip' Uncle. But I'll take your point on board."

"Give my regards to your mother, Clive."

"I'm glad you're feeling okay, Uncle. Take care."

Clive had to hand it to his uncle – he had been soft soaped with praise and talk of legacy, only as a precursor to a rebuke and an exhortation to change with the times. Perhaps his Uncle Terence had developed this Machiavellian streak in the war. Perhaps it was innate. Either way, there was still much Clive Taylor could learn from the old warrior.

CHAPTER 31

PEOPLE LIKE US

"You're buying what?"

Tio did not see why Wyn was getting so excited.

"I've told you once. I'm buying a house about four or five miles away. Why is that so unusual?"

"And this house isn't even built yet?"

"It's being built."

"I've never heard anything so daft. You're running into all these legal problems. You wouldn't be experiencing any of them if you just did same as everyone else – get yourself on the list to get a council house. They're building whole new estates not two miles away from here. I'm sure you could put your name down for one of them, then you'd have it for life."

Ted's interest was piqued.

"I've heard that you lot go right up to the front of the queue for a council house whenever there's one available."

"Shut up, you idiot!" snapped Tio, "I've already said I don't want a council house. And stay out of the conversation anyway."

"Who are you calling an idiot?"

"Sit down, Blister. This conversation's between me and Theo."

Tio barely gave Ted a glance.

"It's just some legal things," Tio continued, "I will go and see my solicitor and he will sort it out."

Wyn laughed. Once again Ted could not resist offering his thoughts.

"You hear that, Rev? He's going to consult with his solicitor. And after this shift, I'll have my butler iron today's Daily Mirror for my delectation and delight. Cucumber sandwiches anyone?"

"He's got a point, Theo. People like us don't normally have to get involved with solicitors and the like. You've got into all this legal mess by the sounds of it, but if you'd kept it simple and rented like the rest of us, you'd have none of these problems. I can't understand why you can't see it, I really can't."

It was not lost on Tio that Wyn had said 'people like us'. Not many years ago, on arrival on these shores, he had been left in no uncertainty that he was people unlike us. Had things changed so much since then? If so, who had changed and when?

Did Tio want to be *'people like us?'* He was not sure. It depended on the people, really.

"Where I come from there is no such thing as council houses. If you want a house, you have it built if you can afford it."

"And that's my point, Tio, you said it yourself. Where *you* come from. But you're not there, you're *here*. Things are done differently here for working people."

"But what if things are done better where I'm from."

"Don't be daft."

"How is he daft? In twenty-five years, I will own a house. You will still be paying rent."

"Look, I'll grant you there's a certain logic to what you say there, but what you don't seem to realise is that you'll be burdened down with debt for who knows how long?"

"Yes, but no matter what, you have to have a roof over your head. So, you have to pay one or the other. That's what I'm saying."

"Okay, so look, I pay thirty-five shillings per week for rent. If you don't mind me asking, how much will the mortgage be?"

Tio gave a cautious glance in the direction of Ted.

"Oh, don't mind me," said Ted, "I can't tell what you're saying half the time anyway."

"The mortgage will work out at about two pounds per week. The rates will be about seven shillings."

"Are you sure it's not more?"

"I have it down on paper. Yes, I'm sure. And my mortgage will go down. Your rent will go up."

"Really…? Are you sure?"

"I have just told you I am sure. What you want me to say?"

"Perhaps I'm missing something, here. Why is it so important for you to buy this house? If you're running into legal problems, surely, it's just better to find something else, somewhere else. Why not just get a council house like ninety-nine percent of working class do?"

"Because it will be mine."

Wyn nodded in silent contemplation. The two men discussed the matter no further. Tio left the snap cabin, leaving only Wyn and Ted, who appeared to want to unburden himself of his thoughts.

"What's up with you? You look as if you've lost a pound and found a penny."

"I'd like to know how comes he can afford to be buying houses here in this country."

Wyn was perplexed.

"You just heard him explain. It will cost him about the same to buy as it will me to rent."

"Aye, but I'd still like to know how he can afford it. There's something not right somewhere if he can afford to have a brand-new place built, and English people can't."

"It's not that English people can't afford it. It's because we do things a different way, that's all."

"No, Rev, it's not all."

"I know a lass who talks to his wife's cousin. She says their house is full of new expensive furniture. She says they've got better stuff in their house than she has, and her husband's in a really good job. I'd like to know how they can afford it."

"I don't understand what you're insinuating."

"I'm saying something's not right. I'm wondering if he's getting special privileges from the government because he's one of them."

Wyn shook his head.

"I tell you what, Blister, next time we see him we'll ask him to tell us exactly how much money he's got, shall we? And we'll get him to bring his passport and all his papers as well."

"I don't know what you're getting stroppy about. I'm just saying, that's all."

"What are you just saying?"

"Ah, you wouldn't understand. You're a foreigner, anyway. Bloody Taff. I'm telling you now, it'll all come out in the wash. It will. You just watch."

"I tell you what, Blister. When you start spending your money on supporting a family and keeping a roof over your head, like he's doing, I might be willing to listen to what you have to say. At the moment, all I see you paying out for is your motorbike, booze and loose women."

"You say that like it's a bad thing."

"I say it as if it's something that gives you no clue about the real world. Come on, I think we've discussed your credentials for Chancellor of the Exchequer quite enough, don't you? Let's get out there and get some work done."

CHAPTER 32

OUTPOST

Today, a rarity. A ride for all the family in a friend's car to see the prospective pride and joy of the Mourillon family, namely the unfinished house at Roxby. Wyn, having recently become the owner of a car, had agreed to take the Mourillon family to see how the house was getting on. His motive was not all altruism. His work colleague fascinated him, so he was intrigued to see this spectacle for himself. Tio did things differently, case in point, having this house built. People below the rank – or, more to the point, the salary – of a foreman would never normally countenance such a thing.

The last person who had ploughed their own furrow to the same extent as Tio was Wyn's father, whom he truly admired. Did he admire Tio? He was not sure. He was frequently exasperated by him. He sometimes thought his working week would be much easier if Tio was not in his life. And yet. The way Tio did things made him look at his own life, made him ponder whether sometimes he ought to be taking a leaf from Tio's book. He could see Tio's emotional attachment to this plot of land. He knew where he had seemingly identified his place in the world. That begged the question of Wyn – where was his?

Upon arrival, Tio was brimming with importance, master of all he surveyed. Tom Cooper was subdued, but greeted everyone. He thanked them for coming and appeared to mean it.

Judith's worry was that Tio, in a sudden blood-rush of assertiveness, would end up quarrelling with Tom Cooper. Thus far, their conversations seemed amicable enough. She knew her husband too well, however, to have any great degree of confidence that this delicate state of affairs would hold.

She busied herself ensuring Andre, her four-year-old, did not run off and treat the potentially dangerous building site as a playground, the remedy to which was to maintain a firm grip on his hand despite tiny vocal protests. Two-year-old Gershom was kept out of harm's way by Wyn, who gave him a ride on his shoulders.

Tio and Tom Cooper conversed some distance away from the rest.

"Have you seen Clive Taylor since we last met?" asked Tom Cooper.

"Of course. He still says you are to blame."

"Does he, now?"

Tom wondered for a moment whether Tio was trying to provoke him.

"Ah, who cares? Let him say what he wants. I know what the truth of the matter is. Anyway, do you want to see the plan of the house?"

The two men pored over the blueprints over the bonnet of Wyn's Ford Zephyr, Tio once again swelling with pride, studying the plan intently. Tom Cooper outlined the rough dimensions of each room, what the trade-offs were regarding space, what Tio would need to do to mitigate flooding of the back garden.

Then there were the changes to the proposed positioning of the coal house. Who on earth has a coal bunker indoors in this day and age? Judith had asked. After all, this was the sixties – everything was bright, new and modern. She had grown up with coal men walking through her family's kitchen making deliveries into the tied cottage she had inhabited as a child, so the idea of going through that type of disruption again with its dust and general havoc was not to her liking. No, the coal bunker was to be placed in the rear garden. She and Tio were both young and strong, hauling the coal scuttle a few yards from the back would be little trouble. Tio talked Tom Cooper through the change, who thought it sufficient of a good idea to suggest the draughtsman replicate it to the symmetrical adjoining property.

Then there was the gas supply.

"I thought there would be gas in the kitchen and the lounge."

"No. Just the kitchen. It says so here on the plan. You can see the line, look."

Tio studied the plan in silence for a moment.

"I don't suppose it would kill me to run the supply into the lounge. I'll do that for you for nothing."

Tio thanked Tom, then continued studying every inch of the building plot. Tom made his way over to Wyn who was still carrying the child on his shoulders. Wyn was busy respecting Tom's earlier instructions not to come too close to where the work was being carried out.

"You chaps friends or are you just the driver?"

"Friends. We work together on the South Ironworks."

Tom nodded

"If you don't mind me asking, do you have any idea why this place matters so much to him?"

"I think it matters to both of them."

"Yeah, but he's definitely got the bit between his teeth, hasn't he?"

"If you say so."

"Oh, come on, he has. Even a blind man could see it. I just wondered if you had any insight into why… ah, it doesn't matter."

"He's over there a few yards away. Ask him."

"I can't really talk to him. Not properly."

"Why on earth not?"

"Well, for one thing, I can't understand what he's saying a lot of the time. Second thing is we got off on a bad footing."

"So I heard."

"Yes but… oh, let's not go over all that again."

"I can offer my opinion, but you'll have to bear in mind these are my thoughts, not his. He might well tell you different."

"Go on."

"I think he wants something a bit like an outpost in a foreign land, like the English did in Wales. And I think he wants something he can call his own, that non-one can take away from him."

Tom Cooper allowed himself a wry smile.

"I think you're probably right about that. Looks like you've really thought this through. You're not telling me you just pulled that out of the air."

"Ah, some of us paid attention at school. Favourite subject, history. Teaches you how to learn from other people's mistakes and not repeat them, hopefully."

"Okay, okay. Maybe it sounded as if I was saying I expected you to have sawdust between your ears."

"I haven't. Neither has he. He's pretty sharp. Not much gets past him. That's for sure."

"No, I don't suppose it does. Thanks for the talk."

Tom shuffled off to continue his work.

Judith, who had been keeping Andre entertained and away from the building site proper had overheard most of the conversation.

"So, does that make Tio an invader?"

Wyn laughed.

"Ah, you heard, eh? It was just something I pulled from the top of my head. Don't be putting words in my mouth, look."

Tio joined them, oblivious to the previous discussion.

"What were you discussing with him?" Tio asked Wyn.

"Would you believe me if I said castles?"

"Castles? No."

"Oh well, never mind. Come on. We'd best go back and invade the town."

CHAPTER 33

THE HEAVENS REFLECT OUR LABOURS

"I've timed you lot in there."

John George, resident poacher-turned-gamekeeper, as described by Wyn Owen and many others, appeared to have decided that his chief purpose in life was to ensure that C Shift was not pulling the wool over his eyes and that consequently, his constant vigilance was essential. As obsessive as he was becoming, he dared not provoke his crew members too much, particularly Wyn, for a variety of reasons. Firstly, because he relied too much on his knowledge of the ironworks. Secondly, because Wyn was respected possibly more than anyone on the whole plant, both by the men and by management. Thirdly because Wyn had known him as a shop steward and therefore knew where all the bodies were buried, in a manner of speaking.

"You're over five minutes past your break time."

"So what?"

Ted was the only one who took the bait.

"Careful, Barnes. There's been a coke spillage behind Anne and Vicky. I know you were hoping for a nice steady night, but I'm afraid it's not going to happen. Barnes, Murray, Bailey, you lot are shovel technicians tonight. The rest of you are on ladle relining, helping the brickies."

There was a collective groan in anticipation of an exhausting shift ahead. Sometimes the job would go quicker if the crew could have a laugh, but that was hardly likely given the three men who had been chosen.

"One more thing. Tom Chandler will be around in the early hours. He's sometimes with his entourage, but it's not unknown for him to go wandering around on his own. Don't let him find any of you lot with your feet up because that will make me look bad. And I don't want to look bad."

As the men dispersed, John George guided the unfortunate three to the scene of the spillage.

"There's the heap. There's the first skip. Need I say more?"

"Yes, you do," replied Ted, "Who's going to empty this once we've filled it and bring us a new one?"

"There will be a couple more coming, so you'll always have an empty one. Enough to keep you busy all shift. Enjoy yourselves."

For thirty minutes or so the three men worked in silence. Philip appeared to be struggling from the outset and looked as if he would not be able to keep up the pace, which would only serve to add an extra burden to Ted and Tio.

"Look, boy," said Tio, trying to catch Philip's attention.

"I'm not a boy." It was the first ill humour he had seen from Philip, who was sweating profusely.

"It's just a saying. It doesn't mean you're a child."

"I still wish you wouldn't call me it. I get hard enough time from everyone else."

"Okay, okay. But I'm trying to help you. What are you getting vexed with me for?"

"Sorry, Theo. It's me. I'm knackered. I'm just not cut out for this."

"That's why I'm telling you. You doing it all wrong. Don't just use your arms and your back. Bend your legs, look. And take your time. And let the shovel do the work."

"To be honest, Theo," panted Philip, "I'd love to let the shovel do the work."

Laughing at his own joke lifted Philip's spirits for a while. Even so, he heeded Tio's advice and eventually managed to break into a steady, sustainable pace.

"Is he going to be alright?" asked Ted, concerned less for Philip than for his ability to do his share of the work.

"He'll be fine. Maybe not in the morning."

Later in the shift, Wyn and two other workmates joined them.

"I thought our illustrious foreman might have a come long and joined the fun too," said Ted.

"I asked him." Wyn smiled, "says he can't on account of his bad back and high blood pressure."

"He sends my bloody pressure high, I know that."

"They're expecting us to hand quite a bit over in the morning to A Shift."

"They would leave it for us. That's for sure."

Bait taken, Ted applied himself to removing the already diminished heap with added vigour.

By 4.30am it was cleared. All that was left was to wash down near the rails. The men needed to rest, but making their way up several flights to the snap cabin required too much effort for the moment, so they placed hessian sacks on the ground and sat back to back. Ted sat with Philip, being as they were of a similar size.

"You do realise that you're sweating that much I can feel it on my back, don't you, Prof?"

"Sorry," panted Philip.

"I'll let you off this once, young 'un. Don't let it happen again."

"That's our new name for you - Prof, on account of you being an educated man and all."

"Okay."

"You did well, Prof. We didn't think you were going to go the distance, did we, Theo?"

"No, the boy did good," said Tio, forgetting that he had promised not to call Philip a boy.

"Thanks."

"I don't think the lad can say more than one word," observed Wyn.

"It's times like now I wish we had a wet canteen like on Lysaghts," said Ted.

"Wet canteen?" queried Philip.

"You not heard of it, Prof?" asked Ted, "it's a fully licensed bar on Lysaghts."

"So can you just drink as much as you want?"

"You can drink a bit, quench your thirst and all that, but the landlord will make sure you don't have too much. Good bloke."

"You've been there?"

"I used to work on Lysaghts when I left school, Prof. When I was knee high to a grasshopper."

"It would save me having to do the beer run at the start of the night shift," pondered Philip.

"Aye lad, it would. We used to have the Station Hotel up here, just a few yards away. It was knocked down a few years ago. Nice upstairs, a bit rough downstairs, though."

"Wow, it must have been bad if it was too rough for Ted."

A sudden cheer went up from the men at Philip's newly discovered bravery.

"Okay. I'll give you a free pass on that one, Prof. Besides, if I thumped you, I'd lose me back rest."

Working through the night shift invariably caused the men to become ravenously hungry, typically from three o'clock onwards. The problem tonight was that only a few of the men possessed sandwiches, for which as always there was only one solution.

Wyn staggered to his feet and took on the role of mother, collecting what there was, pooling them, then distributing them to each man.

As each man sat in silent contentment for the moment, Ted, as ever, was first to speak.

"Theo?"

"What?"

"Tell your missus I prefer cheese on its own next time, not cheese and onion. Okay?"

"Okay. I'll let her know."

Sudden groans from some of the men prompted Philip to search around for the source of the dismay.

"I don't believe it. What's he doing here this time of the morning? I'm not moving. I can't move anyway.

"What's going on? I can't see," asked Philip

"Good morning gentlemen."

Tom Chandler, the Production Manager, was visible to Ted and others, but not to Philip.

The men replied meekly, expecting a tirade at any moment. They knew well enough that they had earned their impromptu rest, but, in the absence of the spillage, also knew that Tom Chandler could easily conclude that they were just malingering.

"I can't believe you've managed to clear all that lot in one shift. I saw it earlier. Well done chaps, well done. I expect you'd all like to get going now. I think you've earned it."

After a pause to take in that they had not been reprimanded, a few languid thanks were murmured.

"Ah, Mr. Mourillon, the man with the French name. I trust there are no problems?"

Tio was by no means reassured by Chandler's renewed attention.

"No. Everything's perfectly okay."

"Good. Glad to hear it. Anyway, don't worry about washing down. I'll make sure the morning shift does all that. You chaps get going."

The men waited until Tom Chandler was out of sight before moving.

"They're slag tipping tonight. I'm going down there for a few minutes to watch it. Anyone else fancy it?" asked Wyn.

"Doesn't sound very exciting," panted Philip.

"Ah, you'd be surprised. You ought to come and see it. It's quite something."

"Ted, Tio? Do you fancy it?"

In the small hours of the morning, Wyn, Ted, Philip and Tio headed along the train tracks in the mild August air over to an elevated point on the far side of the recess. In the distance, a steam locomotive crept towards them from the direction of the furnaces.

"Coming from Anne," remarked Ted.

"Aye."

As the locomotive approached, they could see the heavy refraction of light in the night air as the intense heat rose from the ladle cars. The glow of the molten payload served to brighten the gloom. As the loco eased to a halt, the men, who were a significant distance away from the ladle cars, felt the warmth of their intense heat.

One by one the ladle cars tipped their contents into the recess, each ladle unveiling its torrent of slag merging into a brimming molten river before settling at the bottom of the pit.

Wyn spoke, his face illuminated by the glow of the molten slag.

"*Refulget labores nostros coelum*. It's the only bit of Latin I know."

"What does it mean?"

"The heavens reflect our labours."

"I think I've seen or heard that phrase before."

"Aye," said Ted, "it will have been at the Old Show Ground. It's the motto of Scunthorpe United. It used to be on their badges."

"Ah, okay. I knew I'd seen it somewhere."

The four men gazed upwards to the reflected glow of molten liquid in the heavily clouded sky. It was a glorious and awe-inspiring sight.

"This is what the motto comes from. From the reflection in the sky when they're tipping the slag like this. You can see it for miles," Wyn explained, "Grimsby fishermen have said they can see that glow out at Dogger Bank in the North Sea. Halfway between here and Denmark."

Tio had often seen this glow from the rear of his house on Cottage Beck Road. He had heard various people explain what it was, but this was the first time he had seen the spectacle for himself.

The last time Tio had seen anything that had taken his breath away, it was a sunrise over the Atlantic from his home at Fon Bèlè. How strange that this of all places, should be the next occasion he would experience awesome beauty.

None spoke. All just arched their necks and gazed skyward and absorbed the spectacle, lost in their own thoughts.

Later, in the shower room, Ted mimicked Tom Chandler.

"Well done chaps. Good show."

He gave his ear an exaggerated rub.

"Yeah, I noticed that," said Philip, "what's all the ear rubbing about?"

"He's got some sort of condition," replied Wyn, "I don't know what it is. Very clever bloke, freakishly clever, but it's like he's got no emotion or anything."

"I think I've seen that type of thing in the past."

"Wyn's got him over a barrel," said Ted unable to conceal a large grin.

"Really? How?"

"Saved his life, he did. Pulled him out of the way of a loco when he was about to get struck. He made Chandler promise not to tell any of the blokes or his name would be mud, Prof."

"So you thought you'd tell everyone anyway," said Philip

A sudden cheer went up from the men at Philip's response to Ted.

"That's twice now, Prof," Ted laughed, "don't go pushing your luck."

Each man lingered in the shower a little longer than normal, allowing the lukewarm water to infuse life into their weary and aching muscles.

Cleaned, dressed and something close to respectable, several of the men who lived nearby – everyone except for Tommy and Philip - trudged up Cottage Beck Road, overshadowed by the Four Queens to their rear. The cyclists dismounted so that they could accompany those on foot as they exited the works entrance, devoid of traffic.

"You joining us at the Queens Hotel for an early one, Theo?" asked Brian.

The thought of drinking at such an unearthly time was an anathema to Tio.

"Not me," said Tio, "the only place I'm going is bed."

A few ribald comments and some tired farewells later, Tio left his workmates as he entered his house on Cottage Beck Road. Hopefully, he would sleep solidly through until midday, after which he and his weary co-workers would be back at work in time for the afternoon shift.

CHAPTER 34

OUT OF THE CAR

A knock at the front door. This time, Judith knew it would be Jan.

"Hi, Jan. Is Terry out in the car again?"

"No. Terry's here," said Terry, immediately following Jan through the door.

"Oh, hello."

Judith reddened in embarrassment at her faux pas. Terry appeared mildly and momentarily triumphant.

"Is he in then?" he asked.

"Tio? Yes, he's out the back in the veg garden."

After briefly making a fuss of the children, Terry headed into the back garden to See Tio bent over, apparently doing something meaningful with root vegetables.

"Hello. I'll shake your hand even though it's dirty."

Tio appeared to take a second or two to register Terry's sudden arrival.

"Oh, hello."

"My dad used to do all this lot during the war, you know."

"What's that?"

"Grow veg in the back garden in town. Most of us just do this stuff down the allotment now. Gardens are for leisure."

"Why pay for an allotment, when you have enough space here?"

Terry thought for a second to disagree, but decided otherwise.

"Aye, well you seem to be making a good job of it, anyway."

"Thanks."

Terry considered was a man of temperate disposition and moderate opinions, that was what most people did not appreciate about him, he had protested when quarrelling with Jan two weeks earlier. If she and Judith could only hear the type of terms some of his friends used towards people like Tio, they would realise how reasonable he was by comparison. Alas, his even-handedness and forbearance were as yet unappreciated.

After all, here he was, prepared to go against his sensibilities and do something so clearly objectionable to him. If some people caught wind of it, it could put him in a very awkward position indeed. It was only to be hoped that the penny finally dropped with Jan, should she realise just how great a step he was taking. He was doing it for Judith's sake too. By and by, they would see, they would appreciate it.

He and Jan had agreed before setting off. They would show their faces, perhaps stay for a cup of tea, then leave. They would have done their bit. He would have done his bit.

"Jan tells me you're thinking of moving out to Roxby."

Tio's stomach tightened in expectation of a lecture about not financially biting off more than he should chew.

"We hoping to, yes."

"I think that's a good idea. It's a nice area."

This was a surprise. He had expected Terry to decry the idea, but he seemed to be in earnest. He had first wondered whether Terry was being sarcastic and somehow it was getting lost in translation.

Now and again, Jan and Judith peered out the window. Terry suspected they were probably worried that he and Tio were quarrelling or worse.

Tio spent several minutes talking Terry through their plans to move, explaining how it would be better for the children, how he could let them out to play without worrying so much about traffic, how it was much more in keeping with his old life, how Judith would finally be back in the village in which she had spent her early life.

Terry's interest in the subject was genuine. It was harder to be in enmity with someone in close quarters. And the many reasons he had disliked Tio previously – right now he struggled to remember what they were.

His workmates, those who had been so certain, so strident in their statements about Tio and his like. How would they react if they were here right now, with no audience to play to? He suspected their bravado might just evaporate.

By the time he and Jan finally left, they had spent two to three times longer at the Mourillon residence than they had originally intended. As they journeyed back to their home, Jan purred her approval of Terry's great act of self-sacrifice and that her relationship with her cousin was now experiencing a full-blown restoration.

Jan, happy and relieved to be reacquainted with her cousin, would have to recognise that the relationship had changed, that there was no longer the same degree of dependency, as before. It was now a relationship of equals. It would take some time to get used to it, just as it would take time to get used to the idea of her husband, but Tio was a fact of life, and consequently a peripheral part of her own life.

For the briefest of moments, she cast her mind back to the frenzied meetings and conversations she and Terry and held with her aunt and uncle, Judith's parents. Her Aunt Eva would doubtless have seen Jan's actions as a capitulation. But she was no longer around, Tio was.

Their family crisis meetings, years ago, had all been predicated on the assumption that Tio would have disappeared by now. After all, his type never tended to stick around, did they?

And yet, there he was, at the very least expecting to be around long enough to see his crops harvested. He was a reality, a fact of life. Something and someone with whom she and her husband must find an accommodation.

Quite evidently, her cousin's husband was in it for the long run.

CHAPTER 35

THE HISTORY OF THE POTATO

Enmity tended to have a short lifespan on the steelworks, especially within small crews like C Shift. It was not uncommon for the men to have a furious row one day, only for it to be all but forgotten the next. It was not that they were any more forgiving than anyone else, it was more a case of their having to be pragmatic, given that they were stuck within small groups for long periods of time.

"I tell you what I do like…" said Ted, hoping that someone would pick up the conversation. No-one expressed any interest in Ted's preferences, but Ted pressed ahead anyway.

"Soul music. It's brilliant. Did you see the Supremes on Juke Box Jury? That Diana Ross, I'd give her five points! Definitely."

"I think we can safely say she doesn't know you exist, Blister," remarked Wyn, quickly pouring cold water on Ted's fantasy.

Each man in the crew took a swig from a single bottle of ale and passed it onto the next.

"Aye, I dare say you're right there. Doesn't harm for a man to dream, though. You like her, Theo?"

"Who?"

"Haven't you been listening? Diana Ross."

"Oh yes. She's okay. Good singer. Good looking woman."

Wyn's brow furrowed.

"I can't make you out, Blister."

"That's because I'm a man of mystery, Rev. What exactly can't you make out about me?"

"You liking Diana Ross. You're not exactly renowned as a cultural ambassador. How come you have a thing for her?"

"I honestly don't know what you mean. You couldn't find anyone less prejudiced than me. I don't care if someone's black, white, green or purple."

Wyn raised both eyebrows and said nothing. Tio seemed oblivious, avidly reading the election coverage in the newspaper. He was vaguely aware that a question would no doubt be forthcoming in his direction.

"So, Theo, you know the place where you come from?"

"The West Indies, yes," Tio replied, not wanting to confuse Ted by being too specific.

"Do they have people starving there and everything?"

Tio laughed. He had recently – begrudgingly - acknowledged to Wyn that he could be quite sharp with Ted. He did not want to ruin the outbreak of peace with a sarcastic answer. Everyone, he reasoned, had to obtain their information somewhere. Besides, how would anyone find out these things if they never asked?

"No. Plenty of food there. Bananas, coconuts, yams, pineapples, plantains, sweet potatoes…"

"Sweet potatoes? Never heard of them. Do they have real potatoes?"

Now was Wyn's turn to laugh.

"Of course they do. Potatoes originated in that part of the world. Well, South America, anyway. They were brought over in Elizabethan times by Walter Raleigh."

"Nah Rev, I don't think that's right. Potatoes have always been in this neck of the woods. They must've been. There was that Irish thingy, what do you call it?"

"The potato famine. Yes, that was last century. Elizabethan times were about four centuries ago."

"I'm sure that's not right. How can fish and chips be our national dish if spuds have only been here for that long?"

"Well, first of all, I wasn't exactly aware it was our national dish. Secondly, I'm going to go out on a limb here and hazard a guess that people like Alfred the Great didn't eat fish and chips."

"Ah, what would you know, you're a bloody Taff anyway? Anyway, I wasn't asking you, I was talking to Theo. In fact, ask Prof when he comes in. He'll know."

"I haven't seen him all afternoon. Where is he?"

"He's working as fitter's monkey today. I think they'd like to keep him, with him having two brains and everything. He won't be in anytime soon."

"Looks like we've been dropped in favour of more exalted company," observed Wyn.

"He is wasted here," added Tio, "he needs to finish his schooling."

"Aye, you never hear him talking about it these days," mused Ted, "when he first started, you could never shut him up about it."

Wyn shook his head.

"You mean when you used to take the mickey out of him pretty much every day?"

"He knew I didn't really mean it. Hey, imagine if one of our crew became one of the top bosses. We could get a wet canteen put in this place."

"I can see you're a man of infinite ambition, Blister."

"Life's simple pleasures are sufficient for me, Rev."

"I could say something there, but it would be too easy. Come on, let's go see what young Philip is up to."

CHAPTER 36

THE BRIMMING RIVER

Tom Chandler, whenever possible, liked to escape the confines of a stuffy office in the administrative offices or a control room filled with cigarette smoke. Having changed into attire suitable for a brief tour of the South Ironworks, he set out on one of his many unannounced tours, keen to see for himself what was happening on the factory floor before anyone had the chance to paint the coals black and give him a sanitised report on the state of the plant. His management style differed significantly from that of his peers or predecessors in that he was one of few in the company's upper echelons who had no military background whatsoever. Chain of command was simply not his style. His preference was to be amongst the men on the factory floor.

Sure enough, he was aware of how they mimicked his ticks when they were confident that he was out of earshot, but so long as they showed deference to his face, he was willing to let it pass. Inevitably, however, the men regarded his unannounced visits as an unwelcome intrusion.

Of all those who viewed his presence unfavourably, John George, C Shift foreman, the man before him right now, ranked among the highest. For a man who had once smugly feigned concern for safety in his days as a union representative, his attitude towards the welfare of his men seemed curiously cavalier ever since he had crossed the floor.

John George, in Tom Chandler's viewpoint, was a hack. He was the definitive workplace survivor, and key to that survival was his finely-honed skill of never making a decision. Today, he was complaining about being short-staffed and, as ever, was coming up with a hundred and one reasons not to accomplish whatever task was set before him.

"We've got a problem with the cooling system pipework on Bess. We've got maintenance looking at it, but they're a bit short staffed. I've said they can have one or two of our lads, but that will leave us short."

"Understood. What is it they need to do?"

"They need to work on the gate valves."

"Do they know what they're doing?"

"The fitters do. My men will take their instruction from them."

"What exactly is the problem with the valves?"

"All I know is that they're not fully closing."

"How bad is it? Do you think we'll have to come off production?"

"I'm afraid I can't answer that, Mr. Chandler."

"Why not?"

"Because it's not my call. We don't want to be in a situation where we've got full burden in the furnace with a failing cooling system."

"No, of course not. And there's no way we can fully isolate these valves and replace them?"

"No sir, not without bringing her down."

"But you're saying we can perhaps work around it?"

"No sir, I'm not saying that. We can see if we can get them working live in situ, but the alternative is to come out of production completely. I'm presenting you with the information and asking how to proceed."

John George watched with a quiet sense of triumph as Tom Chandler broke into periodic spasms of ear rubbing, knowing full well that he had unnerved him. Most foremen would have chosen to be being less confrontational, but right now, John George considered his position unassailable. Both men knew they wanted the job done on a wing and a prayer. That was, after all, how things were always done. John George was making sure, in front of witnesses, that if something went wrong, it was clear to all that the responsibility lay squarely with Tom Chandler. It was a dance he had regularly performed over the years, one in which he was now quite adept.

"Are you sure it can't wait until the next outage?"

"It's a risk, sir. The risk is that if we leave the valves as they are. There's risk either way if we're going to stay in production."

That was three times he had used the word risk, thought Chandler, who could think of one or two other words.

"Well George, do as you've said. Get all hands on deck if you think it will address the issue. We're all under a lot of pressure to keep production to a maximum, so no-one will thank us for bringing the furnace down for something like this. If it's possible to sort things out in situ, then all the better."

"Very well, sir. I'm not trying to be impertinent or anything, but just to make sure it's fully understood. Your instruction to me is for us to stay on production while the valves are being sorted? Is that correct?"

"Being as careful as you can, yes. I believe that's what I just said. Do you require clarification on anything further Mr. George?"

"No that's crystal clear, sir. Thank you very much. I'll get the men right on it."

Every member of C Shift, as did all shift crews across the works, had to be recognised and probably named in line with their abiding characteristic, real or imagined.

Ted - Blister – was lazy. Wyn - Rev – was devout. Tio so far was just Theo. Philip was Prof – resident scholar. The maintenance crew had their own nicknames too. Eddie MacArthur, the fitter in his late twenties whom Philip was assisting today, was generally known for his athleticism was either Rabbit or just plain Mac.

As Philip was making a meagre attempt to assist Mac in the repair of a transport ladle using a sledge hammer, Mac felt duty bound to voice his observation.

"Do you mind me saying something, Philip?"

Whatever it was would not be good, so Philip braced himself for the put-down.

"You may as well just go ahead and say it."

"What I can't understand is how a bloke your size has hardly got any strength. I know little nine or ten stone blokes who are a lot stronger than you. I'm not trying to be funny or anything."

Philip rolled out his standard response.

"I've never really had any need to be strong in the past. I sometimes think my size is a curse. I'm sure if I'd been a little bloke they'd have found room for me in the labs. They just took one look at me and no matter how much I protested about studying for my City & Guilds, they just seemed to want to put me down here."

"Aye, the labs is where they normally put the clever ones. Have you spoken to anyone about still getting in?"

"Not recently. Do you think I ought to?"

"You can always try. They can only say no."

"Do you know anyone who you think could put a good word in for me?"

"I'm not sure really. I would have thought your friend Wyn could do that. He's pretty well liked down here."

"Wyn? He's not my friend as such. I mean, I like him and everything, but he's a bit old and grumpy. He's a family friend, through the church my mother goes to."

"Ah, okay. Tell you what. If we get finished on this early on our next job, we'll nip down the labs and I'll have a word with this bloke I know who drinks down at the Crosby. How's that sound?"

"Sounds absolutely perfect."

"Thing is with this place – it's a job for life. Blokes who work here don't often go anywhere else. You can't earn this sort of money elsewhere, you know."

"Well, the money's okay, I can't deny that. But man can't live by overtime alone, you know."

Mac laughed.

"You've been spending too much time with Rev."

"Yeah, perhaps. What's this job we've got to do?"

"Couple of valves on the cooling system. I don't think it's anything that a bit of brute force and ignorance won't fix. Come on, we may as well go take a look now. Might just be a quick job."

Mac emptied much of the contents of his tool bag, threw in a couple of hammers and spanners and then set off.

As they made their way into the cast house they continued their conversation.

"You do realise I'm not promising anything, don't you?"

"Of course. I'm just thankful you're making the effort, Mac. I really appreciate it."

"Well, let's save the thanks until after we get a result, eh?"

The Queen Bess furnace had been tapped and a brimming river of molten metal was flowed into the runner, banishing the gloom of the cast house. Mac made a beeline towards the runner, braced himself, and then hopped over the molten stream. Philip watched in amazement. Surely, he was not expected to do the same?

"Come on. It's less than two feet."

"But there's a bridge I can take up there. Wouldn't that be wiser?"

"Aye, go on then, if that's what you need to do. Everyone jumps over the runner you know. Sometimes you have to be back and forward a dozen times. You can't use the bridge every time. Use it now, though if you need to."

"No, hang on. I can do this."

"Trick is to be quick, that way you don't scorch your legs like your mate Blister."

Philip spent a few seconds working up the courage to jump over the runner, then awkwardly manoeuvred himself over the molten stream.

"There you go. Wasn't so bad, was it? You'll get so you barely think about it."

"If your mate helps me in the labs I won't have to think about it. I won't have to do it."

Mac moved over to one of the offending valves, situated adjacent to one of the furnace's supporting columns. He cast an expert eye upon the valve and respective pipework.

"I'm thinking this may be a smaller job than I thought, Philip."

"That's good."

"You know where I threw those tools out me bag?"

"I think so."

"There's a pouch full of flat punches. Can you nip and fetch them?"

"What does it look like?"

"Philip, it's just a bloody pouch full of punches. How hard can it be for a man with two brains to figure it out? Just go fetch them, will you?"

"Alright, keep your hair on."

Philip continued mumbling as he left. Mac continued his inspection of the valve, which was slightly above head level.

"It should really be a pipe fitter looking at this, not me," mumbled Mac as he tugged and pulled the valve handle, then mumbled a little more.

Amongst the din, the smells, the metal-upon-metal noise, an aroma that did not belong. Then shouting, then a melee of screaming voices.

"Mac! Mac! Your mate!"

Philip had made no sound, and certainly, none that would raise above the background. He had not made it over the runner. Part of his body, most likely his foot had entered the molten stream as he had desperately tried not to descend laterally into the runner. Amongst the confusion, after a seeming eternity, Mac made scrambled over to him, but by the time he had done so the worst of the flames had been extinguished. Two men had been badly burnt trying to smother Philip, and now they were also burnt.

In the office, the desk was cleared in less than a second, and the mass of smouldering flesh that was once Philip was laid on top. His left leg below the knee was missing. His left hand had become detached while carrying him into the office.

Wyn, Ted, and Tio had come into the office by now, having helped to carry the wounded man in.

"Who is it?" asked Wyn.

"I think it's the young lad from your crew, Wyn."

"Is he alive?"

"Yes. Just. I don't think he will be for long. You know the family, don't you? I'm sorry, Wyn."

In the surreal calm of the remaining twenty or so minutes, each man looked on helplessly as the young man succumbed to his injuries. Philip uttered only one discernible word in the time he remained alive.

"Cold."

CHAPTER 37

GOOD MONEY

Wyn, Ted, and Tio assembled in silence by a small rail embankment outside the Queen Bess furnace, Tio and Wyn seated, Ted stood above them, hands in pockets, kicking a stone around.

After what seemed like an eternity, Wyn spoke.

"I'm not sure I can do this anymore. This is no way to live."

Ted, aware that Wyn was trembling, most likely from shock, bent down and placed a consoling hand on his friend's shoulder.

"Ah, it'll pass, Rev. We've known a few blokes who've died here before or lost body parts. It's never nice, but we always get over it. I liked the lad. I really did. I know I took the mickey, but he was alright. He was one of the crew. One of us."

"I promised his mother I'd look after him. She doesn't know. When she does, she'll think I've let him down, her down. I can't do this anymore. I'm finished with it. It's too much."

"That's just the shock talking, Rev. You've got a wife and family to support. You're not like a young single bloke like me. You need the money, and it's good money on here."

"What use is money if you don't live to spend it? How many men do you know who've died within a year of retiring? Slogged their guts out on here, lost limbs, lungs, digits, you name it. For what?"

Wyn who drew patterns absently in the dirt as Ted seated himself alongside him.

"I remember when the boy started on his first day, I thought he would not turn up for his second day, to be honest."

"Me neither."

"I even remember what he said to you when you were trying to scare him off the job in your roundabout way."

"What was that?"

"He said. 'This is important, what we're doing'. I'd never really thought about it properly until he said it."

Wyn dearly wished he had scared him off. He wished he had painted as grim a picture as it was possible to imagine, because however terrifying he could have painted it, it could not possibly have matched reality.

Tio placed a comforting hand on Wyn's shoulder.

"I will come down with you and speak to his mother. It's not fair for it only to be you. We will both go."

Wyn nodded silently.

As they rose, Tom Chandler approached the three men from the direction of the cast house.

"Bad business, this. Awful."

The men nodded.

"The police have almost completed their inspection. I don't think they could make much sense of any of it, but I don't suppose anyone would, really."

Tom Chandler fidgeted, as if preparing himself to say something unpalatable.

"I'm sorry chaps, but I'm going to have to ask you to return to work. There's still work to be done. I know it can't be pleasant for you, losing one of your own, but there it is."

No reply.

"Mr. Owen, if you see Mr. George in your travels, could you please mention to him that we'll need a replacement for young Mr. Bailey. It's perhaps not realistic to have someone in place tomorrow, but we definitely need someone by the beginning of the next shift pattern."

Wyn gave a cursory nod, then scrubbed out whatever he had been etching in the dirt.

"One final thing, if I may, gentlemen. Now that all of the initial investigations have been done, I'd like the three of you to clear the scene of the accident. Otherwise, it could be upsetting for A Shift."

Tom Chandler shuffled off in the direction of the cast house.

"Well, we can't have A Shift being upset, can we?" remarked Ted.

Wyn was oblivious to the topic, his mind still on greater matters.

"You know what I miss?" he asked.

Tio and Ted gave him a perplexed look.

"Singing."

Ted was none the wiser.

"Singing?"

"The sound of a Welsh male voice choir."

"Aye, I heard one of those once. Credit where credit's due, you lot know how to sing. You ever heard them, Theo?"

"No, never."

"Back home. The male voice choirs. It makes the hairs on the back of your neck stand on end," said Wyn, "it's the most beautiful thing you'll ever hear."

"I think I know what you mean, Rev. I sometimes feel like that when I'm out riding on my Beezer."

Wyn smiled.

"I'm going home."

"You can't knock off early. You'll get the sack."

"No. I'm going back to Neath. I don't belong here."

"Course you belong here. Besides, what will you do if you go back after all these years?"

"I've absolutely no idea."

"Well, there you go then."

"Actually, I do know."

"Go on, then. Don't keep us in suspense."

"Sing."

Later, when Tio trudged home up the Cottage Beck Road at the end of his working day, the cacophony of steelworks sounds from the heaving industrial landscape to his rear, Wyn's words once again echoed in his mind.

What indeed was the point of earning good money on the steelworks if you were likely to get killed in the process or die shortly after retiring? Surely it would be better to go back home to Dominica, where his children could swim in the rivers and the sea daily, where the sun would caress their skin, where the background noise would only ever be that of teeming greenery. They would not be alone, nor would he. They would have a vast family support network.

Why had he left the richness of his home country to work in this brutal industrial moonscape? Tio barely need ask himself. The answer was plain for all to see. He could not live on the beauty of nature. He needed substance and the substance was to be found right here.

CHAPTER 38

HOLLIS REMOVALS LTD

"I've been trying to get you all afternoon? Why on earth are you working late one day before we move?"

Tio could tell from Judith's tone that whatever was bothering her was more than just the usual pre-house-move stress.

"Something happened at work so some of us stayed behind. I don't want to talk about it right now. Why were you trying to get hold of me?"

"What happened?"

"We will talk about it another time. Judith, why were you trying to contact me at work?"

"Because the moving company says they won't move us."

"Who, Hollis'? Why?"

"What do you mean why? Because it's you, that's why. Why do you think?"

"Tell me what happened."

"I got Margaret to look after the boys for an hour while I went down the Hollis' with the money you left on the table. They kept me waiting at the desk for about forty minutes deliberately. They weren't busy I could tell…"

"Judith, will you just tell me what happened?"

"They said their vans are booked on another job for the next three weeks."

"But we have the deposit slip and the booking paper. Did you show it to them?"

"I did. They just said the girl who booked us in was new at the time and they said she should never have made the booking. I showed them the slip but the man I spoke to, I think he's the owner, he got really nasty. I tried to argue with him, but he wouldn't listen."

Tio's first instinct was to blame his wife in the absence of anyone Hollis or anyone culpable, but the sheer desperation of plight restrained him.

He remembered Clive Taylor referring to the house moving process in circumstances such as his as a chain. He could not remember all that Taylor had said, but did remember the core message - the chain was delicate, if one thing failed, everything failed. All of this set his teeth on edge and played upon his already brittle state of mind.

Tio put on his work coat and strode out the door without saying anything, a determined look upon his face.

An hour or so later he returned looking depressed and defeated. All he had accomplished was a fruitless and unedifying argument with Hollis. On this occasion, Tio had been the more restrained for no other reason than that he needed something from them that only Hollis and his company could provide. He was hostage to circumstance, and his circumstances were being driven by Hollis.

Hollis had not only denied him, but appeared to glory in doing so, simply stating that another booking had now been made and under no circumstances would he alter the arrangement for *him*. Hollis had a crowd of onlookers, an audience to play to, all of whom laughed in unison to each of Hollis' put-downs. Outnumbered and starved of options,

Tio retreated to try and gather his thoughts, hope of a successful move the next day now all but forsaken.

Tio recounted what had happened with only minimal detail, thus frustrating his wife further by making the situation more opaque and fraying her already shredded nerves.

In Dominica, he would have had a whole community and support network to fall back upon. Nothing of the sort existed here. His friend Brian had a car, but he would be at work, and a saloon car was no replacement for one or more large removal vans. Wyn's protestations about not veering too far from the norm, not following the well-trodden path of renting a house like everyone else was beginning to sound like tried and tested wisdom.

Tio sat in silence at the kitchen table for several minutes more, punctuating the silence by exasperated shakes of the head. Once again, his thoughts deviated back to the land of his birth. How would he deal with this situation had he been back there?

Judith gave voice to her despondency.

"Do you know what I want? I want this all to be sorted, for everything to be covered. I know you're doing what you can. I don't want you to think I'm blaming you, although at times I do think you blame me, or would like to. I just want all of this to be over."

Normally Tio would have reacted angrily, no doubt defensively at her comments. 'Do you not think I want it to be over?' He would have asked. 'What do you think I've been fighting for all this time?' But what his wife had said only mirrored his own weariness. Besides, now was not the time for the two of them to be in conflict. They needed to be united against a common enemy.

The exchange with Hollis had left a nasty taste in Tio's mouth. He had been a little too fast to say no, a little too combative, even hostile in his tone, had taken a little too much delight in denying something he could so clearly see that Tio and his family needed.

But Tio had met men like him before and had sometimes just laughed them off. For every man like him, what did any of them matter? Had any of them mattered in the long run? Up until now, had not Tio been able to navigate round them, sooner or later? But Hollis seemed to have inserted himself into his life at an absolute key juncture. He had managed to get Tio's attention. Tio desperately wanted to prevail over him, because right here, right now, Hollis was the embodiment of everyone who had ever gone before.

Judith, still struggling with her own anxieties, spoke.

"Tio, we've both met dozens of men like Hollis. After tomorrow he'll be out of our lives."

"But that's the point, Judith. He's not in our lives tomorrow because he won't be doing the job for us."

"Can't we threaten him with legal action?"

"I did. He knew I was bluffing because we both know that would take time. And we need him tomorrow."

Tio continued brooding, shaking his head, occasionally cursing Hollis under his breath. Judith cared nothing about him cursing. She cared very much about what the anger was doing to Tio.

"I won't let that man beat me."

She could have told him that the effect was upon 'us'. She could have told him that he was not really beating him or them, that somehow they would find a way. But if they found a way it would be via a huge diversion, Any contention that Hollis was not beating them would have sounded like an empty platitude. No, there would be no going round Hollis, no evading him.

"I'd love to tell him to just…" Tio's voice drifted off.

After a while, Judith spoke.

"You'd be wasting your breath, Tio. It would go in one ear and out the other. People like him never change. I suppose the only thing they do is… well, die, eventually. All we need to do is get to that house with all of our things. When we do, that man won't exist as far as we're concerned."

He rose and headed towards the door.

"Are you going to tell me where you're going this time?"

"I'm going to see the police."

"What can they do?"

"I don't know. Maybe they can't do anything, but we won't get anywhere if we don't try something."

Two-and-a-half bladder emptying hours later Tio returned. Judith was on tenterhooks and very much loath to ask how it had gone, suspecting that she may well be met with an irate response.

"Well, are you going to ask how I got on?"

"I wasn't going to. I figured you'd have said by now if you'd had any success"

"Well," he said, trying to draw out the suspense, "they backed me up. I showed them the papers and they took me down to Hollis and told him they had to move us."

Judith laughed, a mixture of nervous relief and incredulity at the pure bizarreness of the situation.

"The police told him they had to move us?"

"I just told you that, yes."

"I don't know what to say."

"Say? We are moving. That is it."

"I don't know what to say."

Tio sighed heavily and began looking agitated again.

"Oh, keep your hair on."

"Well, you keep asking all these questions."

"Yes, I do. And I've got more to ask actually because it's my life too."

More sighs accompanied by muttering under his breath.

"So, what did Mr. Hollis say after you said you'd been to the police?"

"The sergeant came down with me to his business. The manager argued at first, but what could he say? He has to do as he is told."

"What time are they coming?"

"Seven in the morning."

"Seven?!"

Relieved and exhausted, they both decided they could live with the inconvenience of the early start and the inevitably grumpy children. Tomorrow they would be embarking upon a new phase in their lives.

Judith had spent much of her childhood in the village, had made dens in the fields and meadows in which she shared secrets with her friends, climbed trees, or maybe just watched other children climbing them. She could not really remember having been in the spot where they were about to live, though, close to the church. Nor could she recall whether the site of their new habitation had been an unused extension of someone's garden, or possibly just a patch of meadowland. Whoever had previously owned it no longer did. This place would be theirs.

CHAPTER 39

THE GLOWING KETTLE

Lincolnshire – 2010

What does a man who has fought all his life do when his own body becomes his determined adversary? A man whose strength once defined him, who now no longer possesses it, and he can no longer do the things he took so much for granted in years past. Sometimes he negotiates with the present, saying that for each loss there is a trade-off with wisdom, of doing things better, differently, or, in worst cases, not at all.

Such a man – or woman – may hope to have accumulated enough goodwill throughout their life to support them when they can no longer support themselves, so that they may not be left to whims of the cruel and the uncaring.

When Tio Mourillon arrived in England, of all the things he missed every single day, the luxuriant green of his homeland rated highest. But in September 1956 he experienced his first autumn in his new country and saw a kaleidoscope of colour he had never seen before. And many had remarked over the years, autumn, the prelude to the end of life, could possess great beauty. Now, in 2010, after another torrid, sleepless night he saw no beauty at all, just the biting frost of life's winter.

It is said that Muhammad Ali and Joe Frazier's 'Thrilla in Manila' fight took so much out of them both, neither were ever the same again. The early deaths of Andre, his oldest and Suzanne, his youngest, two of his four children, had extracted too great a toll. The man who had once seemingly had the strength to fight all life's comers in the glory of his youth was profoundly diminished for this, his final battle.

Pain - as it ever does - had made the world look like a very different place.

Judith had driven the Renault Laguna and parked in one of the side streets, not too far from the hospital. If one timed one's journey right, there was usually a space available. With having to visit every day, hospital car parking charges mounted up.

Tio and Judith kissed. A few weeks ago, they had quietly celebrated their fifty-first anniversary.

"Hi. What sort of night have you had?"

He shook his head, just as he did on that humid evening in Lower Penville over half a century ago.

"Terrible. I can't tell you how bad the pain has been."

She knew it would be so.

"Didn't you get any sleep at all?"

Again, he shook his head, his eyes moistened.

"You know what one of the night nurse said to me? She said, 'I'm sick of you pressing this button'. She was just sitting at the desk and was talking all night. I press the button couple times! That's all."

Judith knew that Tio would not have pressed the button to gain the attention of the duty nurse for the sake of it. His fierce independence was impaired, but it had by no means disappeared.

"I'm going to have a word with them about it. Make an official complaint. That's just not good enough."

"I know."

Judith knew that she would probably not make a full official complaint if for no other reason than she suspected that its recipients may just be too adept in nullifying it, too well versed in kicking it into the administrative long grass for anything effective to be done. She also knew that through the stress of her husband's illness that she had limited emotional resources, and to expend them fighting the bureaucratic machine was not wise.

No, her best hope was to try and appeal to good individuals who may actually care, to look them in the eye and hold them to account.

"Gershom will be here in a few minutes. He'll be really mad when he finds out about it."

"Isn't he at work?"

"All I know is that he's got the time off. I think he's explained to them what's going on."

"Did you buy him the kettle?"

"What do you think that great big thing I carried in is?"

"Oh, I didn't see it. Let me see. Was it on sale?"

She raised a bulky carrier bag within which was a large box.

"Yes, it was. Thirty per cent off. Hey, guess who I bumped into as I was coming in?"

"Who?"

"I met Ted Barnes' wife."

"Is he in again?"

"Well, you know he's been in and out a few times, for months now. He's on the Oncology Ward. It'd be nice if the two of you could get to see each other."

"I saw him in the first week I came in here."

"Really, you never mentioned that to me. How is he?"

"He's in hospital, that's how he is. He's okay. He still got plenty to say for himself."

"I've brought the scissors in. What would you like me to do first? Cut your hair or massage your back? Actually, I tell you what, I'll do your hair first or it'll get stuck all over the massage oil."

Tio had now been seven weeks since he had eaten. He was taken to hospital after two weeks of being able to keep nothing down to be fed intravenously, but after a further two weeks of x-rays and stilted investigations, the specialists were saying that they simply did not know what was wrong.

Judith pulled the blue disposable cubicle curtains around the bed as Tio moved gingerly over to the bedside chair and removed his pyjama top. She covered his shoulders with a light towel she had brought in from home, then combed his hair outwards with an afro comb, before cutting his now almost entirely grey hair.

Hair now cut and beard trimmed, he was handsome and presentable once more.

She then manoeuvred him to face away from her, anointed his back with massage oil and began to work it in. The musculature of this once strong man was now just a shadow and a memory of what it once was, his watch spun on his wrist.

"Thank you," said Tio.

"You're welcome."

"No, you don't understand. Thank you."

She nodded quietly.

Footsteps and voices from beyond the curtain, then suddenly a burst of light from it being drawn back.

"Ah, Mrs. Mourillon good morning. I see you are a good wife, there. And how is Mr. Mourillon today?"

"Not good, I'm afraid," said Judith.

"I still can't keep anything down," added Tio with very little strength in his voice.

"No, Mr. Mourillon, so I understand. Still not sleeping? Still not able to eat?"

After a few cursory exchanges, Judith took Mr. Khan, the gastroenterologist aside beyond Tio's hearing. This would at least ensure that Tio did not get too worked up by the conversation, as he was ever prone. After a minute or two conversing with Mr. Khan, she then made her way over to the ward desk for several minutes to discuss her concerns about how slowly they were getting to the bottom of the problem.

At the desk, Judith informed the staff nurse what had transpired on the previous shift. She explained that Tio Mourillon was her husband and her children's father, and said that she wanted them to treat her husband as they would if he were *their* father. She said that she did not want to make an official complaint, but that the offending night nurse needed to be told never to treat her husband in that way again.

Moments later Tio, his mind somewhat put at rest that something was being done, shifted himself back onto the bed, at which point his son Gershom arrived, met with his father's languid smile.

"Hiya Dad."

"You alright, boy?"

"Yeah, good thanks. Where's Mum?"

"She over there telling them off."

"Why, what happened?"

Tio explained the latest controversy at length, before calming his son down and explaining that it was all being dealt with by his mother.

"When you back at work, boy?"

"Dad, work's the last thing I want to be thinking about or reminded of right now."

"I'm just asking you when you back."

"Soon enough. Too soon."

"Look, down in the carrier bag, down there."

"What am I looking for?"

"Look in the bag, boy. Look, you say you like that kettle we bought? We get you one."

"That one that glows blue? Wow, thanks, Dad. You didn't have to do that."

"I know we didn't have to. Tu es ma famille, boy."

For Tio Mourillon, three things gave him more pleasure than anything else in the world. One: to win any battle with the powers that be. Today his wife was fighting on his behalf. Two: anything that could be bought at a bargain. Three: to see his family happy.

In buying the kettle that glowed blue when turned on, number two and number three were accomplished in one fell swoop. Three days before Tio Mourillon died, this day was not turning out quite so bad after all.

CHAPTER 40

I AM HOME

Lincolnshire - August 1964

At 6.55 am, Friday morning there was a firm knock at the door. Tio, who had already been up for close to two hours answered. Two removal men marched into the house without saying a word and began removing items from the lounge.

Judith, having fed everyone and clothed the children, was concentrating on keeping them out of harm's way and making sure they were entertained. All of the preparation work had been done. Tio's chief concern was that all the really expensive furniture was sufficiently wrapped and padded sufficiently for it not to be damaged in transit.

Within the hour everything was loaded into two large vans. They were ready to travel the five short miles north east, destination – their rural idyll.

Seated in the front of the first van with Andre on his knee next to an unspeaking Hollis, Tio's thoughts raced in a dozen directions. He would need to cycle into work now. Not the easiest of routes. He would have a steep hill to cycle up at after completing an arduous shift. Doing so after a night shift would be no fun at all. In time, he would have to learn to drive and buy a car.

Once the house interior was sorted out, he would have to work on the garden, which looked like a building site due to the fact that, until recently, it was one. Judith, now giddy with excitement at what was finally beginning to feel like an adventure, had picked up the keys from the Taylor & Nephew office the previous morning.

Judith handed the keys to one of the removal men, while the other went to the rear to open up the van doors. As Judith alighted the van, a small car wound its way past the removal vans and parked up. A well-dressed woman in her early thirties with short brown hair trotted towards Judith and the children.

Judith's heart sank as Clive Taylor's words about powerful people – or was it influential? – making their lives uncomfortable, played in her mind like a stuck record. They had only been in the village a matter of minutes. Was their first day going to be marred with an unedifying incident – a sign of discomfort to come?

"Excuse me, you used to be Judith May, didn't you?"

"Yes."

"You went to school with Trevor Baker, my younger brother. I'm Pat"

"Oh. How is he?"

"He's okay I suppose. He told me you and your husband were moving here sometime soon. I had no idea it was today."

"No. Well, to be honest, we weren't sure it was actually going to happen today, but here we are."

"Yes, you are. Welcome back, anyway. It's lovely to have another young family here. And who are these two young gentlemen?"

It took a moment or two for Judith to gather her thoughts.

"This is Andre, he's five. This is Gershom, he's three and the noisy one here is Colette."

"What lovely names. How exotic, too. Andre will be at infants of course, but will Gershom be attending nursery?"

"I think so. I haven't really had much time to think about it, to be honest."

"Of course. How silly of me. You've literally just arrived. Anyway, once you've had a chance to settle in it would be nice to catch up again. The nursery school will be restarting a week on Monday. Would you like me to pop by in the car and give you a lift up there? Introduce you to some, reintroduce you to others?"

"Yes. That would be very nice."

"Very good, I'll no doubt see you then."

Pat skipped back to her car, waved, then left.

"What did she want?" asked Tio.

"Just to welcome us. She was really nice, actually."

A moment later, Hollis, dressed in a brown smock coat approached with a clipboard.

"Okay's that's everything. Sign here."

Tio offered Hollis his hand.

"I know we had our disagreements, but no hard feelings."

Hollis did not reciprocate, just as several months earlier Tom Cooper had not done so on this same spot. On that occasion, Tio had offered twice. This time, he would offer only once.

"Yes, there are hard feelings actually. You've ruined my business!"

"I've done what? You exaggerating, man."

"You've ruined my business!" Hollis was shouting now. "You've called the police on me. It's ruined my business, I tell you."

Tio took the clipboard and made his signature whilst shaking his head. Hollis snatched the board and strode away, only to halt, turn around in one final venting of his fury.

"I don't know why you lot don't just…" Seeing the children, he momentarily refrained from cursing. "Why don't you go back where you came from? Bugger off home!"

Tio had no intention of trying to fill the vast canyon that was this man's ignorance. His only concern was whether this man could hinder him. He no longer could.

"I am home."

EPILOGUE

PORTSMOUTH, DOMINICA – 2010

"Bon jou, titja Celestine."

"Bon jou, misyé. Sakafete?"

Clara peered across the street from her veranda to see the arrival of a Toyota pickup, heralding delivery of the post.

"I am very good, thank you. Beautiful day again, Clara. Will you be taking a sea bath in Tanetane today?"

"No. Too many sand flies, Preston. They only like the tourists and me."

They both laughed a lazy laugh as he seated himself beside her.

"You would like some iced tea?"

"Clara Celestine, why would you even ask me such a question? If you ask me this question again, I will stop telling the neighbours you are my girlfriend."

Clara went inside only to appear a few seconds later, tea in hand.

"Anyway, what is all this 'Titja Celestine'? It's a *long* time since I was your teacher. It is a long time since I was anyone's teacher."

"It doesn't matter if I am as old as sixty, you will always be my teacher to me. Look, I have something for you."

"For me?"

"From America. I think it is books."

"But I have not sent for any books."

"Well, someone send you some books."

"It is already opened and resealed."

"Perhaps Customs. Maybe they want to see if they can charge the sender import duty."

Clara opened the package and let out a faint gasp.

"What is he?"

"It's a book."

"I know it's a book. I told you it is a book. What book is he?"

"It's from one of my former students. She is in Houston, Texas. It's a collection of poems about Dominica. A first edition."

She lifted one of five hard backed volumes from the package. Inside, an inscription – *'To my beloved Miss Celestine. My teacher, my mentor, my inspiration.'*

"Is she your student who won the prize in National Poetry Day?"

"But of course. You have a *good* memory, Preston. Rosemond Alexis. I am very proud of her. She was always such a diligent student, always very respectful."

"Just like me, Clara. I am very respectful too."

"Not like you at all, Preston. You are troublesome."

Preston laughed.

"So, read me one of the poems."

"You have time? What about the post?"

"Clara, there will always be post. Read the poem."

"Okay, close your eyes and I will read."

"Okay, my eyes are closed."

Against the sublime azure blue backdrop of the Caribbean Sea, beneath a barely clouded sky, Clara Celestine read to her attentive listener the first from a volume of poems about the mountains, hills, lakes and rivers of her homeland.

ACKNOWLEDGEMENTS

I would like to thank the following people for their help:

My mother, Barbara LeBlanc for her invaluable help, recounting events from long ago when I was too young to remember.

My wife Pauline LeBlanc, off whom I bounced many ideas.

Dr. Irving Andre, with whom I discussed the initial concept, for his invaluable feedback, and casting an author's eye over the manuscript.

Debz Hobbs-Wyatt for her help in the editing process and her encouragement

Philip Emmett who cast an author's eye over the text from a UK perspective.

Sylvia LeBlanc, for her wealth of first-hand knowledge as a teacher in Penville.

Algie and Hescar Charter for their kindness and hospitality and for Algie's many very, very long and detailed anecdotes.

Faustina Charter for her hospitality, her stories of years past and for providing a profound link with a bygone era about which I would have otherwise have struggled to write.

Mr. Gerry Aird for his generosity with his time and for his knowledge of passenger cargo ships in years past.

Mick Hopper for his time and input relating to the blast furnaces and steelworks culture in the early sixties.

Steve Stubbins for his help and resources relating to Roxby village.

Carole Longbone of Scunthorpe Library for her help researching the town's history.

Yvette LeBlanc for her help with character names and for being someone against whom I could bounce off ideas.

Paddington LeBlanc for his anecdotes and recollections of years past.

Charles LeBlanc also for tales of exploits in years gone by.

Made in the USA
Columbia, SC
09 March 2018